THE CUSTOM OF THE COUNTRY

THE CUSTOM OF THE COUNTRY

Tales of New Japan

By

MARY (CRAWFORD) FRASER
(MRS. HUGH FRASER)

Short Story Index Reprint Series

BOOKS FOR LIBRARIES PRESS
FREEPORT, NEW YORK

First Published 1899
Reprinted 1969

STANDARD BOOK NUMBER:
8369-3199-8

LIBRARY OF CONGRESS CATALOG CARD NUMBER:
70-101811

MANUFACTURED
BY
HALLMARK LITHOGRAPHERS, INC.
IN THE U.S.A.

CONTENTS

BEFORE

The ebb and flow
Of Fate's remorseless current fills and lifts,
And floats the stranded off in God's good time.
The quicksand shifts.

The rending breeze
Clearing the way for Love's own summer sun,
That glints across the foam-crowned harbour bar —
The doubt is done.

Shielding our eyes
We watch and wait, until the heart we love,
Drifting in sight, sighs for the chain of peace
Its fancy wove

In dreams of days
Spent before starting, castles in the air.
Facts clash with fancies on the grief-worn steps
Of Reason's stair.

Good-bye, dear Heart,
We meet and touch, and drift apart.   The veil
Drops, fold by fold, until we read aright
Love's tear-stained tale.

H. C. FRASER.

IN TOKYO

In Tokyo

T was cherry-blossom time, and every garden was flushed with a sunrise cloud of bloom. Down the wide avenues of the city, the trees stood thick, and stretched out their branches towards each other, and made arches from street to street, down the banks of the moats and over the bridges till they flooded the palace gardens, and sent silent showers of petals into the very windows of the Emperor's rooms. Tokyo is a garden in which a city has grown up by accident, and the flowers have the best of it still.

Mrs. Nisbet's matted drawing-room was gay with branches of the double rose-like blossoms; outside, in the elaborate miniature garden, which was laid out like a park, and covered perhaps a quarter of an acre, her own three cherry trees were as brave as all the rest, and soared proudly above the shallow stone tank, where the three bronze cranes were always on the point of eating the bronze tortoise. A light breeze wandered past now

3

and again, and then the rosy snowdrifts parted into boughs and wreaths, and shed a rain of petals down on the water, which was already so thick with their fragrant foam that the bronze tortoise was quite smothered and lost to view.

Beyond the cherry trees was the bamboo fence, all pale green, because it was new; and tied together, stake by stake, with neat lover's knots in black string. Beautifully shaped stepping-stones marked the way to a larger tank at the far end of the domain, where irises would wave white and blue flags by and by, when the cherry blossoms had had their day. It was early April now, and Mrs. Nisbet was sitting on her verandah, pouring out tea for a visitor who was in the habit of coming to her almost every day. She was a little hurt because he took scant notice of her garden, which was looking its best in the full sunshine of the eastern spring.

Laura Nisbet was young, and rather shy, pretty and dark-eyed, with a pale face full of the conscientious brightness of the nice American girl. She had been married for nearly two years to Nisbet, of the Kondo Gakko, and was suffering the famishing homesickness which comes to most women in the East. Like many another, she would rather have died than have let her hopeful, hard-working young husband know anything about it. Frank Nisbet was at the school a great part of the day, and found his wife looking so happy when he came home that it never struck him to ask how she looked when he was away.

They had both been kind, as only fellow-exiles can be

kind, to this Mr. Randall Johnson, who had seemed rather lonely when they had first made his acquaintance. Mrs. Nisbet was listening now, for the hundredth time, to his description of " Nita's " home, of " Nita's " accomplishments, of her brothers and sisters, and even of her dog and her bicycle; for Mr. Johnson was engaged to be married, and his future bride would arrive in a few days, to be received and mothered by Mrs. Nisbet, until Johnson could carry her off to the house which he had been proudly preparing for her.

Johnson was a Scotch engineer who had been for some years in the employ of a large Japanese firm. He was not brilliant, not at all good-looking, and was terribly shy and awkward when weighed down by any approach to a social responsibility. But there was a kindliness and modesty about the man which always gained friends for him in the long run, and a gleam of humour in his grey eyes showed that he could be an appreciative listener — at least, before he became engaged to Miss Banks. That event had taken place in the course of a short holiday which he had allowed himself the year before. He had meant to stay at home for a while, and perhaps not return to Japan at all, if he could find employment on the right side of the world. But having persuaded Miss Banks to consent to marry him, his sturdy Scotch conscience would not allow him to bask in her smiles, and gave him no peace till he got back to Japan and put himself in harness again, in order to scrape up a nice little balance at the bank wherewith to welcome her, and to start life afresh in the character of a family man.

Before his engagement he had been working "fine," as he would have said; earning a decent bachelor subsistence, on which he was as happy as the cricket on the hearth. His rather insignificant person looked majestic beside that of Mr. Ikuruke, the head of the "concern." There were several of his fellow-countrymen scattered about in Tokyo, and they took no exception at his multiplied "r's," or his provincial manners, and with them he managed to have many a sober "day off" in the country, when he was not engaged in keeping his principals from running their tunnels out to the sky on the face of a precipice, or bolstering up their railway bridges with bamboo baskets full of loose stones. Since Mrs. Nisbet came he had what every man wants, one sympathetic woman friend, and he was made supremely comfortable in his little Japanese house by O Matsu.

O Matsu was the queen of housekeepers, and her service to Johnson was of that golden kind which never comes into the market. She was a gentle, quiet, little creature, who could work like a beaver, cook wonderful dinners, polish the floor, mend the clothes, keep the jinriksha man in order, and attend to every detail of Johnson's daily comfort, without ever raising her voice or soiling her pretty hands.

When a friend dropped in, O Matsu brought the tea exactly five minutes after she had opened the door, and whatever was the hour of the day or night, she always had on her grey-green gown and her brown "obi," lined with gold colour, her hair shone amazingly black in its twists and wings, and her little sandals invariably dropped at the door on precisely the right spot.

Her method of entering a room was a lesson in deportment. First she sank on her knees outside, and putting her hand on the door exactly two feet from the ground, pushed back the screen just enough to admit her person. Then, having slipped through the opening and saluted the guest with a deep inclination of the head, she would serve him (also on her knees) with the most fragrant tea, while his hat and stick seemed to dispose of themselves by magic, and in their stead a tiny table came to his hand for the tea-cup.

O Matsu had been something of a stumbling-block to the more serious of Johnson's friends, and one in particular, the Rev. Dr. M'Kay, an "airnest" preacher in the Baptist Mission, held strong objections to her existence at all, at least within the wood-and-paper walls of Johnson's house. The good man wrestled with his fellow-being in prayer and expostulation, month in, month out, on the subject of O Matsu, but he "praught" to deaf ears.

"And why should I have no Mats?" Johnson would answer scornfully. "Can I not have a decent, quiet woman-body about the house, but the evil-minded will have it that I am one of themselves? And d'ye think, Dr. M'Kay, that if I cared for Mats the way you seem to imagine, I would not have come to you to get decently married long ago? Nay, nay, I was never one of that kind, having had a very enlightened upbringing, and it's not at my time of life, man, that I'll be misconducting myself. You are entirely mistaken, though I've no manner of doubt ye mean it well."

But like many good people, Dr. M'Kay was more ready to believe in vice than virtue. When O Matsu brought him his tea and smiled as he took two lumps of sugar, his exhortings would cease, for in the face of her calm dignity it was impossible to call her ugly names. But as soon as she had crept away and had run the screen into place, he would lean forward and entreat his friend, as he valued his immortal soul, to put that "pagan stumbling-block" out of his path. At last he prevailed so far as to persuade Johnson to shut up his house and go home for a season; his health was a little run down, and there was an old mother to visit, and Dr. M'Kay and his wife thought that they could get another place for "Mats" while he was away; and planned to provide him with a good "boy" against his return, so that the sad appearance of evil should come to an end.

O Matsu received the announcement of Johnson's departure with her submissive smile, and said that she would take care of the house in his absence. She was perfectly satisfied with her position, although she may, from time to time, have wondered why "Johnson san," who was so kind to her, did not marry her, *à la Japon-*

aise. She had only the ideas of her class on that
subject, and would have felt no more and no less honoured than she now was, by becoming the master's
unacknowledged wife. That anybody could consider
her a disgrace or a stumbling-block was a thought that
never entered her head.

Johnson had been so persecuted by his friend that he
was ready to give in at last. If he ever returned to
Japan — well, he would try a boy, just to please the
minister, though boys were extravagant, feckless creatures, to be sure. But he had not the courage to say as
much to O Matsu, and decided to write to her from
Hong Kong, and to send her money wherewith to get
back to her own people.

Great was the joy of the good M'Kays when Johnson
returned, a little earlier than was expected, with the
news that there would soon be a Mrs. Johnson; according to him the sweetest, prettiest, cleverest girl in the
world. He could not say much about her religious
views, and so talked very little to Mrs. M'Kay or the
minister about her, but poured out his soul to Mrs.
Nisbet, to whom the bride's religious views were a
matter of entire indifference, but who could sympathise
with people in love. She was silently disappointed by
the portrait of Nita which Johnson brought to show her.
It was that of a conscious-looking girl, in a cheap evening dress, which showed thin arms and coarse hands.
The face had a peaky prettiness about it, but the mouth
was poor, and the eyes eager. Johnson explained that
her beauty lay in colouring and expression, but from

that moment Mrs. Nisbet was aware of a tinge of pity which began to shadow her auguries for Johnson's future. It took real women, with true hearts, she thought, to bear the life at all; and as for helping Johnson —

"He would have done better to marry O Matsu," she said to Nisbet, when he came back from the school. "She has one idea in the world, and that is to make Johnson happy. This girl's face is absolutely mean."

"It ought not to be so hard to make a man happy," said Nisbet, unconsciously. "We are very easily pleased, on the whole."

To this Mrs. Nisbet made no reply at the moment, but had a good cry when her husband had fallen asleep. On their small means, with almost no amusement or recreation for herself, it took all her love, and good sense, and energy, to keep his house fair and happy, and then he only said, "We are very easily pleased."

When Johnson first returned from England, the O Matsu question threatened to become acute again. He had written, and had sent her fifty dollars to take home to her mother; but fifty dollars was a large sum in the wise little woman's eyes; her mother had but slight hold on her affections, and the house wanted fresh paper and new mats, and the well a roof to keep the leaves from floating into it, so she took the money for that; and when Johnson came back she had ten dollars in hand for the housekeeping, and there she was in the doorway, knocking her splendidly dressed head on the floor, all beaming with smiles for the

master's return. Then she crept away to see to the
nice little dinner which was cooking on the "hibachi,"
and was so busy taking care of him and unpacking his
things all the evening, that she could not find time to
listen to the story which he was trying to tell her.

When, at last, she understood that an English
"okusama" was coming out to be Mrs. Johnson,
she bowed her head and spread her hands on the
floor, and then stood up again and seemed to be con-
sidering. Johnson felt unaccountably small and displeased with himself when she looked at him and
said quietly : —

"Ar' right, okusama take care Johnson san, my
take care okusama. House clean, dinner cook, no
wantye dollars. Okusama by'm by time glad good
amah, no pay."

Johnson protested a little. Nita had shown evi-
dences of a capacity for jealousy even during their
short engagement, and "Mats" was what Dr. M'Kay
called "ower weel-favoured for a single man's home."
But O Matsu was as obstinate as she was gentle, and
the arrangement had to stand. Johnson hoped that
she would keep out·of the minister's way if he came,
for he was afraid that M'Kay might attack her on the
subject. Those "releegious bodies," as he said to
himself, never took count of anything,· and believed
in no virtue but their own!

Then he threw himself wholly into the happy task
of preparing and decorating the little home for Nita,
and on the day when the cherry blossoms were smoth-

ering the tortoise in Mrs. Nisbet's garden, had come
to ask her to inspect, and, of course, approve of, all
his arrangements.

"Will you come to tea, to-morrow, Mrs. Nisbet,
and tell me what you think of it?" he said. "It is
all very simple, and the house is a wee nest, not at
all what she has been used to, of course."

In spite of the depreciation, he was inwardly bub-
bling over with happiness at having been able to make
it so pretty. It would have been hard to do anything
else, in that commune of beauty. Mrs. Nisbet smiled
as she saw his beaming countenance.

"I am sure it is perfectly lovely," she said; "I will
come to-morrow, if Mr. Nisbet is free. If not, I might
bring Mrs. M'Kay."

She was rigidly proper, in spite of her frank bright
ways, and, like the other married women of her province, always spoke of her husband as "Mr."

Johnson did not want Mrs. M'Kay.

"I'll call in and tell Nisbet on my way down," he
said. "I should like you two to see it first."

As he left the verandah and disappeared through
the little garden gate, his friend looked after him
almost tenderly.

"Poor fellow," she said to herself, "I hope that
girl will make him happy. I expect he has half
ruined himself over the things for her."

Nisbet was free the next day, and, grumbling a
little, went with his wife to Johnson's house. The
owner met them at the door, and led them into the

tiny drawing-room, which was all blue crape and fans, and into the dining-room, which was all red lacquer and bamboo work. The sacred chamber beyond he would not allow Nisbet to enter, but asked Laura to go in alone, and tell him if it was all right. The little touch of delicacy struck her, and when she had left the men outside, and had passed into the dainty room, she realised for the first time that the little Scotch engineer was a lover and a poet!

He had found a white crape with some threads of gold in it, and with this the room was softly draped. The windows, the bed, the dressing-table, were all hung with the creamy stuff; the floor was spread with finest mats, and full white sheepskins lay here and there. The simple furniture was all in harmony; on the dressing-table lay a set of boxes in fine gold lacquer, and in an alcove window hung growing fern wreaths set in wistaria roots. They swung in the fitful April breeze, and tinkled silvery bells that were fastened to them with coloured streamers. All was fine and white and maidenlike, and something like tears came into Laura Nisbet's eyes as she looked round.

"Poor little Johnson," she murmured, "who would have thought of his having so much poetry in him?"

"It is the prettiest room I ever saw," she told him when she came out. "The whole thing is perfect. Where did you learn all that, Mr. Johnson?"

"Well," he replied, blushing with pleasure, "you see, she has had a first-rate home, and I'm not much to look at myself, and it is just incredibly good of her to come all this way to marry me; so I thought I ought to try and make it up to her as far as I could."

"You must have spent a pile of money," said Nisbet, looking round thoughtfully, and returning to a subject which was sadly uppermost in his own mind; "I should say quite a thousand dollars. Did you get an advance from Ikuruke?"

He and Johnson had discussed the question of pay, employers, and advances many a time.

"No," said Johnson, turning away, "I did not do exactly that. 'Twould be a bad thing to start married life on advances. Mrs. Nisbet, will you not come and have some tea?"

Laura noticed that he was no longer wearing a certain diamond stud, whose gorgeousness she and her husband had often laughed at. It was on a removable mount, and Johnson was always changing it from ring to scarf-pin, and then back again to stud. It was gone now, and a modest pearl button had taken its place.

"He has sold it," she said to her husband as they drove home in their double jinriksha. "Oh, if that girl is not nice to him, I shall shake her."

"Why should not she be nice to him, Laura? Oh, I say, hold on!"

At this point the talk had to cease, because the Kuru-maya began to tear down hill at full speed, and as the American couple were light and thin, that meant break-neck pace, and the outrunning of various bare-legged rivals on the road.

That evening O Matsu brought a letter to Johnson as he sat smoking on the verandah. He was afraid to bring his pipe into any of the smart rooms, lest the fumes should cling to "Nita's things." The letter was from the mother of his betrothed, and ran thus: —

"My darling child has left me to go to you. As she is to stay a fortnight in Ceylon with some friends, my letter will reach you before she does. Oh, my dear Randall, although I am sure you love her dearly, you can have no idea of the precious treasure that I am giving to you. It has broken my heart to let her go; but when I think of all the light and sweetness, the high influence and constant help, that she will be in your life, I am already half consoled. She felt the leaving her own dear home most terribly; but you know how brave and bright she is, and she managed not to cry, and to have a smile for us all at the last, besides seeing to all her belongings, for I was too overcome to think of anything. Oh, be good to her, my dear Randall, and Heaven deal with you as you do with my innocent child."

Here followed some motherly recommendations and a list of Nita's boxes, which seemed very copious to Johnson's puzzled comprehension. He did not feel well to-night, and put the letter in his pocket to finish it later. He got up, and came down into his little garden, and breathed in the fresh evening air. It had been a warm day, and he had been running about a good deal in the sun, seeing to various matters connected with the coming event. All was finished now; there was not a touch more needed in the house. Down to the scented soap in the bathroom, he had provided for everything, and now he would take it easy for a few days. The spring was always tiring in Tokyo. It was quite enough to account for a man's feeling dizzy and stupid. He would go to the office, because he must have a month's holiday after Nita came, and it would be — yes, it would be wasted if he began now. How his head ached after that ride in the sun. He felt about fifty years old — fifty, at thirty-two. Yes, it was all this wretched relaxing spring weather. Better give in and go to bed.

.   .   .   .

"I say, Laura," Mr. Nisbet called out, as he came into the house some days later, "have you seen anything of Johnson to-day or yesterday? Some one was saying he was down with fever."

"Oh, *no!*" cried Mrs. Nisbet; "surely it must be a mistake. Do go and see."

"You had better come with me," he said; "I should not be of any use in a sick-room."

So together they went up the quiet road, and down the lane, and across the little stone bridge to Johnson's house. The doors were all shut to the garden. Those were "Nita's rooms"; but the Nisbets found a very sick man lying in a dark, close chamber near the kitchen. O Matsu, pale and tired, was cooking beef-tea over the hibachi on the step outside. The master of the house did not rise to greet his friends; indeed he did not know that they were there. His face was flushed and his eyes glazed, and his hands were pulling at the poor bedclothes. He was lying on a "futon" on the mats, and was keeping up a harsh stream of delirious talk that never ceased for a moment. Nisbet went to him and tried to take his hand, but he drew it away, and went on picking at his blue coverlet. Mrs. Nisbet stood for an instant gazing at him, then she ran and caught O Matsu by the arm, and shook her violently.

"You wicked woman!" she cried, "why is he there on the floor? Why did you not put him in his own bed?"

"He said no, no, all the same no," replied O Matsu, quite unmoved by Laura's anger. "He say, 'my no go okusama pretty room. Japanese room all right,' so he stay here."

"Has the doctor been?" Laura asked; "you should have called him directly Mr. Johnson was taken ill."

"Doctor san three time last night, two time to-day come. Very kind. Say Johnson san by'm by better, nice room take. Plenty beef-tea, medicine give."

And she went back to her preparations with that complete absorption in the duty of the moment which makes the Japanese woman a force in the family. There is neither past nor future for her when to-day has sounded its commands.

Nisbet stayed all night, and towards morning, with the doctor's help, got poor Johnson safely to bed in the one bright sleeping room which the house contained.   Very strange he looked under the white canopies touched with gold, and among all the dainty fittings meant for his bride.   He knew it not, poor soul, at any rate, at first.   Just towards the end he had a moment of peace — peace from the weary rush of speech, from the agonising pressure on the brain. Laura had been sitting beside him, and O Matsu, crouching a little way off on the floor, never took her eyes from his face.   She had not had an hour's rest for five nights, and looked haggard enough, but still calm and alert.

Johnson stretched out his hand towards her.

"And you tell the minister, Mrs. Nisbet," he began, in a weak voice, quite changed from the hoarse cry of his ravings, "be sure you tell the minister that Mats is a guid honest lass, and I will not hear a word contrary to that, and, if it hadna been for her and for you, I'd no have won through this bout.   It's been a sair sickness."

"Don't talk," said Laura, frightened at the change in his face, but hoping it meant that the fever was leaving him.

O Matsu silently brought him a drink and held the bowl to his lips.   He tried to take it himself, but was too weak, and his hand fell heavily on the quilt.   There it met O Matsu's, and he pressed her fingers feebly.

"A guid, decent body," he repeated, "poor Mats. Now I-'ll sleep — a bit.   Lay me down to sleep — I pray —"

He seemed to doze, and Mrs. Nisbet slipped from

the room to speak to the doctor, whom she caught sight of coming up the path. She told him how sensible and quiet Johnson seemed.

"Ay, it mostly ends that way," he said gravely. "It won't be long now. There will be no pain."

Laura sat down on the step and cried bitterly.

"That poor girl! That poor girl!" she sobbed. "She's coming to-morrow — coming to be *married* — and he will be dead! Who can face her? How can God be so cruel?"

.   .   .   .

They left O Matsu in charge of the quiet house the next day, and in sore sorrow and trouble went down to Yokohama to meet Nita Banks. She would arrive in all the glory of expectant bridehood, to be told that Randall Johnson lay dead in his house.

"Who is to tell her?" Mrs. Nisbet moaned again and again, as they sped down through the country all a-blush with the cherry blossoms. "What shall I find to say? How can God be so cruel? We wouldn't treat our worst enemy like that. And they tell us He is love!"

It was rough in the bay at Yokohama, but Laura and her husband hardly noticed how the tender tossed as they steamed out to the black ship, where there would be a broken heart as soon as they stepped on board.

The second officer was standing in the gangway, and stopped them as they passed.

"Mrs. Nisbet?" he said to Laura.

"Yes. Oh, *please*, let me find Miss Banks before any one tells her."

"I must ask you to step this way," said the officer, decidedly, and they followed him to the captain's cabin.

The captain came in a hurry from the chart room, where he had just been welcomed by his wife, and shook hands with the Nisbets.

"Where is Miss Banks? I must find her," cried Laura, in great distress.

"I have a message from Miss Banks for Mr. Johnson," said the captain, with hesitation; "it is not a message he will like, I fear, but these things will happen! Ladies have their privileges, you know!"

"What do you mean?" said Mr. Nisbet, roughly.

He was anxious for his wife, who looked deadly pale.

"Oh, well, perhaps you will tell Mr. Johnson, then," said the captain. "I am sure I do not care about the job! Miss Banks saw reason to change her mind in the course of the voyage, and we put her off at Hong Kong with all her traps, and I was to tell Mr. Johnson that she was really very sorry, but she was sure she could never have made him happy, and — she was going to marry Mr. Baynes of Jake, Paterson & Co., Shanghai, who had been taking such kind care of her all through the voyage."

The captain did not wait to see the result of his message, but ran upstairs again, and Laura sank down on the red cushions of the berth, crying and laughing like a mad woman. Her husband took her in his arms, saying very tenderly : —

"Don't, don't, little woman! It is better so, far better so!"

"Better?" cried Johnson's woman friend, "oh, my dear, it is too best to be true. Think, if we had had to tell the poor fellow *that!* God isn't cruel; it was the one way out, and He opened the door for him. Poor, dear, little Johnson, I am so glad you are dead."

They did not forget him, and Johnson's humble grave was more lovingly tended than many a more pompous one in the cemetery on the hill. Laura never took her tribute of flowers there without finding a branch of the season's blossoms stuck in a hollow bamboo, and well fed with water. Often the little incense sticks were burning, like tender memories, and making much fragrance on the air; and when it came to cherry-blossom time, the low mound was all aglow with bloom, flushing and paling like a girl at her bridal. But that is a word that no one would ever mention within hearing of Johnson's timely grave.

THE CUSTOM OF THE COUNTRY

The Custom of the Country

I

N the early seventies many of the links which now bind the far East to the daily interests of Western lives had not been forged. The world has shrunk rapidly since then, and people know more about it, and no longer hope that one will "see a great deal of my brother in Shangnai," because one is going to live in Peking. In those days the journey was so long that the traveller towards the sunrise came to feel that he had passed beyond the veil with all the other ghosts, who doubtless write letters which are never answered, and peer through their twilight for ships that never come in. It was such a leap into the unknown that the exile often gave up all attempts to bridge the gulf between himself and those left behind; and little by little stopped writing to them from sheer despair at the

hopelessness of making them understand his life. And sometimes the silence, bitter and hard as it might seem to the home-dwellers, had its motive in a sound, if unconscious, conviction of the impossibility of leading two lives at once. A man in whom the sense of self-preservation is strong (women seldom have this sense at all) acknowledges the necessity of adjusting himself to environment, and knows that he cannot do so if he is always reaching out to a vanishing past. Only an accomplished juggler can keep up two contrary movements at once.

Japan was very far from Yorkshire five and twenty years ago. At least so John Thornton felt when his first year of absence from home had passed. He was a very young man still, but he knew fairly well what he meant to have from life. A rover, a thinker, a worker by inheritance, a poet by nature, the narrow existence of his forebears on "t' land" in Yorkshire inspired him with profound and unwavering distaste.

A Thornton had held the farm ever since the Wars of the Roses, and the name was soundly respected in the county. A Thornton had fought under Cromwell, and his old sword still hung over the fireplace in the hall at Thornton Grange. Undazzled by ambition, he had returned to his homestead and had died there in peace, leaving sons of his name to till his acres and stall his cattle. Generation after generation the Thorntons had stood on the soil, taking deeper root on their fair freehold, century by century. Only one had broken away from the traditions of the family, and even now, a hundred years after his death, was spoken of among them as " Roving Jack." He had taken service abroad, and was killed in some skirmish on the Algerian coast. Something of his spirit seemed to have passed to John, old George Thornton's younger son. As a lad he had shown so much quickness in learning that his father had conceived high ambitions for his boy. The great man of the countryside early noticed the bright-eyed lad, and lent him books of travel and history ; eagerly read in every spare moment, they fed the nameless hunger of his mind, and soothed the loneliness of his uncomprehended longings for a wider life. He felt that beyond the walls which closed him in there was a vast army of men of his way of thinking, and the firm resolve to leap all boundaries to join them became the ruling influence of his life.

So John was sent to a good school, then to a northern university, where he came in touch with young fellows of his own age, eager to see, to live, to travel, to be of definite good or harm in the world. The pushing, aspiring northern undergraduate, with his home-made philosophy and clothes, has nothing in common with the majestic denizens of Oxford or Cambridge, who seem to breathe an atmosphere of superb Olympic calm in regard to all the greater questions of life. But then, life can be spelt in more ways than one ; and it may be that there is more heart and philosophy than we dream of behind the immaculate shirt-front and the deliberately vacuous expression of the gilt-edged darling, who is so crudely and constantly described as a "wretched noodle" by one of our urbane women writers.

Even the most fiercely anthrophobic woman would hardly have applied that epithet to John Thornton, and he would have been profoundly indifferent to the calumny if she had done so. He had known few women, and they had not entered into his life to any appreciable extent. His heart went with him quite whole to the East when his first patron, seeing that the promise of his boyhood still held fair, procured for him an opening in the consular service, at which he had grasped eagerly. Old Thornton thanked the M.P. in characteristic words.

"And I thank ye raart well, Sir Charles, for what you have done for t' lad. He's too clever for us, and he's aye restless, and he never took t' farm. And indeed I take it kind of you to help t' lad oot in t world."

The world, to old Mr. Thornton, meant anything south of the Fells. Had John been an only son, his chances of crossing that barrier would have been slight indeed. But he had an elder brother, George, a true son of the soil, who asked no better than to live and, if needs must, die on it. His dogcart and his gun, "t' land," and the market days were enough for George, the last rather too much sometimes, since he did not always return from them sober.

.   .   .   .

John felt as if he had lived a thousand years during the two months that his journey to Japan had lasted, and when he finally landed at Nagasaki he could hardly persuade himself that he was in the same universe which held his early home. Faces too strange to be physiognomies surrounded him, and he could gather nothing of the owners' thoughts from them. Expression had lost its value, form its meaning. These marionettes were pulled by different strings from those which cause the European doll to laugh or weep, walk or run. Some things shocked his untried prudery beyond words. It would be difficult to describe his feelings when, as he was walking, tired and dusty, through a hill village, an old woman, paddling in her bath in sight of all beholders, called out to stop him as he passed.

"What does she want?" he asked of his guide, glancing with a visible shudder at the aged bit of humanity (brown as a last year's oak leaf, and innocent of clothes as a fish in a tank) which stretched an arm to him from the steaming tub.

"She very kind woman," the guide explained: "she say, young gentleman tired, dirty, bath plenty big for two people; please get in!"

"Oh, come along," cried the wayfarer, beginning to run; "what a country! *what* a country!"

Yet the old woman had offered him the one kindness of which he stood in need, according to her lights.

But these were crude impressions, soon forgotten, and he found many things which attracted him; the leisure, the dignity, of Japanese life, where poverty is no reproach, wealth no distinction, struck him as wonderfully sane and beautiful. The more he saw of it the more he felt that it appealed to latent sympathies in his own temperament, which made all its forms easy to him, and immensely lightened the labour of learning the language. Not that he would have wished, for a single moment, to change his nationality. He was far too truly an Englishman for that. But he liked the existence, enjoyed the quiet freedom of the country's ways, and acknowledged to himself, after he had been there for a year or two, that he had never been so happy in his life.

The service was somewhat short-handed at that time, and Thornton rose rapidly, and came to be looked upon by his seniors as possessing excellent brains, a quick grasp of a subject, as well as a correct one, untiring energy, and sound judgment; he had acted with resource and firmness in more than one crisis, and it was augured of him that he would some day get to the very top of the tree.

That nothing less should satisfy him he was resolved. He had discovered the true secret of success, and had taught himself to regard only one obstacle at a time, the next on his path. When that was overcome it would be soon enough to look out for another.

He had been some seven or eight years in Japan, serving first in Tokyo, and then in Yokohama, and finally in Tokyo again. He had just had an encouraging pat on the back for a very elaborate trade report, at which he had been working hard for some months. It had been mentioned in a despatch as " Mr. Thorn-

ton's able and carefully prepared report," and he saw
promotion smiling in the near future. His leave was
overdue; and, in the happiest frame of mind, he packed
up a few books, some provisions (for he had not yet
learned to live entirely on Japanese food), and taking
his jinriksha coolie as travelling servant, he started for
a little town on the south coast, a place of warm
baths and long beaches and wild inland walks, where
an aspiring young man might forget for a time the
intricacies of trade reports, and lay in energy for some
other great achievement.

The coolie's wages had to be raised as soon as
he began to run on the rough country roads, and
he pleaded hard for a permanent colleague on the
journey.

Mr. Thornton san, as Kané called him, was a very
big man, and a fairly heavy one, although there was
no spare flesh on his tall frame. He had managed,
by care and exercise, to keep himself in admirable
training. He had a short, clear-cut face, brown hair,
and grey eyes, very direct and thoughtful in their
glance. It was the countenance of a man who would
be something of a power always, whether for good or
evil it would have been hard to say at that time, but
— and on this all who knew him would have been
unanimous — for himself, first of all. He was then
eight and twenty, and his subsequent history showed
that his friends would have been mistaken on one
point, at any rate, in their classification of his character.

"Rubbish, Kané!" said John Thornton, in reply to

his kurumya's prayers. "You can pull me perfectly well on the flat, and when it comes to hills you can always find some poor fellow who will be thankful to earn a few 'rin' by lending you a hand. Do you think I am going to pay for two hungry men at the inns, besides myself?"

At which Kané laughed and drew in his breath audibly, in token of respect and submission; then girding up his loins with a blue towel, went off to wash and polish his special toy, the master's "jinrikky."

He admired Mr. Thornton's economy, for that is a cardinal virtue in the eyes of his thrifty race, and he consoled himself for the refusal by thinking that at any rate he would reap some nice little squeezes off the bills at the inns. But when he had gone twelve miles or so, smiling and willing, through mud a foot deep and roads flooded by recent rains, Thornton suddenly ordered him to halt at a tea-house, and, jumping out of the grown-up perambulator, put a dollar into his hand, and told him to go and find another man to help him.

"All the way?" asked Kané, mopping his neck with the blue towel, and smiling still.

"Yes, all the way," replied Thornton, gruffly, because he was touched at his servant's good will, and saw that he had been in the wrong.

After that they got on faster, and some days later broke their journey for the last time at a place which seemed to consist of one long street, with pine trees overhanging a beach at the far end of it. There the sea rolls in and breaks in enormous waves, quick and regular as minute guns, and the sea line is seldom broken by a boat or a sail. It was still something of a town when Thornton passed through it on his road to Atami. Now it is all but deserted, in consequence of a cholera visitation, which killed so many inhabitants that of the rest all who could do so ran away and never returned. It is one of the few sad places in Japan.

From there to Atami the road ran up many a weary hill, and then crept along the water's edge, between the orange groves (thick with golden fruit at this time of year) and the white beaches guarded by dark pines. Beyond the white and the dark was a dazzling stretch of deepest blue, touched by the winter sun, and spreading off to the horizon to join the pale rim of the lower sky.

The days were at their shortest and coldest, and Thornton saw little of Atami itself when Kané & Co. raced him up its street to the large tea-house, which was called an hotel in the guide-book. The men rattled up to its steps in splendid form, making little jokes and laughing loud to show their mettle after the twenty miles' run. But the moment after Thornton had unpacked his length from the tiny vehicle, they ran to the water bucket and sluiced their heads well from the ladle which always floats in it. Then the straw sandals, of which they had worn out two pair that day, were loosed, and their feet also carefully bathed, while the red-cheeked maid brought them huge bowls of rice and fish, to be consumed with much noisy talk on the benches of the lower house.

But their master was led up a wide flight of stairs, slippery as glass, to the best room that the house contained, and there, warmed by the blessed hot bath always ready for the weary traveller, fed on strange foods, lighted to his couch by a scarlet lantern pierced on four sides to exhibit the different phases of the moon, he at last fell asleep on a pile of silk quilts soft enough for the real princess of the fairy tale. His slumbers were somewhat disturbed at first by the hoarse chatter of the coolies below, and by his neighbours beyond the next partition wall. They were two men playing a game of "Gobang," and the shadows of their heads went bobbing up and down, backwards and forwards, across the thin white paper of the screens, the light changing and merging them into one for a moment, and then some sudden movement throwing them far apart.

At last they too were still, and Thornton slept and dreamt the long weary dreams of the man who has worked too hard.

II

THE next day burst in a blaze of cold sunshine, white
snowfields, blue sea, and bluer sky, such as made Thornton cover his eyes for a moment when he first looked
out on its intolerable brightness. Snow had fallen in
the night, but now there was not a fleck in the sky or a
cloud on the sea, except the grey plume of smoke which
has hung, since the world began, over Vries Island,
lying far out on the horizon opposite the entrance to
Tokyo Bay.

Thornton was enchanted with the sharp beauty of
the winter morning. It stirred his young blood, and
brought back memories, faint already, of his northern
home. There was a divine strength and freshness in
the still, crystal air. He leaned far out to breathe it
in, and gazed across sloping, terraced roofs, to where
the sea, one dimpling sheet of diamond and sapphire,
laughed softly in the morning sun.

Then he became aware of the strong, humming note
of a samezin near by, and turning his head, caught
sight of a pretty bit of domestic life going forward on
the balcony of another inn, standing at right angles to
his own, on the opposite side of the deep, straggling
street, which led, between crowding houses, down to the
beach. The balcony was on the second floor and on a

level with the one on which he stood, so that he could take in every detail of the opposite apartment. It was all wide open, the screens being pushed back to let in the whole glorious morning, for nowhere in the world is there a race that so feeds on fresh air as the Japanese. But that was evidently not enough to satisfy the lodger over the way, so she had come out on her balcony to sit in the sunshine, while the village hair-dresser woman, with a face of extreme solemnity, pre-pared to make her beautiful for the day. As that is a long business, the young lady had brought out a pile of bright-coloured cushions, on which she had seated her-self, and was beguiling the hour with her samezin. Thornton could hardly see her face, though she sat a few yards away from him in the vivid morning light. Her head was bent, and her hair, a flood of darkness, was spread over her on every side, and lay on the ground in heavy, dusky heaps. Evidently the most tedious part of the ceremony was over — the careful washing and cleansing of those long locks, and now the sun's help was required to dry them before they could be coaxed into some wonderful wing-and-bow structure on their owner's head. The brilliant flower pattern of her robe broke through that black mantle as she moved; and a hand and arm, strangely fair for a girl of her race, held the guitar, whose long white bridge contrasted sharply with the dark strands that blew softly across it, as the breeze lifted now one and now another in its silent play.

Behind her in the room a bronze vase stood near

the wall on a low step, before a hanging scroll painted with reeds and a few bold ideographs containing a poem. On a red lacquer stool, halfway to the window, some brass cups caught the sun and made coruscations of light, which cast a fleeting pattern over the soft wheat-coloured mats; some rich garments were spread on a gilt clothes-screen in one corner.

The hairdresser was crouching just within the opening, pounding some oil and perfume in a bowl; and on a silk cloth, close to her hand, were laid all the pins and wires and ornaments which she would require for the completion of her task. Neither she nor the lady had condescended to notice an inquisitive stranger gazing at them from across the street; and nobody but a stranger would have glanced twice at such an everyday sight as that of a woman having her hair dressed in the open air.

But John Thornton glanced more than twice, and found in long after years that every detail of the pretty picture had been imprinted deeply in his memory. Perhaps his mind was in a more freshly receptive mood than usual, stimulated by change and rest and the sparkling winter weather; he had often watched such scenes in his travels to and fro; but here there was something new, which struck his quick perception at once, although he could not name it in the first moment. There was a touch of fearless grace in the girl's movements, a certain proud strength of outline in her pose, which is rare among Japanese women. Her arm, white and firm, was suddenly lifted to sweep aside her blinding hair; as she pushed it from her brow she raised her head and shook the tresses together, leaning back, and looking out and upward at the morning world.

Then Thornton saw a broad white forehead with the hair growing low in five downward points, eyes dark and full, and a mouth whose proud lips of vivid red were the only touch of colour in the face. The chin was round as a child's, but dimpled by the cleft of power; the skin, in its clear translucence, showed almost bluish in the shadows of cheek and throat. The whole countenance was far more beautiful in its pure strength than the delicately vapid one which the Japanese uphold as the highest type of their countrywomen's loveliness.

Thornton, always able to weigh his impressions, decided that she was a merchant's daughter; indeed, the samezin alone would have shown that she was not a great lady, as the instrument is never seen in aristocratic hands. Also, though she seemed to be surrounded with some luxury, there was no sign of the state which waits on a noble's child.

Suddenly the young man remembered where he had seen women strong and fair like this one, with those same wide clear eyes. It was among the wrestlers' wives in the camps, that gathered the population of a district round them to watch their feats of skill. The type was unmistakable; but why was the girl here, away from any of her clan, in flowery garments instead of in the staring blue and white cotton which was always the uniform of the tribe? He began to be interested in the question of her identity, and softly withdrew a pace or two into the shade of his window, watching for some clue to the situation.

It was not long in coming. The attendant had finished her preparations, and had just begun with her rough comb to divide the girl's hair into various strands, when a scraping sound reached Thornton's ears, and he saw the screens within the room pushed back to admit a tall, middle-aged man, evidently the girl's father. He had a heavy, anxious face, and his eyes seemed to search the corners of the room as he entered. But the colouring — the type — were such as left no doubt of his close relationship to the girl on the balcony.

She turned her head as he entered, and, rising from her low seat with a rapid movement, went a few steps towards him, and then prostrated herself at his feet, her hands describing a semicircle on the floor, and her hair again veiling her face. Thornton did not catch the greeting which passed, but in an instant she had risen again, and, standing beside the man, began to pick some loose bits of wadding off the sleeve of his coat with easy familiarity. Then he came with her to the window, and, pointing to the hairdresser, evidently signified that she was to proceed with her work, for the girl resumed her seat on the cushions, the woman her post behind her, while the father dropped into a Hong Kong chair, left by some passing foreigner, and gravely proceeded to fill his pipe from the green leather pouch in his sash.

There was silence for several minutes, and a very delicate whiff of smoke was wafted across the street to

Thornton, where he stood in the shadow of his doorway. Then the man spoke in the strident voice so common among Japanese men ; every word was audible.

"It is a good day, O Tora san, but cold — yes, cold. My brother has written a letter."

"Is it honourably so ? " replied O Tora, with a polite raising of the eyebrows. Then she took up her small mirror, and examined her complexion critically. The glass was evidently a so-called magic one, for as she turned it Thornton saw the pattern on its back, a character meaning happiness, thrown in full light on the wall behind her.

"He says he is coming to make me a visit here."

O Tora's father brought out the words in jerks, as if he did not like them.

"Why did he never come before ? " asked the girl, looking up from her mirror with a quick glance of curiosity, and then wincing as the hairdresser gave a fierce twist to one of her coils.

"Ah," replied the man, "that is a good question. Why did he never come before ? "

"And," went on O Tora, shaking off the woman's hand and leaning forward, "why did he not come when we were in our house in Tokyo ? Here he will cost you much money ; at least, fifty sen a day. That is not brotherly behaviour, Otott san."

"He will cost me more than that," said her father, gloomily, and then he stopped balancing his chair, and tapped the ashes out of his pipe on the edge of the balcony.

Thornton had now no doubts left as to the wrestler origin of both these people. The father had the heavy form of the race, the round arms, where unheard-of strength hides iron muscles under a surface smooth and white as the neck of a girl. But there was no other indication; the distinctive dress was replaced by the ordinary dark robe and girdle of the well-to-do merchant; the original shock of hair had been trained to lie close to the head, and there was not a spark of the wrestler's fire in the man's troubled eyes.

By some tacit consent no more was said by either O Tora or her father for a full half-hour. The hairdresser is always a gossip, and affairs are best kept to the family, after all. At last she had done, and the top comb was put in and surmounted by an enormous chrysanthemum carved in gold-coloured tortoiseshell. O Tora looked at it gravely in her mirror, and nodded her head in satisfaction. Then out of a purple brocade purselet she took some infinitesimal sum, which the other received with profound politeness. There was a series of finely gradated bows, the inferior head always remaining some inches lower than that of higher rank, and then the hairdresser departed. Thornton hoped now to hear the end of the colloquy, but he was disappointed, for the man sauntered slowly back into the room, and O Tora, waiting to let him pass, ran the window screens together, not without a perceptible pause just before they met. The pause allowed her a long and satisfactory gaze at the tall foreigner on the other balcony, of whose existence she had pretended to be

quite unconscious till now. He came out into the sunshine and smiled boldly at her as she stood, a hand on
either screen, in the narrow opening. But a quick
frown gathered on her brow, and she drew back and
shut the screens with a click, that sounded sadly final
to her admirer over the way.

III

THORNTON turned quickly, and ran downstairs and out into the street. Another sound had attracted his attention — a long, low rumble, like the first news of earthquake visits; the house shook to its foundations, and then a deafening roar was followed by volumes of smoke pouring down the street, and bringing with them choking fumes of sulphur that hung heavy on the air. The great geyser which bursts up in the village square was performing its duty with much punctuality; and it was Thornton's first opportunity of witnessing the portent, because he had been happily asleep when it last called at six in the morning. Four times in the twenty-four hours does the burning deep send a gasp to the upper air in that strange place, and with it comes a torrent of boiling sulphurous water, which is caught in various canals and distributed to all the hot baths in the town; but the steam is collected in a large hall for the benefit of consumptive patients, who sit round on benches, and greedily drink in the mephitic blast, the very breath of the pit. Those who live there feel, of course, that life would be impossible without a good working geyser; and great is the dismay when, as occasionally happens, something goes wrong with the works down below. Then the boiling spring ceases to flow, and only dry rumblings are heard for many days, perhaps ten or twelve, and nobody has a hot bath in all the town, for they have come to depend entirely on nature's steam apparatus. But at last the demons at the mouth of the burning lake below slide back the red-hot hatches that have kept the terror under, and it breaks out in a roar like a thousand geysers in one, and goes on pouring out those scalding streams for days and nights together, till all the reservoirs are flooded, and there is hot water enough to wash Africa white. And at last, deep troughs have to be laid for it down the street, into the sea, whence it came at first.

Thornton stood gazing at the stone-lined opening long after the outburst had subsided. His fancy was following it down to its lurid home, when, through the steam which still hung about, he caught sight of a flowered skirt pausing before the open counter of a confectioner's shop, a little higher up the road. He strode towards it, and in an instant found himself standing beside O Tora san, who was apparently making up her mind about her purchases before entering the shallow doorway. She turned quickly when the Englishman stopped beside her, and that line between her eyebrows deepened when she recognised him. He was quite composed, and looked frankly into her face, which pleased him better now than when he had seen it across the street. He began to speak at once, in fluent Japanese with a barbarous accent.

"If the young lady would buy sweets, there is a finer shop farther on. Those things are not good enough for her."

The girl bowed gravely, and at once turned and began to walk on, her clogs ringing sharply on the stones. Thornton again came to her side.

"Not this way," he said; "may I have the honour of showing the O Jōsan the better shop? It lies quite near."

"Is it yours?" she asked, looking puzzled at his pertinacity.

"No," he answered, smiling down at her as they stood together in the sunshine. "I, too, am a stranger here, like the young lady and her father."

"Well," she said indifferently, "it is of no importance. I have no money with me to buy sweet things now. I have forgotten to bring any."

"I must buy some, however," said Thornton; "will you not come with me and speak to the Kashiya? He will not understand my Tokyo Japanese."

Then she smiled, and a beautiful dimple showed in her smooth cheek.

"Yes," she said, with less constraint in her tone, "the country people are very rough and dull. They laugh at us because we speak properly, and we sometimes cannot understand them. I will help you to buy your cakes."

Thornton bowed gravely, and together they began to walk slowly up the street, he looking before him stolidly, for fear of frightening away his new friend; she glancing at him from under her eyelashes, and taking in, as only a woman can, every detail of his foreign costume, his quiet face, and close-cut hair. She was in reality greatly excited and interested, for he was the first foreigner to whom she had ever spoken; but it would have been against all the laws of good manners to show such feelings; and laws of manners in Japan are the most stringent and the best-observed laws in the world.

They stopped before an alluring show of brightly coloured cakes, laid out in little trays, and protected from the flies by a smiling woman with a rustling paper flybrush, while a fat baby on her back looked out solemnly on the universe from her right shoulder.

"Which shall I take?" asked Thornton, simulating profound perplexity.

"Are they for your honourable children?" inquired O Tora san.

"Oh, no," he replied, laughing, "I have no children. These are for me; I like cakes."

"Then," she said, "take those, and those," pointing to some weird pink and yellow lumps; "they are good for strong men."

"And which are good for pretty ladies?" he asked.

She glanced quickly at him and then spoke to the woman, who turned and drew out a drawer from the wall, in which sugar flowers lay on sheets of thin paper, lilies and peonies and plum blossoms, beautiful to behold.

Thornton picked out a sample collection, inwardly wondering upon what lines the constitutions were constructed which could assimilate such alarming compounds; a symmetrical parcel was made up and tied with straw twist, a nice loop being provided for the finger; and then the shopkeeper, beaming with joy at being some two and a half farthings the richer for the sale, bowed her farewell, and they turned away.

"Not that way!" exclaimed Thornton, as the girl set her face towards the inn. "Will you not show me the road to the Temple? I am a stranger and alone."

Such an appeal could not be refused outright. O Tora san hesitated, and then looking up, said:—

"You speak our language too well for a stranger. Can you really not find your way to the Temple?"

"I am sure I cannot. I shall certainly get lost!" he declared with conviction.

"Then I will come a part of the way," she said, "but I must not stay too long."

"Just till we see the roof," he pleaded. "It is very kind of you to help me. Are you staying long in Atami, O Tora san?"

"No, not long. But how do you know my name?" she asked quickly.

"I heard it from the inn-keeper," he answered vaguely; "a beautiful name. Mine is hard to speak. I am called John Thornton. Can you say that?"

"No, I am sure I cannot," she replied. "I can say the first half, Tchan, but not the other. My father can pronounce all the foreign names," she added with pride. "He has a silk shop on the ginza, and many strangers come there to buy."

"Is he ill, your honourable father?" inquired Thornton, who could not fit the silk shop into his theories about the girl's origin.

"Yes," she said, "he has headaches, and cannot sleep, or eat, and so we came here for the good air. But he will not get better, I fear, for his brother is coming to see him, and he is sorry."

"Why is he sorry?" asked Thornton, surprised at her frankness.

"I do not know," she said. "There! that is the way to the Temple."

They were on the outskirts of the town, and she pointed to a sheet of snow on whose farther verge rose a little hill fringed with dark pines, and crowned by a heavy mass of brilliant green. From beneath the foliage dull grey gables showed dimly, and here and there the sun caught a fleck of ruined gold.

"I see," said Thornton, "but it is a long way off, and you will not care to walk through the snow. I can find it another day, now that you have shown it to me. May I walk home with you, and will you tell me the story of the Temple and the boiling spring?"

"Gladly," said O Tora, turning to go home by his side. She seemed quite reconciled to his companionship now, and looked up at him from time to time, as she told the strange old tale.[1] In sadder days that hour came back to him many a time in vivid reality — the dazzling brightness of the morning, the crisp air, the sharp sound of O Tora's clogs on the rough village street, while her strong low voice told the story of the

[1] See "A Diplomatist's Wife in Japan."

place; and at every pause the long roll of the sea on
the lower beaches came in as a kind of deep refrain that
made the rest more true.

To the man, too, there was the joy, momentary perhaps,
but real, of the close presence of a woman, beautiful in
his eyes, and magnetic to him in the highest degree. As
she told the story he listened to every word, but seemed
to be trying to catch the first faint note of another story,
in which they too were to be actors together. But the tale
that O Tora san told John Thornton was a strange old
legend of prayer and sacrifice, of an old priest's love for
his flock and of his people's gratitude.

When the story ceased they had reached the door
of the inn, walking more and more slowly as they
approached it.

"It is a beautiful story," said Thornton, looking into
her face, "and beautifully told. I thank you, O Tora
san, for so much kindness. When may I see you
again?"

"I do not know," she said gravely, "it is I who
thank you. You are the first foreigner I have ever
spoken to. Good-bye."

"Please allow me to offer the cakes to your honourable father," said Thornton, proffering the small parcel;
"and please also ask him if I may come and see you."

She shook her head doubtfully, and then bent low
in thanks for the present. But she smiled at the last,
and he went back to his breezy rooms with a light heart
and an absurd and unaccountable sense of gain. The
superstitious say that it is a certain forerunner of loss.

IV

THE early winter twilight had set in, and the wind whistled coldly up from the sea, grey and dim now, with one angry line of surf breaking white on the deserted shore. Nowhere does the Pacific boom more loudly and continuously than on the Atami beaches. At first one cannot sleep for that ever returning wave, breaking with a crash of battle on the strand and thundering its echoes through a hundred caves along the cliffs; but soon the ocean music becomes a part of consciousness, the voice of a friend, pursuing the ear for many miles inland; at last it dies away, and then it is as when the music stops in the midst of a dance : people gaze at each other puzzled, and then slink back to their places with a sense of loss—for that which was never theirs.

Thornton had liked the sea song in the hopeful morning hours, but now in the winter twilight it seemed to him the saddest of dirges. He was sitting in his little room with all the shutters closed to keep out the cold wind. A fierce lamp was burning on a small table, strewn already with books and papers, for Thornton could never keep his brain off work for twenty-four hours. Having come here to rest, he had sketched out a programme of study and business which would occupy his three weeks very pleasantly. At least so he had thought, but when he finally sat down to his translation of a Japanese novel, he found that he was restless, the lamp was in the wrong place, he had forgotten to bring his favourite dictionary, and the "hibachi" smelt of charcoal. Then his thoughts went back to his neighbours, to that girl, with her broad brow and wide dark eyes, to the father's troubled face ; and a thousand questions presented themselves to which there was no possible answer.

At last he pushed his books away from him, and they slid with a rustle to the mats from off the other side of the narrow table. He went round and picked them up with all due respect, and then crossed to the window and opened it, letting in an icy breath from the outer air. His lamp flamed high in the draught, so he blew it out quickly. Then in the darkness he returned to his window, whence he had again caught sight of the room in the opposite house.

It was characteristic of John Thornton that he paused to put on his overcoat before taking up his watch for what would happen. With his collar turned up, his hands in his pockets, he stood where he had stood in the morning ; but instead of finding answers to his surmises, he saw that which stimulated his curiosity to the highest point. O Tora and her father were sitting in a room somewhat nearer to his vision than the one she had occupied in the morning. The screens had several glass panes let into their divisions, but one was quite pushed aside in spite of the sharp air. Through it he saw that they were seated on the mat, near a charcoal fire, on which a bronze kettle was simmering. Between them was a low table, and on it was an Abacus, the counting machine on which the Japanese do all their reckoning. The man was apparently doing the same sum over and over again, and Thornton could hear the clatter of the little wooden balls as he knocked them with his long nails backwards and forwards along the wires. Three times did he come to some conclusion, for he looked up and spoke to the girl, and she leant over the table with a troubled face and seemed to be asking a question. Then he would begin again, counting, adding, subtracting, till at last he pushed the frame from him and leant back against the wall, his head sunk on his chest, evidently in deep depression. Then O Tora spoke, and Thornton could hear the words distinctly now, for his ear had become accustomed to the night air and the sound of the sea.

"It is a great sum, father! Will the manufacturer not wait a little?"

"He has waited long already," said the man, raising his head and speaking loud, because O Tora had crossed the room and was preparing to bring him his pipe. "I have promised to pay interest; but he does not care. He, too, has creditors waiting for him. I am a ruined man."

"Oh, surely not, Otott san!" the girl exclaimed, coming towards him quickly; "there is much silk in the shop. It will bring more than five hundred dollars if you sell it."

"Only half is mine," he said angrily, "and that is mortgaged for its value. The rest belongs to the other partner, and he will not lend. I have tried already."

"Perhaps your brother — " O Tora began, and then stopped and ran to the balcony.

A jinriksha had rattled along the street and had pulled up with a good deal of noise at the steps of the inn. A large man slowly got out of it, and the two persons on the balcony (for the man had followed his daughter) turned quickly and disappeared from the room. They had gone down to meet the new arrival.

In a few moments they returned, conducting him with many bows to the cushion of honour, nearest to the hibachi. He was enormously large and heavy, but rather like O Tora's father in countenance, with brilliant eyes, and a jovial smile on his fat, white face. Thornton thought he could hear the beams creak as the huge figure subsided on the mats. He had removed a dark upper garment on entering the room, and the light from a flaring petroleum lamp showed the blue and white lozenges of his kimono. He was a fine specimen of the Satzuma wrestler.

Not a word was spoken till O Tora, on her knees, had served the newcomer with tea, and then her father gave some command which sent her quickly from the room.

The moment after she disappeared, the visitor placed his tea-cup on the floor, and looked up at his companion with a stern expression, quite different from his genial smile of a few moments before.

"And now, Rinzo san," he said, "will you not ask me why I came?"

"For a good and brotherly purpose, I am sure," replied the other, trying to look unconcerned, and filling up the tea-cups with a trembling hand.

"For a better purpose than yours was when you left us," said his brother. "I come to undo the wrong you did, and to offer you reconciliation and friendship from all the family."

"What am I to pay for such precious things, Kato san?" asked Rinzo, eying him suspiciously and stroking his chin. Such an offer from such a quarter seemed more dangerous than a threat.

"There is nothing to pay between brothers!"

Kato spoke as loftily as Confucius could have done.

"There will be his hotel bill," thought old Rinzo; but then he was comforted, for Kato evidently wanted something, and was disposed to be polite about it. That meant, properly managed, an advantage to Rinzo. So he began to look stern, instead of frightened, and offered his guest a fill of tobacco from his pouch with considerable dignity.

"When you ran away," began Kato, "you did what no one had done for hundreds of years — you deserted the noble profession of a wrestler to become a mere shopkeeper, a man of no account, adding up pennies and scraping farthings! Look at your arm, even now, Rinzo san, and tell me if that is the arm of a man who should be measuring silk all his days!"

Rinzo shrugged his shoulders.

"Measuring silk pleased me better than that everlasting twisting and turning with another oiled man in a ring of sand," he said, "and, besides, I could do it no more. Kokichi had crushed my foot. I am now lame."

"Well," said Kato, "it is Kokichi, our elder brother, who sends me. If he did you harm, he is ready to make up to you for it. His son Jurei has lost his wife, and Kokichi asks you to let him marry your daughter. Thus you and she will return to the clan, and all will be well."

Rinzo did not answer immediately. A few months ago he would have refused the offer as unconditionally as he dared. It is never good to quarrel with powerful relations, and the wrestlers were powerful in a rough popular way, swaying their public pretty effectually. But now there were other considerations to be taken into account. The prospect of giving his carefully nurtured daughter to be the wife of a coarse brute like Jurei had nothing alluring in it, and the wrestler's noisy, public life had always revolted him. He was a lazy man, loving peace and comfort and money; and he had deliberately broken away in search of these, when he left his family and tribe to set up a shop in the city. But lately the shop had gone badly. He was in debt — on the verge of bankruptcy — and O Tora might, perhaps, be induced to play the fine old part of the pious daughter, sacrificing herself for her parent, if there was a little money to be made by the transaction. He reflected that fortunately his brothers knew nothing of his money difficulties, so he prepared to hold back until it was made worth his while to consent.

"Kokichi no doubt means to be kind," he said, turning and meeting Kato's eyes with a pitying smile; "but I could not, of course, allow O Tora san to marry his son. She has been brought up with much care, and I am thinking of giving her to a rich merchant in the city. But why is Kokichi sending so far to seek a wife for his son? Are there no marriageable girls among our other relations?"

"Oh, yes, a few, and of course they would be only too glad to become his daughters-in-law, but, you see, in the goodness of his heart he wishes to have an alliance with you."

"The lion roars when he is hungry," thought Rinzo, but he only said: —

"I had heard that Umé Matsuida died, and that there has been trouble in the house of our other cousin, because his daughter was going blind after the smallpox. Which are the other girls whom Jurei could marry?"

"Now we shall come to business," thought the messenger.

"In truth, Rinzo san," he said, with a look of great frankness, "they are not many, and there is not one like your O Tora. She is a wrestler's daughter indeed, strong and tall and white. She and Jurei would be well matched, and you would have many handsome grand-children to wait on you when you grow old."

"I had all but promised the merchant," said Rinzo, appearing to relent, "and he was going to put some money into my business."

"How much?" asked Kato, falling into the snare.

"Five hundred yên," said Rinzo, with a gleam in his heavy eyes.

There was silence for a moment, and then Kato spoke again with a note of profound dismay in his voice.

"Five hundred yên, my brother? But it is a fortune."

"It is much money," Rinzo answered. "O Tora san is worth it, though I should not say so, she being my daughter."

"And if — Kokichi . . . offered you two hundred, would that not do as well?" inquired his brother.

But Rinzo knew the value of his wares. A wrestler's daughter must be obtained to be a wrestler's wife, otherwise the race would deteriorate. So he held firm.

"Why should two hundred do as well as five?" he asked with scorn. "Besides, my daughter is not for sale like a Geisha, and the arrangement for her marriage is almost concluded. Kokichi must look elsewhere."

"And if by any possibility Kokichi were able to pay a little more?" Kato inquired.

His instructions were to promise anything in reason, in order to secure the proper bride for Kokichi's hopeful son.

"Ah, then, of course, my brother should have the

preference," said Rinzo, with a kind smile; indeed, his heart was bounding at the prospect of saving his business.

"Of course I did not bring a large sum with me," Kato continued; "but I will see what Kokichi says."

"It will have to be now or never," replied Rinzo, yawning. "We return to Tokyo at once, and, on the whole, I think I prefer the other arrangement for the girl. After all, that young Jurei has a very bad temper, and he might make her unhappy."

"He is a dove!" cried Kato, seeing his negotiation melting away in failure, "and any girl would be happy with him. I could pay some part of the sum down, if you like."

"As you please," replied Rinzo. "Of course, that would bind me to Kokichi."

The astute trader could afford to be calm now, for he felt sure that he had succeeded.

"I could pay —" Kato hesitated.

"Yes?" Rinzo inquired soothingly.

"A hundred down, and the rest later, when I have seen Kokichi again," Kato said. "Of course it is a great deal of money."

He looked at his brother and sighed, but Rinzo was not to be moved.

"Two hundred down," he repeated firmly, "and the rest the day after to-morrow. I will wait for you here. Why do they not bring your supper? O Tora cho!" and he clapped his hands.

There was a little noise in the passage, and O Tora

pushed back the screen and bowed her head as she knelt on the threshold. When she raised it her face was very pale, and her eyes shot angry glances at the two men. Then she rose and entered, followed by the red-cheeked musume of the inn, laden with trays and little dishes. When they had been placed before the guest, O Tora slipped away, leaving the maid to wait upon him. Such a breach of family manners meant something serious, and a constrained silence followed her departure.

The conversation had lasted over half an hour, and Thornton, straining his ears to catch its import, had heard enough to make the situation clear to him. So had O Tora san, who had listened to every word of it. She knew that it would probably be about herself, and had not left the other side of the screen till it was ended. As for Thornton, he felt no more remorse for his eavesdropping than if he had been listening to two crows cawing in the elms of the compound in Tokyo. He could not regard Japanese of the lower classes as men and brothers yet.

O Tora's shadow was thrown for a moment on the white paper of a window, and a few seconds later Thornton saw a dark figure come out from the inn door and walk rapidly down the street.

He darted out in pursuit. She was walking fast, but he soon reached her side. She glanced up at him quickly, but would not stop, and he had to keep up with her.

"Whither so late?" he asked.

She did not answer except by quickening her pace. They were already in the lower part of the village, and the roar of the rollers in the bay filled the air.

"You must not be displeased with me for following you," he said, coming close to her. "It is late and cold, and your father will be angry."

The Japanese woman's instinctive obedience to a man made her pause, but she answered coldly: —

"You are a stranger; and I know what is right for me to do."

The light from a little fruit shop near flared in her face, and he saw that she looked defiant and miserable. She was in her thin house dress, with no mantle over her shoulders, no little crape hood on her hair. The wind whistled chill up the street, and she drew her sleeves down over her hands.

"I know what is right for you to do," said Thornton, with a new sense of power. A sudden pity filled his heart for this girl, shivering in the night wind, and flying from those who should have been her protectors. "Here," he said, slipping off his overcoat and putting it round her shoulders, "you have forgotten your ahori. You must wear this, and come with me to a sheltered place where you can tell me what is the matter, and how I can help you. I shall help you whether you wish it or not."

She made no resistance when he wrapped her in his heavy coat; then she looked up at him and spoke.

"You are kind. I thank you honourably. But you cannot help me. Nobody can — except the sea. I will go and throw myself into it now. But you must keep your coat."

"Why will you throw yourself into the sea?" cried Thornton, who was not prepared for such an announcement.

"Because my father sells me to Kokichi for his son. I will never marry Jurei. He is a brute — he drinks saké all day — he strangled his first wife. I will not marry a dirty, murderous wrestler!"

Then she began to shake all over, and hid her face on the rough sleeve of John's coat and wept. His heart grew hot within him.

"No, by Heaven, you shall not marry a murderous wrestler!" he repeated slowly. "Come this way," he said, taking her hand and leading her forward. "Do not let these common people see you weeping, O Tora san. Come with me."

Together they went down the steep street toward the wind and the sea. They passed a few more houses where the cheery light shone through the white screens, and shadows of mothers and children were fleeting back and forth.

One house was open, and a very old man and woman crouched by the side of the square fireplace sunk in the floor. The old man was smoking his pipe, the old woman nursed a cat in a frilled collar, and all three were staring gravely at the flame.

The little picture of humble married faithfulness

seemed to open Thornton's eyes, and in some unaccountable way showed him his road.

Then they had left the houses behind. Sand was blowing in their faces, a little salt spray, too. Under their feet were the heavy pebbles of the Atami beach, and just in front of them a long wall of angry foam thundered against the land. A little to the right was a deserted shed, whose timbers creaked in the blast. Thornton drew O Tora towards it, and made her sit down on the broken bench inside. Here they were sheltered from the wind and spray, and could speak more quietly.

John seated himself beside the girl, whom he could hardly see. He drew the coat closer, put his arm round it to keep it in place, and said : —

"You need not trouble to tell me any more, because I heard them talk. So Jurei is a murderer, and they want to make you marry him ? Why do you not refuse? They cannot force you to do it against your will. That is not lawful now."

"There is no law like a father's will," said the girl; "and they are his kinsfolk, and my mother is dead. Unless I die they will make me do it. And then he will strangle me as he strangled O Miné san, in a tipsy rage."

Thornton felt her shudder. He paused for a moment and then said : —

"Can you see me in this darkness, O Tora san ? "

"No, only a very little," she answered. "Why ? "

"I want you to look at me and tell me something,'
he said, loosing her and moving a little away. "I am a
foreigner, and I forget what I look like. If you were
my wife, would you dislike me very much?"

There was no answer and he could not see her face
in the darkness.

"Very much, O Tora san? You would not let me be
even a little kind to you?"

Suddenly she was at his feet, weeping and sobbing
for joy; and then her hands found his hands, and she
beat her forehead on them wildly, and bathed them in
tears, and held them close to her heart, so that he could
feel its happy beatings.

"Oh, you shall be as a god to me!" she cried. "I
will serve you and obey you, and use all my life to
make you happy! But I can never show you gratitude
enough. Is it really true that you are meaning to save
me from this?"

"But I am doing very little, O Tora san," said John,
stooping down and raising her face to his as she
crouched at his knees; "and by and by you will see
that, and get tired of being grateful for a small service
long past. And then will there be some love for me,
little girl? Will you be glad then to be my wife? Say
the truth, please."

A soft cheek lay on his hand for a moment, and then
she raised her head and said earnestly, in her own
strange tongue: —

"I will give you all the love and honour that can be
found in a woman's heart. And the women of my

country know how to honour their husbands.   You shall be as a god to me."

"Then," said Thornton, rising and lifting her from her knees, "let us go and talk to your father, my dear. I have a little money saved up, and I dare say that it will do quite as well as Kokichi's."

V

THORNTON's chief had been away when the young man went down to Atami in the winter; and Thornton was still in the country when Mr. Hardwicke returned, bringing Mrs. Hardwicke with him. She had not accompanied him before, having remained in England to attend to the education of her children. There was a general feeling that her coming would cause the strings of things to be tightened up to extreme propriety point, and make an end of much bachelor enjoyment in her husband's domain. She was known to be strict in her ideas, evangelically inclined, "dour," regarding heathens and papists with equal, though distinct, aversion. As a matter of fact, her horror of a Catholic was the more acute of the two.

Mr. Hardwicke, like many a man who has lived long in the East, had an easy tolerance about various details of life which run on different lines in Japan from those traced out for them in England. Many people are inclined to think that the Japanese methods are more respectable than ours, because, though they cannot wholly abolish vice in the country of the rising sun, they, at any rate, prevent scandal. As long as there was no scandal, Mr. Hardwicke had not been accustomed to inquire very closely into the private affairs of the men who worked under him, and they in turn regarded him as a kind and tactful chief, who, having passed to his present post from their own ranks, might be supposed to be more in sympathy with them than a hall-marked diplomatist fresh from Europe could possibly have been.

But Mrs. Hardwicke was quite another kind of person. There was a sort of authorised smartness about her dress, it was true, but this was evidently put on for duty's sake, and protested against by a deplorable method of doing her hair, which she brushed crudely back from a high, narrow forehead. Her eyes were brown and piercing, and her long nose turned up instead of down, a serious mistake. She had quite tamed her husband on the way out, and he greeted the men who went down to meet him at Yokohama, in a timid, deprecating way, with occasional glances at his wife, as if to make sure that she did not disapprove of some of his old favourites. It did not seem as if Mrs. Hardwicke were likely to be very popular with her husband's juniors.

About three weeks after their return, Thornton appeared, and took possession of his little bungalow in the compound. He did not come alone. The Japanese servants whom he had left behind, cook and houseboy, smiled many a smile of welcome to their fair countrywoman, whom they were told to address as okusama, and who was to be called in general, Mrs. Thornton. When they had shown her into the drawing-room, and brought her some tea, they retired to pack up their bundles and ask for a holiday at once, a holiday from which there would be no return. Who would care to serve under a Japanese mistress who would be sure to know the real value of everything?

Thornton left his wife to have her tea and explore her new house alone, while he went to report himself to Mr. Hardwicke. When he announced that he had brought back Mrs. Thornton with him, the other man rubbed his eyes and sat straight up in his deep arm-chair.

"Why, when were you married?" he asked; "you always seemed to me to be a confirmed woman-hater."

"I don't think I ever was quite that," said Thornton, slowly. "Anyway, I am converted now. I was married six weeks ago, sir, in Atami."

"Then you weren't," said Mr. Hardwicke, quickly; "no marriage is legal unless a consul is present. Who performed the ceremony? Some meddling missionary, I'll be bound."

He was angry that one of his own men should have fallen into such a mistake. Thornton's face set in very unpleasant lines.

"My wife is a Japanese lady," he said stiffly, "and we were married according to the custom of the country. We are quite satisfied."

"I have no doubt you are," Mr. Hardwicke replied with something like a sneer; "a good many Europeans get married according to the custom of the country, as you call it; but they don't have the confounded impertinence to call the lady Mrs. Jones or Mrs. Brown."

"Sir!" exclaimed Thornton, jumping up and looking dangerous.

"Well, they don't," repeated Mr. Hardwicke; "and if you take my advice, Thornton, you won't do it either. You cannot keep her in the compound. It is simply impossible. Go and take a nice little house for her outside, and I will say no more about the matter. I don't want to be hard on you, Heaven knows."

And Mr. Hardwicke sighed.

"I'll do nothing of the sort," Thornton replied; "if she is not Mrs. Thornton now, she shall be by dinnertime. I will step over to the Vice-Consulate with her at once. I dare say I ought to have thought of it before, and I am much obliged to you for reminding me of it, though you did so rather roughly, sir, and I got angry."

"I wouldn't if I were you," said Mr. Hardwicke, looking at him doubtfully; "you are sure to regret it later. You will meet a nice, pretty English girl, and then, there you'll be with that millstone round your neck. Of course, I am entirely against all such connections; but if they must be, well, keep them quiet and don't make them permanent."

Thornton rose, looking very black.

"I am much obliged for the good advice, sir," he said. "I shall hope to bring my wife to call on Mrs. Hardwicke to-morrow."

"Stupid, stupid!" sighed Mr. Hardwicke, when his visitor was gone. "A good fellow like Thornton to be caught like that! Emily would not dream of receiving her. Dear me, what a pity!"

Nevertheless he tried, being a kind man, to persuade Mrs. Hardwicke to hold out the hand of patronage to Mrs. Thornton. He glanced into the register the next day, and found there the marriage of John Thornton and O Tora Yakumichi duly entered and attested. Then he did all that he could to soften his wife's heart, hoping at any rate to extract a promise that she would not be openly rude to the alien bride, should Thornton carry out his threat of bringing her to Mrs. Hardwicke's reception that afternoon. Emily listened to his tale without a word of comment, and when it was done, she turned away her head and asked a question.

"Did you say they were married this morning, my dear?"

"This morning in the Vice-Consulate. Jimmy Hayes performed the ceremony. I believe it was his first."

Mr. Hardwicke laughed nervously. What he could see of his wife's face did not look pleased or kind.

"And you say that the Japanese marriage took place before? How long?"

"Oh, not long! A very few weeks, I think," said Mr. Hardwicke, who saw that he had told his wife too much.

"A few weeks! Oh, Robert!" Mrs. Hardwicke raised her head, and spoke in accents of reproach, "and you ask me to receive into my house these people who have been living in sin for weeks past. I am amazed at you, amazed and hurt. It is my duty as a Christian woman to show the strongest disapprobation of such goings on."

Mr. Hardwicke was roused into speaking rather severely.

"Well," he said, "perhaps you know best. I cannot say, I'm sure. But—two things strike me forcibly. I had a kind of idea that it was my house that I was asking you to receive the Thorntons in, and another kind of idea that Christian duty would lead one to help sinners into the right way, and be nice to them when they got there. But then, I am not sure that I set up to be a Christian myself."

Mrs. Hardwicke made no reply to her husband's speech, but she sat down and wrote a grim little note in the third person. It ran thus:—

"Mrs. Hardwicke thinks it right to let Mr. Thornton know that it will be quite impossible for her to receive him or the person residing in his house. Mr. Thornton's conduct is a scandal to the whole community and puts him beyond the pale of ordinary consideration."

O Tora, beautifully dressed in grey silk lined with pink, sashed in her best brown and gold obi, was sitting in her drawing-room, waiting for Thornton to take her to see Mrs. Hardwicke. He came in with a piece of paper in his hand, and she saw for the first time a look of intense annoyance on his face. In an instant she had thrown herself down on the floor, entreating in the gentlest tones for forgiveness. She was sure that she had offended him in some way, and was ready to plead guilty to every accusation except the one of having intended it.

Thornton was a man whose thoughts ran on lines of their own — special trains which did not pull up at the customary junctions. He had married O Tora almost without reflection, convinced in some unspoken argument of heart and brain that she was — his woman, no more and no less. There was no thought of intellectual companionship, no wild passion of sudden love, but just the sane, mature conviction that she was for him and he for her. If her loyalty was that of a devoted slave, his took the form of tender protection; her very ignorance and helplessness in all that touched the backbone of his life filled him with a warm chivalry of feeling for this child of strangers, whom he had brought out from among her own people to stand by his side forever.

He crumpled Mrs. Hardwicke's note into his pocket, and touched O Tora on the shoulder. She looked up quickly, and her dark eyes searched his face.

"Oh, you are not angry!" she cried joyfully. "I was so frightened! I could not live if you were angry with me," and she rose slowly to her feet.

"Why should I be angry with you, dear?" he said, returning her gaze. "You are always the same, gentle and sweet and — mine. Thank God for that!"

He drew her close to him, and felt her tremble for happiness in his caress. Then he put her a little from him, and said, smoothing a fold of her sash : —

"You look so beautiful in the new dress, O Tora, that I think we must go out to Meguro and see the plum blossoms to-day. Would you like that?"

"I would indeed," she replied, with quick gratitude;

"but will there be time after we have been to Hardwicke san's okusama?"

"We will not go to her to-day," said Thornton, "she — is not very well, I hear. Come, I will take you to Meguro."

O Tora was disappointed, but would not let him see it for a moment, and he had the satisfaction of watching her enjoy the fresh air and the gay sight in the flowery meadows, apparently with all her heart. As they sat under one of the snowy plum trees, looking out on the blue bay, with the air of spring blowing balmy in their faces, Thornton told himself that they two had no need of Mrs. Hardwicke and her visiting list, no need of anything but leave to live in this beautiful world. He cared little for society, and since his work and ambition remained to him, would live for them, and find all the solace he needed in the love and kindness of his wife. As for O Tora san, there was very little doubt as to her object in life; it was Thornton. From the moment when he saved her from marriage with her cousin, all her affection and gratitude went out to him. Where he was concerned all the strength or weakness of her character spelt one word, worship. As the sun went down over the quiet bay, her hand slipped into his and she looked up into his face and sighed for happiness.

A true Japanese wife, she never asked a question or troubled him with reasonings on matters which he must decide. He did not again refer to Mrs. Hardwicke, and a few days later told O Tora that she had better not wander about the grounds outside of their own little garden, although she could always have the "kuruma" to go out for shopping or visits. Since Mrs. Thornton was not officially recognised by the wife of his chief, he would not allow his men friends to visit her. Gradually he came to have very little to do with his colleagues except in the way of work. He had never been a sociable man, and they did not miss him greatly.

O Tora had a few friends — Japanese women of her own class — who came to see her, and whom she visited occasionally. Her father had wisely disappeared, leaving a foreman to manage the business and give vague answers to any of Kokichi's people who might come to inquire after him. O Tora often received little presents from him, and was inwardly glad that he left her alone with her husband. She could hardly believe in her own good fortune when she found that Thornton had no parents to be waited on, and that her married life would be free from that hourly slavery to a mother-in-law, which is the hardest part of a Japanese woman's existence.

"You are happy, indeed, O Tora san," her friends would cry. "Nobody but Thornton san to wait on. I wish I were you."

"Yes, I am happy," O Tora would reply, with deep conviction; and yet — it hurt her to see that the great lady of the place turned her head the other way when she passed her in the grounds, and took less notice of her than she did of the rough country women who were called in in numbers, about this time, to help the gardeners in relaying the turf on the lawns.

The disfavour of her relations — the wrestlers — troubled her less than it did her father. Thornton was such a tower of strength, the flag under which he served such a panoply of safety, that fear seemed pure foolishness.   Who could frighten or hurt her now ?

Months passed on; the plum blossoms were long gone by; pink cherry clouds and purple trails of wistaria were things of the past; July, hot and blazing, had opened all the red and white lotus cups in the ponds, and the scarlet death-lilies were blowing on every green bank.   The weather was warmer than usual for the time of year, and O Tora began to look weary, and pale with a pallor quite different from her usual clear whiteness.

"You have been doing too much, little woman," said Thornton, one breathless evening, as they sat on their verandah in the short twilight.   "I shall have to forbid you to go near the kitchen in this warm weather.   The cook is quite capable of managing by himself, and you shall not make yourself ill."

"The cook is a good man," said she, fanning away a huge humming insect of some sort that came blundering out of the jessamines at her side.   "But he is extravagant if I do not look after him ; and why should I let him spend your money uselessly ?"

Thornton's expenses had diminished by half since he had brought this little sinner into his house.

"Besides," she went on, looking at him proudly, "you are much better and stouter since I took care of your food.   That is a joy to me."

"Do you ever think of yourself, my dear?" he asked, putting back a little stray lock which had crept down to her cheek.

"Very often, to remember how happy I am, and what an easy life I have," she answered. "Oh, I am sorry for my friends who have unkind mothers-in-law. But may I really ask for something for myself?"

"Of course. What is it? Why did you not tell me before?"

It suddenly struck him that he was taking all her devotion and giving her very little in return. Was he becoming a selfish brute, like so many men he knew?

O Tora mistook the feeling, which made him look grave, and said earnestly: —

"It does not matter; pray, do not be angry; I want nothing."

"Oh, please understand, dear girl," he burst out, "that it is my greatest pleasure to give you what you want. You must know that by this time. I am only sorry that you did not speak before."

"You are kind," she said, reassured; "then — this is what I desire, if I can have it. To go for a little to the country, to live in a Japanese house, away from the brick walls, and to see woods and rice-fields. I want to feel the soft mats under my feet, and to open all the rooms to the fresh breeze. Ah, it is beautiful in a Japanese house in summer; though, of course," she added politely, "European houses are far the best — really."

"You poor little thing," said her husband, looking at her, "I believe you are half-choked in our stuffy rooms — all carpets and upholstery. And you do not look well, dear; what is it? You used to be so strong and bright, like a white lotus with a lamp inside. Now it is the lotus without the lamp. And you tremble for the least thing. What is wrong? Tell me."

He drew his seat closer to hers, and put his arm across her shoulder, turning her face to his; she looked very troubled, and was really trembling.

"Do not speak of the flower of death," she said; "what an evil omen!"

"Rubbish!" said Thornton, laughing; "I don't believe in omens. But tell me true, O Tora, you are not unhappy? Would you rather — no, I won't ask that, and you shall not be troubled with questions. Of course I will take you away at once. It is getting frightfully hot here; I ought to have thought of it sooner. Where shall we go?"

"Would your friend lend us his house at Dzushi?" she suggested; "he is not using it this summer."

This was a cottage on the seashore, belonging to a friend of Thornton's — a European working at the university. He had once invited him to bring O Tora down for the day. The place was remote, sheltered, free, and the sea rolled to the garden steps.

So to Dzushi they went. It was sufficiently near to Tokyo for Thornton to get backwards and forwards, as his presence there was required for work; and he was thankful to get O Tora out of the inimical atmosphere which seemed to hang round Mrs. Hardwicke. Her treatment of his wife had inflicted a terrible wound on the man's pride; and though he told himself that she had less to do with his life than the snow on the summit of Fuji, yet he felt sick and sore when he saw her pass in her pretty carriage, carefully looking away from his little house. He thought that O Tora must feel the insolent neglect as keenly as he did, and was glad when a great stretch of country was put between them.

She brightened up at once in the soft sea air, and the return to her own way of life gave her hourly pleasure. The cottage at Dzushi stood on a kind of dune, where the sand was held together by a group of old pine trees, whose dark arms had tossed and waved through a hundred years of storm and sunshine. The few rooms all looked to the sea, and as one entered the little dwelling a perfect view of Fuji filled the eye — Fuji across the bay, Fuji through the pine branches, Fuji beyond the crested rollers of the shore, ever present like a loved ideal in a sheltered life.

A few hardy flowers grew by the doorstep, and under the pines the grass was green; but with all that sea and sky there was little need for a garden. It was enough joy to sit in the pine shade and drink in the song of the ocean in the morning sun, or at night to count the stars gathering in ones and twos to crown the silent mountain; and then to fathom the faint mystery of the moonrise, and let the spirit wander away to paradise on the silver bridge, without pier or stay, hung between earth and heaven.

Thornton saw it all.   To O Tora the beauty was second nature; her dower and inheritance, sweet and unmysterious as a parent's smile.   But for him it was different.   He felt the delicate edge of all this loveliness with a keen aching of appreciation which she could never know.   To a tongue-bound poet such indescribable perfection causes a thrill of joy too sharp to be separated from pain.

One divine evening they were standing on their doorstep, silent in the hush of the sunset.   O Tora slipped her hand into her husband's and said, with her eyes on the sea:—

"Do you remember the winter night and the wind roaring round the shed on the beach at Atami?"

"Indeed I do," he said, as his fingers closed round hers.   "How you cried, poor little soul.   But there was perfect peace as soon as we understood each other, wasn't there?"

"Perfect peace," she replied; "and how good you were to me.   I have never shed another tear since."

"And you never shall, my dear — you never shall."

But who was he to promise away the decrees of fate?

VI

It was the end of September and the days were beginning to draw in, the nights were growing chill, and the time had come for Thornton to get back to Tokyo and stay there.

"We must move home next week, O Tora," he said one morning, "but I shall go first and get the house put in order before you come. I cannot have you over-tiring yourself now. Shall you be afraid to stay alone for a few days?"

"Not afraid, but sorry," she said, in her direct way. "May I not come? I will promise to be very lazy, and to let Kiku do all the work."

"No," said he, "Kiku will stay here and take care of you, and when everything is nice and pretty I will come back and fetch you."

Kiku was a maid whom O Tora's father had sent to her just before they came to Dzushi. She was a member of the clan, a kind of poor relation, and proud to wait on O Tora, whom she now regarded as quite a great lady.

"Very well," said O Tora, in answer to her husband's remark. "Of course it will be best if you wish it. Only please do not be long."

"Perhaps only a day or two," he said as he moved off, for he was starting to catch a train at the little station some three miles away, "and you must keep Kané to guard the house. I will tell the policeman to take extra care of you."

"There is so little to steal," said O Tora to herself as she turned back into the house, "why should my husband speak to the policeman? But it will be very lonely."

And so she found it when, a few days later, Thornton carried out his intention, and left her and Kiku by themselves in the cottage on the dunes. Kané pulled him to the station and did not return till very late, having stopped to enjoy himself at more than one tea-house in the little town after his master had departed. There was a festival of some kind going on there, and the place was full of shows and processions. Kané had stood a long time to watch some wrestlers performing their feats of strength, had talked to the people in the ring, and had taken a little more saké than was good for him.

"Has Kané not come back?" O Tora asked of her maid, as the latter began to close the shutters round the lonely house at twilight.

"Yes, he has come back," the woman replied, "and much running must have made him tired, for he has gone to sleep on the kitchen doorstep, and I cannot wake him up."

"Much saké," said O Tora, shaking her head. "You must get him to come inside, and then shut the amados, Kiku. This is the first night we have been without the danna san,[1] and there are thieves everywhere."

[1] The master.

So the wooden shutters were rattled into place all round the fragile fortress; but O Tora kept one doorway open to the sea and Fuji till all the stars came out, and the mountain was less than a cloud on the shadowy horizon. Kané was sleeping heavily on the earth floor of the kitchen, and Kiku was rattling her pots and pans in the tiny wash-house behind the bathroom.

The night was very still, and the roar of the sea beyond the steps most musical and regular. The village was hidden behind a spur of the dunes, and no sound came from thence. O Tora, standing in her doorway, turned and looked back into the narrow room, where Kiku had lighted a rather unsuccessful paraffin lamp. It seemed hot and close inside. O Tora was not really at all timid or frightened at the loneliness. She had looked grave when she spoke to the servant, in order to prevent her from running off to gossip in the village. For herself she had no fears, and sauntered slowly along the path under the pine trees, and, when she reached the end, sat down on one of the stone steps which led to the beach, and mused in the gathering darkness.

The danna san must have finished dinner by this time, she thought, and would be sitting smoking in their favourite corner of the verandah, sheltered by the jessamine of the trellis from all curious eyes. The jessamine would be over-blown now, and all the other creepers would be rioting wildly after the late rains. How bitter sweet the pine boughs smelt with the salt wind blowing over them, for a wind had arisen which was driving little rags of cloud across the sky and the near sea, where she could see it was whipped into foam. Suddenly she sat up straight, and listened with straining ears. Some one was talking in low tones on the other side of her pine tree.

"There is only a maid in the house. I made the kurumaya so drunk to-day that he must be asleep on the road."

"Still, we do not want noise and screaming," said another voice, which was not quite unfamiliar to O Tora's ears. "Better go quietly to the front door and say we have come with a message. Once inside she will give us all she has to get rid of us."

O Tora remembered the voice now. It was that of Kato, the uncle who had visited her father in Atami. She was terribly frightened, and the blood was beating in her ears and darkening her sight; but she kept her presence of mind and sat motionless, knowing that her one chance of safety lay in escaping their notice now, and in flying to the village the moment that they entered the house. Then rough tones fell on her ear as the second man replied to his companion.

"I do not want all she has. I want her. Her father took my money, and then gave her to this devil of a foreigner."

"Suppose she won't come, Jurei?" sneered the other. "You cannot marry her by force, and if you try, you will get into fine trouble. Remember Gojiro, who was beheaded for killing a foreigner."

"Be quiet," said the rougher voice, with anger in its tones. "I mean to kill no one. She is not a foreigner. I want my wife."

"Much better take her money and make off," said Kato. "We must say we came to collect a debt. Her father owes it to us. Come on."

At that moment Kiku came to the door, and stood looking out.

"Okusama, mistress!" she cried anxiously. "It is cold. Come in."

The two men glanced round, hesitating for an instant, and then went boldly up the garden path and confronted her. O Tora heard a scream and a slight scuffle, and then she herself had dropped on the soft sand, and was running for her life in the direction of the village. The men would not harm Kiku. It was herself they had come to seek. Running was painful over the heavy sand, and her heart was beating to bursting point; but she kept on bravely, knowing that safety lay before her. Then, looking back, she thought that she saw a dark form chasing her on the distant sands. If they sighted her she was lost. The storm seemed to be rising now, and the wind was beating her back.

Then the cunning of a hunted animal came to her aid. She turned aside and plunged into a deep sand-hole under an overhanging ledge, fringed with gritty long-tailed weeds. There she pulled the creepers down over her, and shovelled the grey sand in loose heaps over her feet and skirts, and hardly dared to breathe for fear of shaking it off. But she was safe. There were long stretches of these ledges along the border of the dunes, and the men would not think of searching that particular spot. She was almost covered, too, and they might have passed close to her without seeing her. As it was, they came pounding along the crest of the dune, not two feet from where the sea grass waved above her head. She heard their angry voices, felt the ground shake under their feet, and narrowly missed being buried indeed, for a heavy fragment of the over-hanging ledge gave way with a soft rushing noise and fell just beyond her, scattering her sand nest with dust and pebbles. Her poor heart stood still then, and an icy shudder went through her, followed by a sword of such pain that it wrung a sharp scream from her white lips. The wind was shrieking shrilly now and drowned the cry. Then she lay for what seemed hours in the darkness, and once and again that sword went through her; again she heard voices and footsteps, but lay still as a buried shell till she recognised Kiku's tones calling for her. Then, slowly and with gasps, she freed herself from her rough shelterings and staggered to her feet. The others saw her and rushed to catch her in their kind faithful arms, Kiku, and the benevolent policeman, and, very shamefaced in the background, Kané, carrying an enormous lantern.

.   .   .   .

So Thornton's little daughter was born just before sunrise on the last morning of September, when the sea was rosy with the coming day, and the storm had gone off in the train of night, leaving one small blind wind to bring the first sobbing, shuddering breaths to the tiny lungs, the untried lips, of the little creature just dowered with immortality.   There he found them, mother and child, when he came rushing down from Tokyo in an agony of apprehension, bringing nurse and doctor to watch over his treasures.   The colour had already come back to O Tora's lips, but her eyes looked dark and frightened, and she could hardly greet Thornton when, pushing every one aside, he burst into the room and knelt down beside her where she lay low on the mats, the tiny crimson bundle on her arm.

"Forgive me," she pleaded, looking up in his face, "my lord must forgive me, it is only a girl."

"Oh, you blessed little goose," he cried, trembling all over, "as if I cared, so long as you are safe.   Come into my arms, the pair of you, and stay there forever."

Then happy tears welled up in O Tora's eyes, and Thornton gathered her and the little one somehow into his arms, and sat there rocking them a little and crooning over the two as his mother had crooned over him long years ago in the grey north country.   And when the Angel of Thanksgiving at the gate of Heaven bids him remember the crowning moment of earth's bliss, he will think, but hardly dare to speak, of that one, when he sat for a long sweet hour on the floor of the poor little house at Dzushi, holding wife and child to a heart that seemed full to breaking with happiness.

Perhaps it was due to the unmixed air of love and kindness in which they breathed, perhaps to the clearness of those early autumn days and the constant floods of pure sunshine which set the little cottage a-blaze with golden warmth, that mother and babe seemed to gain strength every hour, and all danger from the somewhat premature birth of the child appeared to have passed away. The doctor came down to look at them for the last time, and gave Thornton his formal permission to bring them up to Tokyo.

"Wrap them well up, and get to town early in the day — the evenings are bitter," he said, looking at O Tora critically.

"But I am so strong, doctor," said O Tora, who laughed at the idea of being coddled, "and we have the windows open to the sea all day here."

"Tokyo is not Dzushi," said the doctor, shortly. "Don't let me hear of your catching cold."

So one golden October day the little party, increased by one, slipped back to its old quarters in the compound. In the shortening days the warm cosy rooms looked inviting enough; but John and O Tora had left Dzushi with regret, with a kind of nameless fear that such peace would not return. The baby — happy mite — had no such fears. Mother's bosom, father's arm, the dear light to stare at, and the kind darkness to sleep in, these were all that the baby wanted, and she did not know that she had, besides, undisputed sway over the whole household, from danna san down to Kané, who had been pardoned his delinquencies and taken back into grace at O Tora's especial prayer. He himself had quite forgotten his sins, and when he was allowed to carry the domestic empress for a few minutes, stalked up and down in the sun, a proud man with a beautifully clear conscience. But that task generally fell on Kiku when the baby was to go outside her own garden. O Tora never showed herself; her position in regard to Mrs. Hardwicke was clear to her now; she was looked upon as a "mékaké," one who had no claim to the name and position of a wife. Even the poor baby fell under the ban. When she was about three months old, Kiku dressed her in her best, and planted herself proudly in Mrs. Hardwicke's path one morning; the little one, a dazzling flutter of colour, sat up straight on her arm and gazed at the lady with solemn eyes. But she pretended to have gone suddenly blind, and passed them without changing a muscle of her cold, hard face. The baby, frightened at the first sight of hatred, burst into cries, and the nurse ran back full of indignation to tell her mistress how ugly and disagreeable the "Number One okusama" was, and how the child had cried out at the sight of her.

"She shall not see her," O Tora exclaimed, in a sudden heat of anger; "nobody shall look cross at the danna san's baby. Do not take her out in the grounds again, Kiku."

But "danna san," thinking more of the future now, both for O Tora and the child, felt that he had not done enough to regularise their position. He reproached himself, too late, for the selfishness which had caused him to shun publicity, and take his happiness silently, as so many a man longs to do but cannot. The gentle world had mistaken his reticence for shame, his silent ways and his love of his home for the enforced privacy of a guilty life where silence as to one's sins is the only condition on which they may be overlooked. It would not have hurt him in himself, and alas, he was but pagan at heart, and cared little for scandal given to his neighbours. But his wife was more to him than any one dreamed. Her entire unasking devotion, her absolute purity of intention towards him, had kindled a great fire of love in the man's unused heart, and every ray of light and heat was focussed upon her and her child. O Tora was the first to love him in all his life since the forgotten days of infancy, and she reaped to the full the stored affections of an exceptionally strong and tender nature.

His silence as to his marriage, his apparent unsociability and love of solitude, were instinctive defences, taken up against the chattering, meddling world. It seemed to him as if his happiness would lose its bloom, O Tora herself something of her delicate, crystal simplicity, if he and she should have to throw their doors open to all comers ; if they were obliged to go day after day to weary, gossiping receptions and dinners, where their own moral atmosphere would be sucked away and absorbed in the stale air of social ambition and rivalry. Then, according to the conventional view, O Tora, a shopkeeper's daughter, would not be considered a lady, and it would only be after long years of struggling and climbing that she could gain that coveted height. He thought it all out, over and over again, and always remained convinced that the game was not worth the candle. They were happier in their obscurity.

But now it was O Tora herself who, to his amazement, protested against the situation. The insult to her baby had roused fires of wrath which no hurt to herself could have kindled. When John came in from the office on that day, she came to greet him for the first time with tearful eyes and no joy in her voice.

"What is the matter?" he cried, as soon as he saw her face, "has something happened to the child?"

"The child is well as yet, my husband," O Tora replied, with a great effort at self-control. "The child is well, but my heart is heavy lest harm come to her. The Number One okusama looked at her crossly in the garden and she wept much. I have a great fear that she may have thrown an evil charm on my daughter. We must not live near people who hate her."

Thornton ground back an imprecation which rose to his lips. The sight of his wife's trouble and little Umé's wails in the next room made him feel murderous, but he kept his composure.

"Do not be distressed, little mother," he said; "there are no charms that can harm the child. Get her to stop crying. I will come back directly."

And he strode away to find his chief. As he passed the central gate he saw two strangely dressed figures enter and turn towards his house. They were sisters of charity, popularly known as the "black sisters," and they came on little begging expeditions from time to time, to collect money for their crowded orphanage.

Many a five-dollar note had Thornton given them in times past.

He stopped for a moment to receive the sisters' greetings, and then walked back with them to his own gate, deep set in the hedge of yew and japonica. They spoke little English, and his French had never existed, so few words were said after they had asked leave to pay their respects to his *bonne dame*, but there was that in their mere presence as they paced beside him, which hushed his irritation and allayed his anger. The elder of the two Sœur St. Ephrem, had a beautiful white face, with eyes like warm stars. It was impossible to be near her without wanting to see things from her point of view. When John had shown them into his house and turned to go back and fight Mr. Hardwicke, he found to his amazement that he had no angry words left to say.

Meanwhile O Tora received the sisters with her baby in her arms. Little Umé was quiet now, safe in her rightful throne, and did not even whimper when she was smiled at and admired by the two strange ladies. O Tora, who knew nothing of Christianity, felt the soothing influence of their presence, and, full of curiosity about their work, drew them on to talk in their clear French Japanese, none the less fluent for its thin U's and Marseilles R's. Little by little, as they told of their sick people, she spoke of herself and the child, and the fright she had had lest it should have been "overlooked."

"*Mais* — Madame is not then a Christian?" Sœur

St. Ephrem exclaimed, with a sudden covetous pity illuminating her face.

"No," said O Tora, looking puzzled. "My husband has not told me to be one. He lets me go to the temple where I always went."

The sister bent towards her companion, a younger nun, who had hardly spoken yet, and said quickly, in French: —

"Then this poor lamb is not baptized! Pray, while I talk to her."

"*Bon, ma sœur,*" the little nun said, and she turned her head towards the window and obediently sent her soul to storm Heaven for a conversion.

Then, while the child fell asleep in its mother's arms, Sœur St. Ephrem spoke long and earnestly, and told O Tora the happiest things about the children's God and Mary Mother, about the eternal preciousness of the wee lambs, and of how no charm or spell could hurt those who were signed with His mark. When at last she rose to go, the young mother's heart was all aflame with hope and love, and she begged that they would come again and tell her more of the happy story. Was it all indeed true? she asked, searching the sister's face with anxious eyes. It seemed too good; surely it must be a fairy tale?

No, it was no fairy tale, but just a little bit of eternal truth brought to her that day because she was in trouble. The sister gave her a tiny medal and told her to hang it round the baby's neck as a sign of her desire that the great Mother should protect her; and she bade her take off the silly charm bags — they could neither help nor harm.

When Thornton returned (having found that he could expostulate quite gently with Mr. Hardwicke about his wife's unkindness), O Tora met him with tremulous smiles, and an eager light shining where he had seen tears an hour ago. He was pleasantly surprised when she said that she had some wonderful good news to give him.

"What is it, dear?" he asked quickly; "has your father sent you another piece of silk?"

"No, better than that," she replied confidently, "better than a thousand pieces of silk! Come and sit down by the fire, and I will tell you everything."

She was very much in earnest, and made him sit in his favourite chair while she knelt on the rug beside him. The day was nearly done, and there was only the firelight in the room; it danced and flickered cheerily as O Tora told her wonderful good news.

"Is it not beautiful?" she cried at the end. "Oh, danna san, I am so glad to be the one to tell you what will make you so happy. We will worship the children's God together, and our little Umé will grow up the best and most beautiful daughter that parents could dream of. Why do you look so grave? Are you not glad?"

Thornton had hidden his face in his hands, and his fingers were clasped tight and hard. He even groaned a little. He had done so well without any religion, he had made up his mind never to be troubled with that sort of thing, and now it was his wife, a pagan, a Japanese, who came to preach it to him! No, this must be stopped at once — he would not be unkind, but — he raised his head.

O Tora was kneeling in the firelight, with little Umé lying on her bosom. One hand held the baby fingers to her cheek, and her eyes were resting in possessive tenderness on the small face that smiled up from her arm.

"Yes, dear," said John, speaking very low, "it is good news. We will worship the children's God together."

VII

Mrs. Hardwicke had her way, as women of a certain kind generally do. She would not recognise Mrs. Thornton, and Thornton would not expose his wife to insult, so there was nothing for it but to take her away and live elsewhere.

"I should think you could easily find a nice little house quite near," said Mr. Hardwicke, delighted to have come to anything like a solution of the difficulty, "and you can claim allowance for rent, of course. Your bungalow really should be occupied by the other two men as it is."

"Thanks, sir, you are very kind," said Thornton; "but I shall not think of claiming any allowance. I have brought you my resignation."

Mr. Hardwicke bounded on his chair.

"My dear fellow," he began, "but this is madness. When you are getting on so well, too. I'll move you down to one of the ports if you really wish to leave Tokyo. I cannot let you break your neck like this. It is perfectly absurd, just because —"

He stopped, flushed and angry.

"Yes, it is just because," replied John, wearily; "it would be the same wherever I went, in the Service. There's my resignation. I have accepted a post as teacher in the Nobles' School. And now that you are

94

no longer my chief, Mr. Hardwicke, I'll say two things.
You have always been very nice to me and I want to
thank you. That's one. And my wife is the best and
purest woman in the world, and there isn't a d——d
hypocritical British matron of the lot who can hold a
candle to her. That's the other. Good-bye."

Of course after that it had to be good-bye. The
Thorntons were allowed to depart in silence as far as
the Hardwickes were concerned. The other men spoke
their regrets aloud, for every one was sorry to see such
a straight man and good worker leave the Service.
Every one, except Mrs. Hardwicke, who, poor thing,
was cursed with a peculiar moral colour-blindness
which prevented her from recognising true men and
good women when she met them. She breathed more
freely after the Thorntons were gone, and resumed her
walks about the grounds, free now from the polluting
presence of O Tora and her child.

O Tora also breathed more freely when she found
herself arranging their furniture and little valuables in
a purely Japanese house, remote from the street, with
its own small garden already lit with the first plum
blossoms, which came so early that year that at first it
seemed as if they must be merely belated snowflakes
caught in the bare branches. Soon a leaf or two followed, and some pink camellias, which had been holding on bravely since January, fell to the ground, and
lay, fold upon fold of rosy shells, on the dark soil,
whence Kiku gathered them all up for Umé to play
with.

The little girl began to crawl along the verandahs now, to develop a fine taste for mischief. The first soft murmurs of language found their way to her lips, the "mum mum" and "da da" of nursery history all the world over. Day by day she seemed more bright and winsome, day by day she wound herself more closely round the core of Thornton's heart.

At first he missed his old status, his old work-fellows, but as time went on and he felt the charm of being his own man, and, out of fixed hours at the school, absolutely free, he ceased to regret the change, and set about turning his ambition into other channels. His admirable knowledge of Japanese and his thorough mastery of the one or two subjects which he undertook to teach, soon obtained for him the offer of a history professorship in the University, thus giving him a permanent footing in the scientific and literary aristocracy of the country, an aristocracy almost as much respected among the Japanese of to-day as that of birth. Some of the other Europeans on the staff were married to Japanese women, and these were kind to O Tora, who, at home once more among her own people, received and returned the few visits with distinct pleasure, much augmented by the pride of showing off her little daughter, dressed in silks of dazzling colour and design, periodical presents from the paternal establishment on the Ginza.

The affairs of O Tora's father seemed to have been going extremely well since the crisis in which John had come to his help. But he still kept away from Tokyo,

leaving a sharp young man in charge of the shop; and
if he came, as Thornton suspected, at fixed periods, to
look into his accounts, he did so unnoticed and un-
announced.   Once or twice he visited his daughter
towards nightfall and on foot.   He was evidently in
fear lest he should be followed, and all O Tora's wiles
and John's dutiful invitations never could persuade him
to stay the night.   In truth he was mightily afraid of
coming across the terrible Jurei or his father, whose
money he had pocketed as well as Thornton's.   Their
wrath (as described by a confidential eye-witness) when
they found that he had disappeared with money and
daughter, had been quite awful to behold, and they had
sworn to have full revenge on their faithless relative.
Of course, he might have sent back the money, but,
even now, that went bitterly against the grain; two
hundred dollars was what he had wrung from them,
and why give money to a lot of drunken, gormandising
wrestlers, he said to himself.   It was better and safer
invested in the shop.   They would not go to law, for it
was against all the traditions of the clan to settle their
family disputes in that way; but — he might get a
terrific beating if they caught him alone, and on all
counts it was more prudent to keep out of their path.
He had been much impressed by the attempt to disturb
O Tora at Dzushi, and on the one or two occasions
when he did pay his daughter a visit, uttered repeated
warnings about the inadvisability of young women ever
leaving their homes, and the necessity of closing the
amados or wooden shutters round the house before dark.

But that fear seemed to have passed out of O Tora's life now. All around her was peace, and most of all in her own heart. At first she had entreated John not to do anything for her sake which could injure his future. She would leave him if he desired it — if his friends did not think that she was a suitable wife for him — but he must please do nothing unwise for her sake. She said this with a breaking heart, her head on his feet; but his answer was quite conclusive, for he lifted her up and clasped her to him for a long space in silence. When he did speak it was to forbid her ever to revert to such a possibility, under pain of his heavy displeasure.

So now, seeing him serene and happy — seeing that his men friends came more than before to visit him in his cheery study looking on the garden, seeing that he and she were at any rate none the poorer for the change, and that money was always forthcoming to satisfy their modest wants — O Tora rose up and lay down in peace, and thanked God daily for her sweet life.

Yes, thanked God, for she had heard all the rest of the good news from the sisters, and their straightforward, sunny teaching had gone home to the woman's simple heart, all warmed and opened to happy influences by the love of husband and child. Thornton, poor timorous heathen, had been pitifully anxious at first lest this new element should bring change and disturbance into their daily lives. Why could that which had answered so far not suffice any longer? Who wanted the fuss and friction of modern Christianity (early breakfast and morning prayers, of course) let into the idyllic peace of the little home? It was like setting up a board school in the Garden of Eden!

But after having looked these fears in the face, and having consented to live with them because he would refuse nothing to the beloved mate, he found that they were groundless. Fuss and friction did not enter into O Tora's methods, nor into those of her teachers; and little by little Thornton began to be proud of his wife's goodness and intelligence, to take interest in her comings and goings to church or school (always with wee Umé in her arms), and he would often get her to talk about the small charities which she began to exercise towards poor neighbours or sick people, and found the reward of his patience and forbearance in actually being able to look up to the gentle being whom he had only loved and protected till now. Once he took her to Sunday Mass when the faithful Kiku was ailing, and having gone once he went again. The service was incomprehensible to him, but one thing needed no words to explain it. Every soul there was lifted up in intensely believing prayer; the strong man who loved peace suddenly felt himself folded in its very heart.

After that, just to please Sœur St. Ephrem, there was a quiet little ceremony one morning in the sisters' chapel. O Tora stood beside Thornton with the white veil (always worn in church) over her hair, and the Missionary Father joined their hands, and O Tora became quite speechless with delight over her thick gold ring. This was at once taken off and given to

Umé, well secured by a ribbon, to distract the little maid's attention from the enormous beard of the good priest who poured water and said holy words over her unconscious head. When all was over the three came back very soberly, in the morning sunshine, to their fragrant, airy home, and O Tora, handing the baby to Kiku, instantly set about making Thornton's tea.

O Tora had a tiresome little cough in these days, which disturbed her husband at his writing, and her breath seemed to come and go for nothing at all.

"You are not well, my dear," he said, one morning, stopping her as she passed, and looking long into her face. "What is it? Ought you to have a change, or is that little monster Umé wearing you out?"

She laughed.

"I am not ill, and even you must not call Umé san a monster," she said. "I suppose I am getting old; everything makes me tired, as if I were an O Bassan."

"Awfully old," Thornton replied, with mock gravity; "twenty next week, isn't it? But you cough," he insisted; "that must mean something."

"Oh, no," she answered; "Japanese people always get a cough after they have lived in European houses. You have big fires, and shut-up rooms, and it makes us catch cold afterwards. It is nothing; the warm weather will soon come."

"I shall tell Doctor Herz to come and see you," he said, "and you would tell me if there were anything wrong, wouldn't you?"

"What should I have to tell you, beloved?" she

replied, laying his hand against her cheek, and looking up into his face with eyes all truth and tenderness, "except that I am too happy, and God is too good. Life is so sweet."

And she sighed without knowing why.

"I told you on no account to catch cold," said the doctor, irritably, the next morning, as he folded up his stethoscope and stuffed it into his pocket, whence a snaky black coil or two emerged rebelliously.

"I did not catch it on purpose," said O Tora, picking up Umé, who had been crawling over the mats during the previous part of the interview.

"Do you think it hurts you less because you don't do it on purpose?" asked the doctor, with fine scientific scorn.

"Do lecture her, Herz," said Thornton; "she will get up at unearthly hours, and run in and out of the kitchen, and tire herself to death over that little tyrant. She doesn't mind a word I say!"

"We will have a little talk in your study directly, Thornton," said the doctor, who was still looking critically at O Tora. "Now, Mrs. Thornton, please listen to me. You must get up late and go to bed early, and only go out when the sun is up, and drink plenty of milk, and eat Mizu-ame, if you like it, — it's as good as cod-liver oil any day, — and wean that child at once. And then," he muttered in English, "we may possibly pull you through."

O Tora's face fell at the last order, and she bent low over the baby that the two men might not see the tears come into her eyes.   She seemed to be losing her self-control.

But poor John had caught the doctor's murmured words; he said nothing, but laid a heavy hand on Herz's shoulder, and led him away to his own study.

"I heard what you said just now," he exclaimed hoarsely; "it is impossible! You have made a mistake. She is as sound as I am!"

He sank down into a chair, and looked up at his friend with a haggard countenance.

"My poor friend," said the doctor, "I do not like the look of it. She was sound, I have no doubt, until the child came, and that pulled her down — and — how long has she been coughing like this?"

"Oh, I don't know," groaned Thornton. "A month or two, perhaps."

"Too long. The Japanese have no lungs. One heavy cold, and then — "

Herz thought that Thornton had been negligent, and was inclined to punish him pretty severely. John suddenly rose and said unsteadily : —

"Herz, if you talk like that — I'll shoot you! There, I'm hard hit. Have patience with me, and, Herz, you will save her — you will?"

"I will do my best," the doctor answered, and there was more sympathy in the tone than in the words. "After all, she is young, and it may not have gone so far as I think."

.   .   .   .

Perhaps it had not, for O Tora was long in dying.
The whole strength of her youth was thrown into the
struggle, and was only vanquished by slow degrees.
Her sound frame and untainted nature made a gallant
fight for life; but the result showed that Herz had been
right in his estimate of her people. They have no
stamina to help them withstand the inroads of slow
disease, and, the lungs once seriously compromised,
they rarely recover.

She was always calm and quite happy, never believing in her own danger till near the end, and beguiling
long days of pain and weakness with a hundred happy
plans for what she and danna san would do when she
got well. There was to be a cottage in the hills for the
summer, and even a little pony carriage, and flowers and
toys always for Umé. She was only sad when, fearing
for the child's health, Herz told John to keep her away
as much as possible from her mother; but by that time
O Tora was so easily tired that she was satisfied to
have Umé merely trot in and out, or to lie and listen
to her ringing laugh as she played in the garden. She
loved to watch Thornton carrying the child from flower
to flower, and busied herself almost up to the last in
making her little gowns, whose brilliant coloured patterns made the mother's fingers look more white and
transparent than ever.

It was only when she had to give up the pretty work
that O Tora felt that she had lost her hold on life. She
had a bitter hour then; but no one knew it, except perhaps Sœur St. Ephrem, who used to come and go a

good deal, and whose eager longing for the joys of Paradise puzzled O Tora greatly.

"What a pity that we cannot change," she said to her one day towards the end. "For me, Paradise is here; for you, beyond! But you must stay, and I must go — must I not?"

"That is as God wills," said the sister, with her radiant smile. "Perhaps you are the pet, and are wanted first; but we will all come, you will see! Mr. Thornton and the baby, and even I!"

"Oh, to take them with me," cried the woman's heart; "who will take care of them when I am dead? Could not the children's God have made us immortal? Mothers ought never to die."

Towards this time Thornton received a letter from his father, begging him to return to England, to fill his brother's place. Poor George was dead. He had gone once too often to the market town. The old yeoman pleaded with John to come home, and stand by him on the land for the few remaining years of his life. Mr. Thornton's letter ran thus: —

"THORPE OLD FARM,
"BEDALE,
"YORKS.

"MY DEAR JOHN, — It is a long time since I wrote you but now I feel it right that you should know how things are going, John I want you home as soon as you can get back, your brother George is dead. It came about this way, he was coming home from Bedale

Fair a week ago, he had been a-drinking with a lot of them drover chaps and I think he had more than enough, poor lad a steady lad as ever was — he was driving a young mare that he chopped some beasts for with old Bob Harrison of Thirsk, and being a bit muzzy like he mistook turning it being main foggy and drove the mare and all into a sandpit, he was quite dead when he was picked up by some lads in the morning. We buried him yesterday in the Thorpe Churchyard next to the mother and amongst us all. Now John my lad I am a getting old and what with rheumatism and such like I can't get about the farm as I did, and I'm thinking it won't be long afore I join him and her, so lad come home it would grieve me sore to let the old farm pass to strange folk. I heard as how you had gone and married some foreign lass I hope that is not true but I'll welcome her for your sake John. There is not much to tell thee, Sir Charles is dead and Sir James is living at the Hall now, he's been and married one of these here short-haired lasses who is a trying to alter everybody's ways, she better by far stop at home and mind the bairns, I'm thinking — but never mind that John its you I want my lad. If you want money I have a bit in Pease's Bank you can have. — Your loving father,

"JOHN GEORGE THORNTON."

John could not promise to live in England, but he replied that he would come, at any rate for a visit, as soon as his wife should be a little stronger and able to

bear the journey. That day never came. His martyr-
dom was long drawn out. For three sweet agonising
years the pure flame of her life rose and fell, and
fought with the winds of death; seemed almost spent,
and then burnt up so brightly that John drew breath and
told his own heart that love had won its victory. But
a sterner Lover than he, and one who is never denied
at the last, had desired her for Himself, and slowly,
surely, step by step, led her out from the sunny home
on the hillside, from John's arms, from the baby's
kisses, and at last, through the silent ecstasy of death,
to learn the secret of life.

.   .   .   .

And the day she was buried the child was stolen.
The grey-faced man who came dragging leaden feet
up to his silent doorstep noticed nothing at first; and
three precious hours passed by ere he raised his head
and looked round like a wounded animal who hears its
pursuers. The silence had suddenly become terrible,
full of menace — where was Umé? He listened and
realised that he had indeed heard a sound. A stifled
breathing came from a room near. When he reached
it he found Kiku lying face downwards on the mats,
her head muffled in a cloth, through which a little blood
was slowly trickling. The child was nowhere to be
seen. Thornton raised the poor woman's head, tore
the stifling folds from her mouth, and quickly fetched
water to dash in her face. Just then Herz, wishing to
bring some little comfort to his friend, appeared in the
doorway, and Thornton left him with the servant while

he, in a cold sweat of fear, searched every corner of house and garden — in vain.

This new terror filled his consciousness to the exclusion of every other idea. The two or three neighbours into whose houses he rushed to ask if the child had been seen were dismayed at his ghastly face, and thought that his trouble had driven him mad. When they understood what had happened they were full of readiness to help him in his search. One went off to the police-station to warn the authorities, and others divided into little parties and sought for the child in every house in the surrounding streets.

Thornton came back to his stricken home, and found that Herz had succeeded in restoring the woman to consciousness; but at the sight of her master she turned faint again, and the doctor motioned to him to stand where she could not see him. Thornton passed behind a screen.

"What happened, Kiku san?" said Herz, kindly. "The danna san must know, but he will not be angry."

"He will kill me," said Kiku, gasping. "Two men came in — right into the room where I was putting away the poor okusama's things. . . . Umé san was with me . . . and one of them took her up, and I cried out and tried to pull her away, and something struck me. . . . I know no more. Umé san is stolen. Let the master kill me. Miserable wretch, I deserve to be killed."

"Rubbish," said the doctor, hard-heartedly, for she was beginning to sob, and he and Thornton must hear more. "Nobody wants to kill you. We want to find the child. What were the men like?"

"Big, strong, terrible," wailed the poor nurse; "but their faces were wrapped in towels. I could only see their eyes. They looked like some of our people . . . like wrestlers."

And she fell to weeping bitterly.

"You keep quiet, Kiku san," said the doctor, "or the bandages will come off your head. Lie still while I go and speak to the danna san."

Thornton came towards him, stumbled, and would have fallen had Herz not caught his arm. He made him swallow some brandy, and together they went into the next room, the poor little deserted nursery. A few well-worn toys were scattered round a cushion on the floor, and halfway to the door a little shoe had been dropped in some hasty toddle. John picked it up and put it in his pocket. Then he snatched down a print of the Good Shepherd from the wall, and tore it across and across, cursing heaven and hell, and in his anguish renouncing the God who smote him.

"Now," he said, in despair too tragic to be grotesque, "there is no God. Come to the police-station."

Everything was set in motion that could in any way help to clear up the pitiful mystery. Every one assured Thornton that in a day or two at most the child would be restored to him. But day followed day, and not the least trace of her had been discovered. The authorities were in despair. Mr. Hardwicke raged at the insult to his flag (for John's child was a British subject), and at last, when two weeks had passed, threatened to demand an enormous indemnity if she were not forthcoming, alive and well, within three days.   Then the authorities became incredulous, suggested that the nurse had been drunk, and that the child had fallen down some well; and finally, having really done all that in them lay to help the bereaved man, folded their hands, and said that they would look upon the incident as closed for the present.   The police force, both of the towns and provinces, had instructions to continue the search indefinitely, and anything they heard would at once be communicated to Mr. Hardwicke.

He, kind soul, was so full of sympathy for his old favourite in his awful trouble that something very like a reconciliation was effected between the two men. They did not mention Mrs. Hardwicke, who was away on some little journey.   She had taken no more notice of O Tora in her lingering, heartbreaking illness than she had done when she was living close to her in all her fresh beauty and sweetness.   It was strange that the rough clasp of his old chief's hand should have brought Thornton a minute of comfort in that blackness, but it did; and when, a few days later, he resolved to go and search for Umé himself, he came down to tell Mr. Hardwicke of it, and to say good-bye.

"I dare say you are right," said Hardwicke.   "It will occupy you at any rate, and I am sure you could not do any work now."

"Well, no, I don't think I could," said John, almost smiling at the idea of going up to lecture students on history . . . while there was that brown grave at Shiba and that empty cot at home. He had shouldered the burden now, and could carry it quietly without any more curses — could reason clearly, and tell himself just how much hope there was for him.

"But will they keep the place open for you at the University?" inquired Mr. Hardwicke. "Won't you find yourself . . . inconvenienced by the loss of the salary?"

This seemed the most delicate way of introducing a proposal to lend him money if he needed it.

"My expenses will be smaller now," said poor John, his face twitching suddenly. "I shall be quite able to meet them."

"Well, good-bye, then," said Mr. Hardwicke, "and God knows I wish you good speed with all my heart."

"Thank you, sir; good-bye," Thornton replied. "It may take a long time, but I shall succeed in the end."

He had put the whole question down in black and white, as it were, in his mind, and he felt that, if Heaven but held its hand and let him have his way quietly, he would succeed. The child was alive, of that he was convinced; for if they had meant to kill her, merely as a piece of revenge, they would have done so on the spot. Since they had gone to the risk and trouble of carrying her away, they evidently wanted her, and in their own rough way would be kind to her, for no Japanese is ever cruel to a child. He winced miserably when he thought of his dainty floweret in those rough hands, when he thought of the coarse food, the ugly sights, the low, brutal atmosphere of the wrestlers' camp. But two points he kept steadily before him, and at last refused to look at any others — they would be kind to her, and he would find her before she was old enough to be contaminated by any impurity. The intense respect felt for children in Japan would keep her safe for years to come, and, thank God, she was but a baby yet.

But a baby, just a baby, oh, poor little darling, torn from all she knew and loved. So his heart wailed in spite of all his philosophy, and he fiercely took back the "Thank God" which had risen to his lips. What had he to thank God for? he asked himself. Better to have lived on as he was before, light-hearted, self-seeking, prosperous, alone, than to have had such happiness and be bereft of it. Then, as he sat in the gathering darkness in his empty home, his wife's face came back to him, with the wistful, child-like eyes that always seemed to be asking if he were happy, if he were pleased with her; and he laid his head down on the table and broke into a storm of dry, tearless sobbing, while his hand crept out as if to clasp hers, shadowy though it were, once more; and the poor soul took back all his blind blasphemies against love, dear sweet love, that gives life even while it murders us, and makes us sure we are alive by the very edge of our agony.

VIII

So John went out from his old haunts, and his pleasant life, and the work which he loved, and if, from time to time, he returned to Tokyo, nobody noticed the gaunt man in Japanese dress, who was only seen when a popular festival was going forward, or where the wrestlers were drawing crowds to look at their feats. In his constant wanderings his skin became deeply tanned, but the grey, northern eyes made it impossible to take him for a native of the country. He chose to wear their dress because in it he could pass almost unnoticed, and his fluent, colloquial Japanese was of immense service to him. Sometimes, as he passed, people would nudge one another and whisper, "There goes the mad Englishman, seeking his dead child." Something of his story was known here and there, and he met with a good deal of kindness and sympathy on his weary way.

Months grew to years, and he had not found his little daughter; but he sought her still, and still told himself that he should succeed at last. Sometimes, when he saw a tiny child dressed in brilliant colours, his heart would leap wildly, and then he had to remind himself that his Umé would have grown much by this time, would be, ah, so much taller and bigger than father or mother had ever seen her. And his two terrors came

back and made him cold.   The first, that he might pass
her without knowing that it was she ; the second, that
he might not find her until — too late.   That was the
point in his mental journey at which he involuntarily
began to pray for her safety — defiant prayers which
were more like threats than supplications.   He had
come to stake everything on that.   Would heaven
restore his child to him, then heaven should exist,
and John Thornton would forgive, and acknowledge
heaven and its Master.   If not, no heaven for him
— and why hell in another world ?   He surely would
have found it in this.

And now, for the first time since these wanderings
began, he turned his face towards Atami.   Nothing
had led him thither as yet, and he had avoided the
place carefully.   He had never heard of any festival
there which was likely to attract the sort of people
among whom he might hope to find his lost baby, and
— the beginnings of his lost happiness had come to him
there.   Those bitter-sweet memories made the place
painfully sacred.   He was thankful not to have been
obliged to visit it again.

But now, a whisper had reached his ears, through
Sœur St. Ephrem, that one of the " good pagans " in
the country, whom the sisters paid to foster the tiniest
of their nurslings, had seen a child with blue eyes pass
through his village with some pilgrims, as he said.
There was to be a great Matsuri in Atami, because the
boiling spring had ceased to flow for several days, and
the gods were to be propitiated by processions and fire-

works, so that the honourable hot water might return. Many companies of strolling players and wrestlers were also going there, for it was to be a great Matsuri. The man had noticed the little girl because of her blue eyes, and also because round her neck she had a bit of brass on a string, with the image of the "holy woman," like those which the children from the convent always wore. And this is what made him tell Sœur St. Ephrem of it, when a day or two afterwards he presented himself in Tokyo to receive his monthly wage for the foster child.

The good sister had never ceased to pray and hope for the safety of the lost lamb, and at once communicated with Thornton. He, knowing that her heart was in the quest, and that she was acquainted with an immense number of the poorer people, always left some indication with her as to where a letter would reach him. She reminded him that the little medal would be probably regarded as a charm by the persons in charge of the child, and would not be taken away. It was an indication worth following up, and he hastened down to Atami, trying all the way to persuade himself that he should still not lose heart if the ray of light went out in darkness, as so many had done in the eternity since O Tora's death.

That ·had seemed to be the insupportable sorrow when it fell; but now, compared to the gnawing terror, the heartrending compassion for his little girl, her mother's death was peace to think of — a sorrow lifted by its greatness into a hallowed radiance of quiet glory. He had almost sworn not even to visit her dear grave

until he could bring her darling with him ; he could not
face the calm green mound, with these live fiends of
anxiety tearing at him night and day.

No wonder that a party of English people passing up
the long Atami street in the hot twilight (for this happened in the heart of summer) did not recognise the
ambitious John Thornton, who used to write trade
reports, in the worn man in common Japanese clothes,
who sat on the steps of the inn among a crowd of chattering girls.   They were asking him how a man with
foreign eyes came to speak Japanese so well.   He did
not answer, for he had caught sight of Mrs. Hardwicke
walking between her husband and another man, with an
interpreter behind them.   A certain kind of state seemed
to hover round the little official party.   Mrs. Hardwicke
looked cool and prosperous and superbly contemptuous
of the common crowd.

Suddenly, however, she stopped as if some one
had struck her, and she touched her husband's arm
sharply.

"Who is that man — on the steps ? " she said quickly.

Hardwicke, of course, turned the wrong way, and
then answered : —

" I don't know one from the other, it is just a crowd
of Japanese.   What is the matter ? "

"I am certain it was Mr. Thornton," said Mrs.
Hardwicke ; " I never saw any one so altered, but I was
sure it was he.   Oh ! " she exclaimed, looking back
nervously, and then hurrying on.   " He looked as if he
could kill one ! "

Thornton had recognised O Tora's enemy, and met her glance with one of living hatred such as she had never before beheld.   Then he was ashamed — being too great to hate without suffering for it — and as she looked back after him, he turned and answered something said by one of the girls, with a bitter laugh.   He looked the wreck of his old self.

Mr. Hardwicke started when his wife mentioned Thornton's name.

"Where?" he said, "show him to me; I must speak to him."

"Oh, there at the tea-house door," cried the woman, in whom a sudden revulsion had been worked by the sight of the man whom she had helped to cast out of his birthright of dress clothes and English food, sitting dusty and haggard, in poor cotton garments, among an alien crowd.   She caught her husband's arm as he turned to go back, and spoke hurriedly.

"Tell him . . . I am sorry. . . .   Robert, get him to come back into the Service!   It is too horrible to see him like that!"

But when Thornton's old chief reached the door of the inn, the man he sought was gone, and the people looked at him suspiciously, and would tell him nothing.

"He was gone away," they said; "he had never been there; it was all a mistake."

Thornton rose quickly from his seat, after the Hardwickes passed, and strolled away down a side street, where he was at once lost to view.   He was very weary, for he had visited every Chaya in the town that day,

without finding a trace of his lost child. In his bitter
depression he had no wish to shake hands with his own
countrymen again. Some situations were too painful to
be faced uselessly, some contrasts so sharp that it was
better not to dwell on them. As he came towards the
end of the town and found himself on the road leading
to the Temple, where, seven years ago, O Tora had told
him the story of the old priest and the boiling spring,
he felt himself sinking down in a bottomless abyss of
loss and loneliness, and — for the first time — felt as if
life itself must be made to hang on his success now; it
was impossible to carry such a burden indefinitely.

For a moment he let himself go to the dream of
ending his misery; for the devil's last lie to his victim
is always that one about finding peace by the high
treason of suicide. But then John's only dogma rose
up in terrible singleness before him — he must meet
O Tora. She was the future life to him. Since she
had died there was for him one living soul in the silent
realms, and he would meet her again. Meet her without the child? look into her questioning eyes, and tell
her that he had left Umé alone on the battlefield with
their foes?

He raised his head as a scream of discordant music
came up to him from the village. The night had fallen
now, and strings of lamps and coloured lanterns were
climbing up the high poles and the gables of the houses,
here red, there white, swinging wildly as the sea-breeze
caught them in its dance. What was he doing out here
in the silence, when his little one might be passing in

the crowded streets? It was only after dark that the great procession of the Matsuri would form, and many women and children who had not been out before would hurry to catch a glimpse of the wonders of the show.

So he went back to his post with a sudden hope lifting the burden for a minute, and a wild prayer sent out into the blackness above him. Surely to-night would end this living death!

Where were all these people coming from? He must have been sitting longer than he thought out there in the darkness, for now the streets seethed with an undistinguishable mass of humanity, and the hot air was heavy with scents of camellia oil, and tobacco, and camphor, while drums and gongs were drowning the roar of the voices. All were going towards the shore, and a man in the crowd told him that the great cars were already on the beach, where red fires were flaring up between land and sea.

So with the rest, gazing eagerly at the faces which the many lights now showed distinctly, Thornton slowly made his way to the beach, where an amazing sight met his eyes. Five enormous cars were sunk almost to the axle in the heavy sand; raised in double and treble tiers, they were hung all over with thick flower garlands and flaming lanterns; in each tier was a crowd of girl musicians magnificently dressed, singing and playing on instruments of strange shapes, which assumed a weird vitality, and moved back and forth, twisting like snakes and dragons in the dancing light. Every car but one was crowned with a gigantic figure of hero or goddess;

on one Benké waved his standard of rattling gourds, on
another the fairy woman-bird spread her bewildering
plumes as the wind came in over the leaden sea, which
moaned sullenly, and rolled away in heaving blackness
behind all this gorgeous, futile glitter on the narrow
strip of shore.

As Thornton came nearer, he saw that the cars were
harnessed to huge teams of naked men, forty or fifty
for every one, some straining at ropes thick as a man's
arm, others pushing with poles from behind, all wild
with saké, and screaming and leaping like things possessed. They were mostly lean, brown fishermen, with
a sprinkling of sturdy peasants from inland; but one
car, the farthest from him, was surrounded by a crowd
that looked whiter than the others. He caught glimpses
of huge forms among them, and there the shouting rose
higher and higher, and at last rent the night with a long
yell of triumph as the wheels slowly turned in the clog-
ging sand, and the car tottered into movement, swayed
and rocked, and seemed to be unwillingly dragged to
the very water's edge. It carried no gigantic image,
but a little figure of a child, dressed in stiff purple and
gold, for its crowning ensign.

The look of the men, and that wild anxiety to miss
no slightest chance, made Thornton eagerly fight his
way through the crowd towards the far end of the beach.

"Do not be in such a hurry," said one man to him
good-humouredly. "You have plenty of time to see
them when they come up again. They will not stay
in the sea!"

"Are they going into the sea?" cried the English-man.

"Yes, of course," said the other; "to get the sea-spirits to help them, and also to bless the water. That is a very holy car, for it belongs to the Satzuma wrestlers. There, they are in!"

Thornton reached the spot, he knew not how; when he got to it a long space of trampled sand and deep ruts showed where the trophy had passed. Now it stood well out among the leaden, uncrested billows, but in a few moments the sea itself was alive with human beings, whose efforts to drag their burden farther out churned the black waves into angry foam. The water must cover the wheels and the men's shoulders, or the ceremony would not be complete.

By this time the four other cars were also in the water. In the strange struggle many of the lanterns fell, and floated for a moment, lost lights on the waves; garlands came loose, girls stood up in their places and flung baskets of fruit and fish out to sea, the deafening choruses clanged out their shrieking music, and earth seemed to be defying sea and sky, taking possession of the universe in its bursting pride.

Suddenly something fell. No one saw it, but each felt the pall of fate, and turned in a mad effort to reach the shore. The sea was growing deeper, and those who had been standing safely on their feet found that they were out of their depth, and shrieked for help. The giants round the wrestlers' car tried to rally, tried to wrench the monstrous thing back towards the land. In vain! The tallest were not able to stand now. Many struggled to shore, others scaled the sides of their ship of earth, fast bedded in the sand. The sky, which had been of inky blackness, parted in a long white rift from end to end, and by its light Thornton saw two things — his little daughter in a blown cloud of flame, from which her mother's face seemed to be bending over her, her mother's hands seemed to be holding the child's arms out to him — and a mile away on the black face of the sea, a solid wall of water, the tidal wave rolling steadily to land.

He never knew whether other lives paid for Umé's that night. There were still a few seconds to spare when he reached her — just time to fold her in his arms, to wrap her in his robe, to hide her eyes on his heart from the death that was close upon them, and then to call on God and O Tora as the ocean thundered by.

By, not over, those two. The heavy car, the ship of earth, with all its clinging freight of terrified humanity, was lifted slowly from its place, and borne onwards to the shore, past the shore, to the upper shelf of the pebbled beach, where it sank against a grove of pines as gently as a little child is set down on the ground from its mother's arms. The sea would have none of the ship of earth.

That one slow wave broke down dykes and defences all along the coast, flooded fields and farms, took many a life, but those two it spared.

When day broke it found John on the road to Tokyo, with his little maid in his arms. As the morning sun touched her she woke with a shiver, and turned startled eyes up to his face.

"I thought the sea was coming back," she murmured. "I was so frightened."

"There will never be anything to frighten you any more, my little one," he replied, drawing her closer to his heart, "nothing, ever, any more.   Go to sleep."

Umé smiled dreamily, and then, with a happy sigh, nestled down on his shoulder.

.   .   .   .

"How did you know it was I, father?" she asked, long years afterwards, when they were all in all to each other.   "And, if you found me then, how was it that you did not come before?"

"I could not find you before, my own, though I sought you night and day.   I suppose the time had not come . . . and I found you then . . . because your mother showed you to me . . . in a wing of flame . . . when the wave rose."

"How strange," said O Tora's child.   She was silent for a moment, and then went on: "Dear, pretty little mother, I remember her so well."

"I am glad you remember her, dear," said John, laying his hand on his daughter's head.   "I don't think she is so very far away from us, after all."

SHE DANCED BEFORE HIM

She Danced Before Him

I

 REDERIC CHARTERIS had been in Japan for two years and a half, working hopefully at the wonders and terrors of the most amazing language in the world. It was to be his stepping-stone to a berth as assistant interpreter in one of the consulates, and finally, perhaps, in the dim future, to a consulship for himself. He had already scrambled through a rather severe competitive examination in order to enter the Service at all, and having done that, was inclined to take it for granted that the rest would go smoothly enough. The time of probation had been passed in Tokyo, in the cosy students' quarters in the great compound which has been the cradle of a very hard-worked Service.

Alas! something seemed to have interfered with the going smoothly of all the rest; and poor Charteris, on a certain warm, soft afternoon, had to hear some rather bad news.

"I fear you are a bit weak on the written language," said Mr. Murray, gravely.

He had been giving Charteris a preliminary canter over some columns of hieroglyphics written backwards on very thin paper, supposed to represent that new growth in Japan — public opinion.

"I am afraid I am weak all round, sir," replied Charteris, in profound dejection. "I had no idea that a man could work so hard and learn so little. I shall never pass."

"Oh, yes, you will," said the examiner, in a voice whose coldness belied his words. "We have all been through it. But it takes grind, you know. That was an extra bad piece in the *Nichi Nichi Shimbun*. You need not be down about that."

He was sorry for the young man, but felt small hopes of him officially.

"Oh, hang the *Nichi Nichi Shimbun!*" cried Charteris, savagely. "What right has any nation to run a newspaper like that?"

He held up the smudged and rustling sheet by one corner and glared at it. The printing was so small and pale that the complicated characters had the appearance of delicate spattering work. Charteris had been studying them with a large magnifying glass.

Murray was inclined to laugh at his despair, but, mindful of seniority and the expletive, decided to look stern instead.

"I can read it all right," he said, "and your eyes ought to be better than mine."

"I believe my eyes are going, like everything else, sir," wailed the examiner's victim; "I shall give it up, and go and break stones in England! You have been awfully patient with me, sir; but even you cannot tell me that I have the ghost of a chance — can you, now?"

"You certainly would not pass at present," said the other, looking critically at the afflicted junior, and then beginning to draw elaborate patterns on his blotting-paper.

The two were sitting at opposite sides of a much abused Government writing-table, in the dingy room set apart for purely Japanese work in the Chancery. It was a fine April afternoon, and through the open windows came twitterings of the first songs, and faint perfumes from freshly burst peach blossoms, that were waving low against a rose and amber sky.

Charteris looked out bitterly on the unbought beauty of the great gardens in the sunset light, and then bowed his head in his hands and stared moodily at the worn carpet. Life seemed all one stretch of useless work and baffled hopes. His brow was aching, and his eyes were burning with the strain of reading those horrible characters. After months and years of what he thought close work, he seemed no nearer his object than when he started.

"No," said Murray again — and Charteris lifted his head and met the examiner's glance fixed upon him, not unkindly — "no, you could not pass now; you are tired

and overstrained, and what you know is not at your command.   But I suspect you know a lot more than you
think.   Look here, Charteris, you drop the written language altogether for six weeks, and go up country and
do 'Colloquial.'   It will rest your eyes, and set you up
generally, and when you come back we will see what
you make of this rag!"

He pointed to the anathematised newspaper, which
was lying in a crumpled heap on the floor.

Charteris sprang to his feet and shook himself, like a
spaniel let loose from the chain.

"Oh, come!" he cried, "you are a trump, Mr.
Murray!   I have been just longing to get away up
country.   They say the jonquils are in bloom.   Do you
think the chief will let me go?"

"Oh, I don't see why not," replied Murray; "there is
not much work on just now.   I will ask him to-night."

Charteris walked back to his rooms at the far end of
the compound, feeling like another man already.   The
languid beauty of the spring evening was no longer an
insult.   He was going to be his own master for weeks
to come, and he marked his exuberant sense of liberty
by pitching a grammar, and then a dictionary, across his
tiny courtyard at a head whose top just appeared, wag-
ging up and down a good deal, at an open window
opposite.

The head took no notice of the grammar, but the
dictionary caused it to look up, and a pair of mild blue
eyes peered out through very strong glasses at the
assailant.

"Hullo, Charteris! Back already? Don't kill me because you have won in a canter. I always said you would, you know."

"Well, you said wrong," replied Charteris, coming down from his verandah and across the narrow strip of garden, till he could rest his arms on the window and look into his friend's room. "I've mulled the whole beastly thing so successfully that old Murray says my constitution wants building up, and I'm ordered off up the country to do 'Colloquial.' What do you think of that?"

"You don't look particularly shattered," said the other man. "Think I'll try shirking, too, and see if they won't give me a little holiday. I need it more than you do."

"They can't spare you, Jimmy, old boy," said Charteris; "your handwriting is too magnificent, for the copying. But I wish you were coming all the same."

"I don't," said his friend, shortly, and his head went down again into his work.

Jimmy Hayes was a pale, slight man, with a hesitating manner and a fierce light moustache. He and Charteris had entered the consular service at the same time, but Jimmy took every fence first, and was looked upon as a very promising, hard-working young fellow; while Charteris, who had irrelevant tastes for sketching and flower collecting, was always lagging behind and being exhorted to "buck up and put some steam on, — look at Hayes, there's a worker for you."

Charteris did look at his great colleague, and admired him quite as much as his seniors did, with a kind of awe which they could not feel. But, notwithstanding this admiration of Hayes, poor Charteris was ever the hindmost. No one could quite say why. His fresh young face looked intelligent enough, and his eyes were of misleading brightness, causing unreflecting seniors to expect great things from him, which they never got. But there! some people are not born to learn Japanese.

Murray took advantage of a quiet moment in the smoking-room that evening to report to the chief on Charteris's poor progress, and to suggest that he should be sent away for a time.

"I can't make that boy out at all," said the Head of Things, testily; "he is not stupid, and he is not lazy, but he never does a bit of decent work. What is the matter with the fellow?"

"I don't know about the not being stupid, sir," replied Murray, remembering Charteris's hopeless floundering over quite simple characters that afternoon, "but we shall have to give him time."

"He's had six months over time now," said the chief; "but you do as you think best, Murray; send him up to the hills by all means, only tell him to find somebody to talk to, and to *talk!* I hear he wastes no end of time over Japanese flower painting, and botany, and all that sort of rubbish."

Charteris stayed in Tokyo for one day more, after getting his leave. There was an entertainment to

which he had been invited for the next evening,
and it seemed a pity to miss it. A rather famous
dancer had been engaged to amuse the guests, and
Charteris knew that he was fortunate in having been
included among them. Such diversions were enormously costly, and it was the first time that he had
had an opportunity of attending one on such a scale.
Surely this might count for a necessary part of his
Japanese education!

The garden of the Maple Club was crowded with
jinrikshas when his man dropped the shafts with
a jerk, close to the steps which led to the first
vestibule. A slight spring rain was falling, and all
the outlines of the trees were blurred and shadowy
around. Within the wide-open door all was brilliant
and clear. The hanging lanterns swayed in the
draught, and their light was reflected on the dark
polished floor. A crowd of girls, gay as tulips, were
standing a little within the opening; and two of them
ran, with smiles, to take Charteris's hat and coat,
while a third knelt down at his feet, and tried to re-
move his shoes, stooping over their fastenings till all
the nape of her neck was bare, and the three-cornered
spot, untouched by powder, at the roots of her hair,
was seen to great advantage. Charteris felt quite hot.

"Arrigato, thank you so much. Oh, please don't!"
For the Musumé had succeeded in loosening both
his shoes, and now looked up into his face with
laughing eyes, as she held out, one in each hand,
the enormous felt slippers which are always kept in

readiness for a guest. Charteris shook his head, but had to submit at last, as all the others had done before him.

He found the great room upstairs half full of people, who were seated in a semicircle at one end. Charteris was a little late, and the rest had begun the indescribable meal which is called Japanese dinner. All the strangest products of earth, regardless of precedence, hustle each other on the small square table before the guest, and little by little overflow its bounds, and are placed on the floor around him — a growing nebula of tiny plates, many of which he will not touch if he be wise. What strikes him first, perhaps, is the uncanny familiarity of some of them. If this is really his first visit to "little Japan," where could he possibly have seen three pink shells lying on golden straw in a scarlet plate? Or a large white fish, with beseeching countenance, comfortably put to bed among sprouting rushes, all apparently growing out of the meshes of that fairy basket-work? Where, in the name of sanity, has he had sugar peonies and chrysanthemums done to the life double their natural size, or octopi and red crabs artistically chasing each other on plates of corrugated glass? Are these the stuff that dreams are made of? Then he remembers : of course they have all come out of the embroideries and off the lacquered tables of his childhood. The dinner is an object lesson in exquisite arrangements of form and colour, and should be regarded as such. Viewed as food, it is distinctly unsatisfactory, and far, far too satisfying! The impression on rising, stiff and dizzy, from the floor, is that of having watched a kaleidoscope, and swallowed Mont Blanc.

Charteris's host was indulgent to European weaknesses, and early administered bumpers of champagne to his guests, to keep up their spirits for the second course. Charteris felt better after he had tasted the wine, and forgot his troubles so far as to smile back kindly at the pretty girl who was waiting on him. She sat on her little heels exactly in front of him, watching every mouthful that he ate, and laughing at his efforts to manage macaroni and pigeons' eggs with chopsticks. When he had nearly swallowed one, she gravely took them from his hands, and produced from her sleeve a well-worn fork and spoon in Britannia metal, which she handed to him, saying:—

"More better! *Ingirishu urashi.*"

She was a quaint little figure, in her gown all over star-shaped leaves, to match the house; everything there is marked with the maple, from the tea-cups to the dancing-girls.

But Charteris was taking little notice of her now, for the screens at the end of the long room had opened, hoarse music began to sound a halting, expectant measure, and people seemed to be holding their breath. They caught it audibly as the screens ran back into place, and a wonderful vision floated towards them as soundlessly as if wafted up by the night wind from the bay.

Was it flower, or bird, or woman, or all three in one? Soft golden pinions rose from her shoulders, and as she spread them a shower of dewdrops flashed upon the air. Folds on folds of melting rose and crimson and carmine swathed her round, and were flung wide like opening rose-petals in the soft rush of her entrance.   As she swayed and turned, her limbs were wrapped in a swirl of silk, from which her body seemed to rise as a flower bursts the calyx, while her arms reached out to the light, and her face, in its tender paleness, said that the rose had found its soul and must break from earth at last.

"The bird of paradise who seeks her mate," explained a Japanese, sitting beside Charteris.

The man he addressed did not even look an answer. What were eyes for but to watch this revelation of beauty, this first miracle in his half-fledged life? Ah, she was coming nearer, seeking, returning, darting hither and thither, as the music rose and broke and wailed for loss.   Her whole being seemed to be answering to its palpitating motion, now reaching upward as for sudden flight, now bending, shrinking, all but falling in a wild backward curve, as if uprooted by the wind; hanging for an instant in lines of dreamy grace, then carried past in a rush of perfume, in a whirling storm of scattered drapery and dazzling colour as an inner robe of scarlet was caught up and spread to the light — one seething, blinding burst of red.

It paled and folded down, the gleaming wings sank out of sight, the music ceased, and a slender girl in a gown of grey knelt and touched her forehead to the ground.

There was a burst of applause from all the men, Japanese and Europeans. Charteris was crying for joy, and never felt the tears streaming down his cheeks. He would not have cared. He knew the reasons of things at last, and tidings, inarticulate still, but breathing of divinest happiness, had been brought to him by the dancing of the Geisha girl, O Haru Takayama, in the upper room of the Kwoyo-Kwan.

II

FOR some nights past Charteris had been unable to sleep; why, he knew not, for, indeed, sleep was the last thing in his thoughts. They had suddenly broken away from his own control, and instead of going over the same well-trodden ground — his work, his expenses, the next mail, and the sins of his "boy" — were now running wild races through storm and sunshine, setting his heart beating and his eyes shining, and anon plunging him in depths of moody wretchedness never sounded by such woes as wrong roots and mistaken finals, or even "mulled" exams.

Yes, argue it out as he might, it came to that: a man was to pass all his youth in poring over blinding characters and odious translations; was to live in the fine hope of getting more and harder work to do by and by, and, even at last, of turning into a dried-up old mole in a consulate somewhere; and all the while beauty in its most ravishing form was all around him, and Life's high time had struck, and the first notes of Love's pæan were sounding in his ears. Was he not a man, and young, and unspoiled, and strong ? And was there never to be a leaping at heart, must he never look at a fair woman or clasp her to him till he was too old to know or care? He had never troubled himself much about such things' till now; he had grown up slowly, in a small family

circle when he was not at school, and had thought himself fortunate to get a nomination to compete for a post
in the consular service at nineteen. Since then, his
work, and the quiet life led by the other student, Jimmy
Hayes, had framed in his existence; and all that side
of his being which might otherwise have reached out
for colour and excitement, for love or adventure, had
been lying dormant, or caged, too long. Poor Charteris
had been taught in his narrow home that beauty was
mostly wickedness, anyhow it was safer to think so;
and, as for love, of course that was a question which it
was almost immoral to discuss, until a man was earning
enough to keep a wife and family — say, five hundred a
year !

And Charteris, always ready to accept others' conclusions, had acquiesced lazily, and crept along in the dull
furrow marked out for him, dissatisfied with himself and
the life at times, but reconciled to it on the whole by
seeing his seniors with homes and incomes, and believing that it would all come right in the end if he could
only hold on and pull through.

That was before he had seen the bird of paradise
seeking for her mate. O Haru had not said one word,
had hardly let her eyes rest upon the young student,
sitting at the end of a row of great people; but sweet
youth had called aloud in every motion of her dance,
love had shone in her dark eyes, and the very witchery
of woman's dearness had laid its spell on the poor boy's
untried manhood. The official ascetic was suddenly
but completely overcome by vague, intoxicating possi-

bilities of happiness; his refined home circle would have trembled at his temerity, and would probably have cast him off forever, could they have realised his mental condition for the next few days.

Unwillingly he had left the town, longing to stay and try to see the dancer again.   But he knew that that was all but impossible.   He had no claim on her notice, no money to pay for her dancing; and had been told, besides, that her employers had let her go away for a time, on a visit to her parents; so, reluctantly, he gathered a few things together, and let Hayes, who had some experience of travelling, send him off to this little place above Hakone.   As for "Colloquial," — oh, how he hated the whole thing!   He should never try to pass the examination now.   What could it possibly lead to?

The little inn where Hayes had advised him to spend his holiday was remote from the village, lying in a narrow gorge some way back from the lake.   Only two or three other dwellings raised their grey roofs among the pine trees, and on an eminence nearer to the water a Buddhist temple made a bit of red colour in the scene. A tiny stream ran down past the temple's foot and emptied itself into the lake, and the trees — firs and larches — were everywhere.   Charteris had spent two days in these solitudes, and began at last to feel something of the eternal leisure of the woods.   The ferment in his heart was lessening, but it seemed to have brought him something which could not be taken away.   He felt hopelessly poor — and yet immensely rich.

The nights were already rather oppressive, and he

rose on the third morning, while it was still dark, to push back the screen window of his upper chamber and step out on the worn wooden balcony.

Divinely fresh seemed those early airs, and Charteris leant on folded arms and gazed out on the slumbering pine woods. There was dawn behind the hills to the east, but night lay in the valley still. Tardily the darkness seemed to rise from its dewy bed in the hollows. The stream murmured as in sleep on its way to the lake, past the upright black stones, each crowned with a little Buddha showing dimly in the darkness against the spray that keeps him forever wet. Then, off in the woods to the right, the sweetest bird-voice in the world broke out in its first song. "You sweet, you sweet, you!" sang Japan's nightingale, ever faster and faster as the joy of life burst on him in the growing light. Out of the wistaria tangle on the hillside a hawk rose slowly, and stretched his brown wings against the thin silver of the sky. Soon the stream showed less white, the trees less black, and away at the end of the valley day was floating on the bosom of the lake.

Downstairs all was quiet still, and no rattling of the wooden shutters gave signs that the household was awake. It would have been hopeless to try an exit that way, for the fastenings of the domestic fortress require skilled fingers to undo them. But it was not far to the ground, and Charteris thought that he could slip down to the lower verandah easily enough. He dressed quickly, threw his shoes over the railing, and, with a slide and a drop, rejoined them where they had fallen; in a few minutes he was following the grassy path by the stream's edge, with his face towards the opening of the valley below.

A kind of awe came over him. In all his life he had never been so alone with Nature. No one ever sees her truly in the full glare of day, when all her subjects are hustling each other on a million roads to good and evil, fortune and misfortune. But in those silent, thrilling hours between darkness and dawn, go out and listen: you will hear the very pulse of the world, whose delicate beatings have only lately been made known to us. You will feel what an atom you are, how small and unnecessary, and yet how integrally you belong to the heart of things, how closely you are folded in the robe of a Love that means to count with you forever, that calls to you in ineffable whispers among the forest leaves, that sends divine messages of eternal peace from the wild lily's heart into yours, that kisses you mutely in the wind, and lures you by a thousand silent charms to climb one easy step higher on the road to Life.

Charteris felt the wonder, and looked round from time to time as if some one had spoken to him. When he reached the widening in the path below the temple he stood still, and then turned up a green footway in the woods, where white jonquils with golden cups were swaying on their stalks in the wind. The road was hollowed out, and the banks rose on either side, fringed with wild flowers; overhead the trees met, but the day was almost come now, and the tiniest leaves and buds were visible in a tender haze of green.

The path had turned suddenly, and stretched far before him into the seclusion of the woods. And coming towards him from those solitudes, with both hands full of flowers, was the woman who had made him love and loathe his life for days past. O Haru did not notice him at first, and for one breathless moment he gazed, unbelieving of what he saw.

Alone, gowned like the dawn, in rosy crape, she was wandering after wild flowers in the first hour of the day. For untouched freshness she and they might have sprung up in the night together. She had drawn back her long sleeves with a ribbon that crossed her bosom twice and held her thin robe to her form in classic folds. Her arms were bare to the morning dews, and on one side her dress was drawn up through her girdle to the knee, showing the close-fitting white silk gaiters that the Japanese women love to walk in, and bare feet in little straw sandals, creeping through the grass. On her arm was cradled a sheaf of slender jonquils, and she was stooping to pull blossom after blossom and add it to her store. Her cheeks had a tinge of colour now, and her eyes were less languid than when she had danced her way into the young man's heart.

She was drawing nearer, and he could see the tiny pattern of rose-flecks in her *kimono*, could note the fine moulding of elbow and wrist, as she raised her arm and buried her face for a moment in her fragrant burden. As her head sank into the piled sweetness, he caught sight of a nodding jonquil blossom that she had stuck in her hair. Then came a moment of intense suspense, for O Haru raised her head and met his eyes.

Would she be furiously angry? the poor youth asked himself, arguing from what would have been the mood of a European woman surprised in such a costume. No, O Haru looked startled, but not displeased, and his courage began to return. He advanced a step, and still she did not scream or run away. On the contrary, she stood still, laid her flowers down on a flat stone, and with the grave simplicity of a race for whom the word impropriety does not exist, slipped off her binding ribbon with a single turn of the hand, and shook her long sleeves out like wings; then she drew her skirt down from where it had been tucked beneath her girdle, patted it all into place, and gave a critical glance at the folds of her *obi*. In her country clothing is a matter of respect, individual and mutual. Foreigners are known to be sensitive on this point, and great concessions are made to their prejudices; but even the most delicate and refined persons do not pretend that they were born in full dress.

When O Haru was satisfied as to the dignity of her appearance, she gathered up her flowers and came towards Charteris without the slightest sign of embarrassment.

He almost ran to meet her, and she smiled a composed greeting. Then, in the elation of the moment, he found more "Colloquial" than he dreamed he possessed, to tell her how he had seen her dance at the Maple Club, how he had thought of nothing else ever

since, and how overjoyed he was to find her. There is
no lion so bold as a shy man when once he has discovered that he can speak. The girl did not perhaps
understand all that he said, but she smiled and thanked
him for his praise, replying, as in duty bound, that her
dancing was awkward, her appearance mean, and her
dress "dirty." Upon which Charteris, not understanding the purely conventional nature of the phrases, tried
to convince her of her own loveliness and perfection, in
inspired terms which would have caused surprise and
joy to his teachers and seniors. Alas, nothing was
more improbable than that they would ever hear him
speak Japanese with the masterly fluency which came
to his aid that morning, when talking to O Haru in the
Hakone woods.

He walked by her side, carrying her gleanings, which
he had taken from her; and in a few moments she
turned into a side path which he had not noticed, and
pausing, held out her hands for the flowers.

"You are going home? May I not come too?" cried
he, his eyes on her face.

"Oh, yes, if you like," she replied, smiling, "but the
house is small and dirty, not at all fit for a great foreigner like you to see."

"I wish I were a great foreigner," said Charteris,
moving on beside her; "I know what I would do!"

"What would you do that you cannot do now?"
inquired O Haru, looking up at him with a puzzled
expression. "You are rich, you are free, you are a
man. Ah!"

She sighed, and there was a touch of bitterness in the tones.

"Ah, my dear, that's all you know about it," Charteris replied, in English.

And then he forgot that he was carrying flowers, and tried to put his hands in his pocket, and O Haru's jonquils fell in a scattered heap on the wet ground.

She laughed aloud at his crestfallen face.

"It is nothing," she said. "They are of the ground, they seek their home. So shall we some day."

But she gathered them up carefully, and shook the soil off their petals, and would let him carry them no more.

The path had been rising, and now came out on a little plateau or shelf in the hillside, shut in by thin fringes of larch trees and natural stockades of last year's undergrowth, except to the front, where it was open to the lake and — Fujiyama.

Charteris uttered an exclamation as they emerged from the woods into the full glory of the morning. Before their feet the ground dropped in a green precipice to the water, and a level wash of blue and gold spread away between deep-bosomed hills, following one another in soft succession, and seeming as if they must float out and meet on the still flood. But they were only the lowly ranges that guard the waterway to Fuji's footstool, and beyond them the world's queen of mountains rose from her misty bed — rose and towered in dreamy perfection, hyacinth-tinted in the sunrise, against the cloudless crystal of the upper sky.

"Fuji san," murmured O Haru, and she threw a flower towards the wonder.   The flower fell and floated on the water far below.

"Will you come and rest?" she said to Charteris, and pointed towards the house that stood in the clearing.

He turned, and saw one of those small homes in which beauty, comfort, and simplicity seem to be one at last, — such little homes as make the worried and weary traveller wish he had been born a Japanese. The grey thatched roof bore on its crown a waving fringe of iris leaves.

Once there was a famine in the land, and it was forbidden to plant in the ground anything which could not be used for food.   The frivolous irises only supply the powder with which the women whiten their faces, but their little ladyships would not be cheated of that. "Must we look like frights as well as die of hunger?" they cried.   And every woman set a tiny plantation of irises on the roof of her house, and there, in most country places, they are growing still.

The upper windows of O Haru's dwelling were open, and a gorgeous silk quilt was hanging over the balcony. On the ground floor the shutters were still in place; the carved pillars and fine wood of the verandah showed that it was not an abode of poverty, and on one side the steps led into a tiny garden, with stone lantern, pond, and goldfish all complete.

Casting a quick glance at the front of the house, O Haru led Charteris to the side that looked on the garden.   Flat velvet cushions lay on the polished wood of the verandah, and she placed them where he could sit and see the view; then she disappeared into the interior by the little earthquake door.   Charteris obediently took his seat on the step, and gazed round him as if afraid to wake from a happy dream.

"Good heavens!" he thought, "does this kind of thing come to everybody? No wonder some men are happy in Japan!"

Presently, after a sound of talking within, the shutters began to jump and drop out of their places, and an old woman, dressed in dull blue, ran them all into their closet at one end of the building. She passed Charteris with an indifferent glance, and also disappeared.   Then the screens were pushed apart, and in the half light of the room beyond, O Haru, kneeling on the mats, invited him to enter.

"But I must not come in," he said ruefully, looking at his shoes, which were heavy with wet soil. "I shall spoil your beautiful mats, O Haru san."

"Take them off," said the little lady, smiling at his dilemma.

"Can't!" wailed Charteris.

He had suddenly remembered that the jinriksha man's wife had had a holiday before he left home, and that his stockings were terribly in want of darning.

"I will do it for you," said his hostess; "my servant has gone out."

"Oh, no, no, no," cried he; "do come and sit with me here. It is so lovely in the open air," he added, with duplicity.

So she pushed the tray, carved like a lotus leaf, out towards him, and came and sat on her heels on the farther side of it, and gave him tea in tiny blue cups, out of the smallest and brownest teapot he had ever seen. She seemed amused when he emptied three of the cups one after another; and then he was made to eat white squares of peppermint mixed with glycerine, and pink rice biscuits.

"Mayn't I have some more tea?" he asked, remarking mentally that it was rather a "rum breakfast." He was not in the least frightened now, and was sunning himself in her presence as a lazy, happy dog basks before the fire.

"What do foreign ladies make tea in?" asked she, suddenly, watching him drink it. "It seems to me that it would be better for you to have some made in the bath if you are so thirsty."

Charteris wondered if he could turn his reply into a declaration, — something about thirst produced by burning love, — but it did not go, so he only said : —

"Do not laugh at me, O Haru san. It isn't fair, because you can say so many sharp things in Japanese, and I cannot answer you."

"I will teach you," she said, looking at him kindly ; "but they will not be sharp things — only very nice, polite ones."

"Will you really?" he cried, the colour rushing to his face. "Oh, you do not know what it would be to me!"

"Yes," she said; "you can come every day, and I

will be glad.   I stay here to see my . . . mother.   She is very sick with the old sickness, and sleeps much, and I am lonely in the morning."

Charteris did not stop to ask what the "old sickness" was.

"Oh, how can I thank you!" he cried.   "I will come every day, very early.   Oh, you are good, O Haru san."

The sun was high and hot when he crossed the open space and plunged into the woods again.   They were dumb for him now, but he needed no more comforting or soothing.   He was quite happy, quite satisfied, and not inclined to ask what would come to-morrow.   The sleep that he had lost at night he found again in the warm afternoon hours, and with it came wonderful dreams, perhaps not too fair to be realised, after all. At sunset, he ran down to the lake and found a boat, and rowed far, and then rested on his rough oars and floated hither and thither.   He would have climbed again to the grey-roofed nest on the hillside, but that O Haru, who was a very decided little lady, had said that he must only come in the early morning and never at any other time.   She had " business," as she vaguely said, during the rest of the day.   How on earth, he asked himself, should he drag through the empty hours till the next day's dawn ?

It came at last, and Charteris rushed through the dewy paths, unheeding of many things which had thrilled him yesterday.   This time O Haru was leaning over her balcony, and when he came to the gate ran

down to let him in.   There seemed to be more to say
to-day than yesterday, as they sat and chattered on the
step; and by the time that Charteris went down the hill
on the second day he had added a large stock of new
words to his "Colloquial," and he felt almost as virtuous
as he was happy.

And so the happy days went on; he always came
early, but he very often stayed quite late.   Sometimes
it was midday before that harsh voice called from the
other side of the house, "O Haru Cho!"   Then O Haru
would dismiss him with a quick signal, and glide away
to answer the summons; and after that, however bright
the day was, he always felt that the sun had set for
him.

Yes, he loved the dancing-girl.   How fine and wicked
it sounded, he thought; and he smiled as he pictured to
himself Murray's middle-aged disapproval, Hayes's cold-
blooded "Such rot!" his pious family's horror at the
confession.   Love! that was too cold a name for the
passion which consumed him!   How absurd it seemed
to call her a Geisha!   He knew, of course, that the
name was not necessarily a term of reproach; still it
implied a kind of stagey publicity, and the girl with
whom he wandered in the woods or sat on the hillside
in the mornings was the incarnation of everything gentle
and modest and refined.   No princess could have shown
more dignity in all her ways; and yet, she was only a
dancing-girl!   He had persuaded her to tell him something about herself.   As far as he could make out, she
would belong for years to come to the master who had

had her educated, at great expense, as she explained, and who was now reaping golden profits from her accomplishments.

"He is a very kind master," she said simply. "I had no father, and he found us, very poor, when I was a little child. Then he took me to have me taught, for my people had been dancers for many generations, and he said I should do it well. My mother was with me then, but . . . now . . . she lives here, because the air is pure. And once in two years he lets me come to see her. He says I dance better after I have been in the hills! He is a good master. Not all are like that. But I shall not come again to this place."

"Why?" asked Charteris, taking her hand and laying it, finger for finger, on his own. "See, O Haru, your hand looks like ivory fallen on rough earth. Tell me why you will not come back to Hakone?"

"Because my . . . mother will be dead in a year," she answered, lifting her fingers one by one, and letting them fall lightly on his. "The sickness has lasted long already. There is much suffering. It is better to die."

She spoke as calmly as if she were telling him the best news in the world. He was greatly shocked.

"But are you not sorry?" he asked. "You do not seem to love her at all."

O Haru cast a reproachful glance at him.

"I love her very much," she said. "Japanese people always love their relations. But why should I make you sad? My trouble is for me, not for my friends."

"Forgive me," cried Charteris; "of course, I understand. Oh, how I wish I could take you away and keep you for myself. Dear, dear O Haru, if you could only dream how I love you."

He was holding her hand to his cheek, and she did not take it away.

"I cost a great deal," she replied; "are you a very rich man?"

He dropped the hand as if it burnt him, and started back, shaking the little tray of cups behind him.

"What do you mean?" he gasped. "Cost? Rich?"

"Yes," she went on stolidly; "many persons have wished to buy me, but my master asks more than anybody will give for one ugly little dancing-girl. So I must stay with him till I am an 'O Bassan,' and then nobody will care to see me dance."

"But you said for some years," protested Charteris, trying to see things from her cool point of view, "and then you would be free!"

"And I am not young," said she, despondently. "I am already twenty, and at twenty-three the younger girls will call me 'O Bassan' (grandmother)! I shall be still more ugly than I am now, and nothing will matter any more."

But she laughed as she said it, and seemed to take comfort from something in Charteris's eyes. They were lingering on her face in burning protest against her words.

"You are the most beautiful thing in the world," he said, half choking. "Oh, why am I not a rich man, to free you from this slavery?"

Before she could reply, a crawling sound was heard on the mats behind their screen, and that horrible muffled voice called, nearer than it had ever called before : " O Haru Cho ! "

The girl looked frightened, and sprang to her feet.

" I come ! " she cried, and she pushed Charteris quickly away.

" It is so early ! " he pleaded ; " let me stay a little. May I not see your mother ? "

" No," she said, more sharply than she had ever spoken before ; " condescend to go at once ! "

He could but obey, and strode off, sore and angry. All that day he tasted the full poison of O Haru's words — " . . . many have wished to buy me." The day might come when the great sum would be forthcoming, and she would be sold into new slavery — and she would not mind it. There was the sting. Poor Charteris hardly knew why it hurt him so much. He had dragged all his anchors, overthrown all his standards ; and Right and Wrong, instead of lying in one white stripe and one black one, before his moral vision, as heretofore, had got wildly intertwined, and were dancing mad reels in his consciousness. Right? It would be right for him to marry O Haru, to carry her up to Tokyo and make a British subject of her on the spot ! There would be no more question of dollars after that !

No question of dollars ? Why, he could not even buy clothes for her out of his small student's pittance ! And again he thought of Murray's grim amusement, of

Jimmy's half-cynical condolences, of that interview with the Head of Things, in which he would certainly be told that, not having passed his examination at the proper time, on the whole it was undesirable that he should remain any longer in the consular service. And then? No, he could not ask O Haru to become Mrs. Frederic Charteris. And that being so, of course, the only right thing to do was to go away and never speak to her again.

Arriving at conclusions does not always mean carrying them out. When Charteris saw his duty clearly before him, he looked it in the face, found it amazingly unattractive — and turned his back on it. He was rather a weak creature, and had to find an excuse to face his conscience with.

"'Colloquial' — gaining every day," he murmured, as he went downstairs almost on hands and knees, for the steps are steep and slippery in country inns, — "million pities to lose it all now."

III

THAT night there was a full moon, a great yellow spring moon, that would not be gainsaid. All the hares on the hillsides were springing about like mad things, trying to think that their big ears had grown into wings and they could really fly at last. The little children fell asleep on the verandahs, and sucked dream lollipops noisily with their little kissing mouths. The bonze in the temple felt disposed for prayer, and made his acolyte put fresh flowers at Buddha's feet and light the incense sticks, and strike the gong industriously, while he sat and gazed at "O Tsuki sama," and found himself heretically fancying that Nirvana was in the moon — Nirvana, of course, being a state and not a place! More than one village girl crept down to the shore, wondering if the boys would soon come in from the fishing; and the blind "Amma," feeling his way slowly down the street, put quite tender notes into the rhythmical call of his reed pipe, as he sang out his prices for rubbing away all the different pains of aching bodies. The day's work was over, even in busy Japan; and the brown countrywoman sat on her doorstep, looking at the Mother light in the sky, and hoping that the babe at her breast would grow up strong as Benké who could fight the gods, and wise as Hideyoshi who taught men the arts of peace.

Was it likely that when Charteris, all unbidden, strolled up to the bamboo gate of O Haru's domain, he should not see the little lady herself, leaning from her balcony, and gazing out towards Fuji and the moon? And, since the light was full on his face and he gave a low call, was it likely that she would not bestow a glance on her friend of the sunrise? Of course she turned her head, then disappeared within the house.

Suddenly she was close to him, having skimmed over the grass on her quaint clogs without a sound. He leaned across the gate and caught her hands. She looked up into his eyes and laughed.

"Foolish one!" she said in low tones, "if you do that, how can I come out?"

"I will lift you over!" said Charteris, boldly; and before she understood what he meant, he had raised her lightly and swung her clear across the gate, not to set her on the ground, but to throne her on his shoulder instead.

"I shall carry you right away now," he murmured, looking up into her face as it hovered above him.

"That is quite necessary," she replied, kicking out one little foot from under her bewildering draperies. "I have left my *gheta* in the garden."

Her clogs had fallen to the ground when he lifted her.

"I shall carry you down to the water, and we will swim away in the moonlight together, you sweet!"

She did not answer, but only put a hand on his curly head, to steady herself as he took the path to the lake. Once she gave a slight cry, for a bough caught her hair and one of the gold pins fell from its place. Charteris stooped for it without displacing her from his shoulder, and as she took it from his hand she said:—

"You can carry well! What a good coolie you would make! Where are we going?"

"Out, in the moonlight, on the water. There is a boat just below here. I had it this morning," he replied.

"Can you row, Chiata san?" she asked. "They say the lake is full of evil spirits at night. I am afraid."

"No evil spirits will come near us, O Haru san," he answered; "your face and my heart—will keep us safe together."

Charteris felt as bold as a lion, and as strong as Benké. He drew his arm closer round his light burden, and rubbed his cheek against the soft *kimono*. The crape smelt so sweet of sandal-wood.

When they came out from the bushes the tiny cove was all aflood with moonlight, and the water beyond was a rippling sea of silver. Charteris set the girl down on a mossy stone while he pulled up the boat, which was rocking idly a few feet away. It was rather a heavy craft, with a sort of deck at one end, and stout oars were lying along its length.

"I am afraid you must walk a step," he said, looking towards O Haru. "If I loose the rope to come to you, it will float off again." He reached out his hand to help her.

"I will try," she replied, "but I have no shoes. I hope the stones are not sharp."

"It is all soft sand," he said; "only two steps — so."

Her bare feet made a few tell-tale marks in the dark sand, and then she stood beside him. He held out his hand as if she were mounting a horse, and, springing on it, she was over the side of the boat in a moment. He followed, pushed off vigorously, and felt the craft buoyant on the water. Then with a few long strokes he shot out into the open, and the black barge seamed the sheeny surface with a thousand converging ripples.

O Haru had perched on the edge of the deck and was dipping her feet in the water. It dropped from their whiteness in a rain of diamonds, and she wantonly splashed a little in Charteris's face.

"Do you think I mind?" he cried. "I would have swum the lake ten times across to see you sitting there in the moonlight! If the world were mine, I would give it to you, O Haru san."

She turned and looked at him gravely.

"Oh, no; I think not," she said. "You like me to amuse you, because there is no one else here, and I am teaching you to speak much Japanese."

"O Haru!" exclaimed Charteris, leaning forward on the oar, "don't say such dreadful things! You know you are the one treasure in the world for me! I never, never loved any one before, and I never shall again! But I am only a poor man, with no money, and I can do nothing for you!"

"I want nothing done for me; I have all I want," said O Haru, proudly. "But I think you say true,

Chiata san, and that you do like me a little — but we will not talk of that.   Shall I sing to you now?"

She leant back against the socket of the mast, and began a low song like a death march.   Her voice was young and sweet, but the strange intervals of the music made Charteris shiver.   There was an ominous thrill in them, and a night bird woke and answered from a clump of trees in the black shadow of a bay into which the boat seemed to have drifted of itself, for Charteris's rowing was very fitful.

Singing, for O Haru, meant dancing, and almost unconsciously she began to sway in time to her own weird music; her hands waved and met and parted; and then, as the boat passed out from the darkness, she sprang up, light as a cloud-wreath, and moved in a slow step to a wailing song in time with the oars, and her shadow danced beneath her on the silver flood.

Charteris held his breath, leaning far forward to gaze at her, his arm moving just enough to steady the boat.

O Haru had forgotten him.   The pure ecstasy of the night had taken possession of her blood, and the intoxication of genius was upon her.   None had ever seen her dance as Charteris saw her now, carried away by the maddening spell of the freedom and the mountain air, and that bath of warm moonlight.   On the rough wood of the deck her bare feet flashed, noiseless as falling snowflakes, and the few drops that still clung to them slid, round diamonds, on the poor planks.   Her thin draperies moved slowly round her in changing clouds, now wrapping her close like the whorls of a shell, now dipping up a rain of gems from the water's kiss as she bent far to this side and that in curves of reckless grace. Her dark eyes shone with triumph, and then were veiled in languor as the fever of passionate life shook her in its might, and she bent like a flower in the storm. She seemed the very spirit of wind and water, whose mystic beauty is embodied in the highest symbolism of her people.

Suddenly her sash came loose, and trailed its heavy lengths of green and gold over the boat's edge. She caught it back with a whirl, which brought a dripping bow of silver in its wake, and threw it up on the air, where it flew from her hand and curled round the mast, like a live thing at bay.

She bounded after it, with white arms outstretched, and as she sprang, her upper robe fell to her feet in a foamy heap, leaving her one white-veiled line of beauty against the mast.

Charteris reached her side in a leap, and caught her in his arms as she sank down in the utter abandonment of reaction. Then he knelt by her and made her rest her cheek on his shoulder as he held both her hands in his. His arm was around her, and she did not push him away. There was a happy smile on her mouth, and her eyes were dewy with unspoken joy.

"My little one! my little one!" the man murmured again and again, with an infinite tenderness in his voice. The climax of life had come; and they sat together, these children of East and West — she dumb with the woman's certainty of loss, knowing well the hour would

not return; he triumphant, sure that it would last forever.   And it seemed that æons of peace were passing
over their heads as they two floated alone, silent, safe, in
the blessed freedom of the night, under the shining of
the Spring moon that would not be gainsaid.

.   .   .   .

At last she made him turn and row her back to the
little bay.

"I have been out too long," she said anxiously, looking at the moon, which was beginning to dip towards
the hills; "they will have been looking for me, I fear."

As the boat grated on the beach she sprang out unaided, and fled, without waiting for him, up the shadowed path between the trees.   Already the early dawn
was sending cold shivers along the air, and a bluish
light rested upon the temple and the grove.   Charteris
made the boat fast and ran quickly after O Haru,
though he had little hope of seeing her if that invisible
tyrant indoors had really called for her.   It was some
distance up to their dwelling, and the path twisted and
turned more than once, so that the daylight was fairly
full when he breasted the last rise and came out on the
little plateau.   The gate was open, and he ventured in,
stepping gently so as not to be heard.   All was quiet at
the front of the house, and he crept round one corner,
making for the verandah where he always sat with
O Haru over their fairy breakfast.

She had her back to him, and was stooping over
something that had crept out from between the open
screens, and now lay, a hideous form, close against

her feet. It had been a human being, but all features were obliterated from the poor face upturned to hers. With a tender gesture she was caressing the tumid cheek. The rest of the countenance seemed to be one awful wound, and the hand that caught at her arm was eaten away to a stump by the devouring famine of that disease.

"O Haru Cho,"—the muffled accents were just recognisable—"you left me. Why?"

"Only to wash my garments in the lake, beloved! See, I am in time to make the tea."

She turned to the little tray, and took one of the blue cups from which Charteris had drunk many a time, an hour later than this. As O Haru moved to reach the tray, the creature's arm fell by its side, and it leant back against the pillar of the verandah. The cold light showed all, forgave nothing. Charteris saw that the form, colossal in its ruin, was that of a man. The breast was bare, and the coarse blue gown which fell away from it was held to the purple, perishing limbs by a man's narrow girdle. O Haru's "beloved" was a leper.

Charteris shrank back, trembling, with ashy cheeks. Then he crept away, passed the gate without touching either lintel, and stumbled like a drunken man, on, into the woods. There darkness came over him; he sank down against a tree, and his senses went out in a sick swoon.

IV

In six months Charteris went up for his examination again.

"Really, my dear fellow," said Mr. Murray, lifting his glasses delicately off his nose, "it is too little to say that I am amazed! When I begged the chief to give you another six months, I had very little hope that you would make such good use of your time. Go on; you are reading quite fluently."

Charteris seemed less delighted with the praise than Murray had expected. His fresh face had changed and grown older; his eyes had lost their foolish brightness, and seemed shadowed, as with some sadness or terror looked on too soon and — too long.

"I am glad you think I am getting on, sir," he said quietly, and then continued to read aloud : —

"'Local News. — *The Cholera*. We regret to say that the popular dancer, O Haru Takayama —'"

Charteris stopped, and the paper rustled, for his hand shook violently.

"Yes?" said Murray. "O Haru — the girl who danced at the Kwoyo Kwan the night we were all there. Surely you remember? Go on: what do they say?"

Charteris pulled himself together with a strong effort, and continued : —

" ' O Haru Takayama . . . died . . . at the Uyeno Hospital . . . last night.   She had been slightly unwell for some weeks with a swelling of the ankles, . . . which prevented her from dancing.   She has now succumbed to the prevailing epidemic. . . . Her loss will be much felt . . . by her employers . . . and the poor, to . . . whom she was most generous.' "

The reader's voice had broken halfway, but he had struggled to the end.

"Is that all?" asked Murray.   "What is the matter?"

Charteris was leaning back in his chair, very white, and his hand had fallen by his side.   He got up and walked to the window, muttering something about his head being "funny."

"We may as well knock off work for to-day," said the older man.   "As for your Colloquial, it will really about do now, it seems to me.   That time in the hills was the making of you, my boy."

A SON OF THE DAIMYŌS

"No need to tell how young I am and slender, —
A little maid that in thy palm could lie!"

(*From a Japanese poem by the Lady Sakanouhe, 8th century.*)

A Son of the Daimyō

I

IONE was an only child. No brother or sister ran races with her in the gardens of the Mæda Palace, no little playmates disputed the possession of her costly toys in its wide low rooms. Alone she ruled over every creature in the place, from her soldier father down to the lodge-keepers and the stable-boys. Her mother, still a young and beautiful woman, would sometimes shake her head, and say that it would be hard for the child to give up her own will when the yoke of marriage should be laid upon her neck; and she took advantage of every occasion to preach the necessity of submission and self-annihilation before husbands and parents-in-law. O Ione would listen humbly and with downcast eyes, but in her heart she was thinking that the new teachers at her school said nothing about submission, and a great deal about independence and the

equality of the sexes, and of how good and clever women (of whom she certainly intended to be one) should make their influence felt, and should help to govern the world.

O Ione was sixteen when the sovereigns of her country celebrated their silver wedding, but she still went every day to the Peeress's School, and did all her lessons with great exactness and zeal. Her teachers — intellectual English women, new to the East — were delighted with the girl's enthusiasm for learning, and pushed her on, perhaps a little recklessly, not realising how great a strain is put on the unfolding powers by having to learn the science of two worlds at once, by the attempt to assimilate the mathematics and ologies and statistics of Europe, and at the same time to become possessed of the language, history, literature, and maxims of a system so enormous, and so absolutely divided from Western thought, that no European has ever yet mastered it in its entirety.

When the Empress came, once a year, to visit the college of little noble ladies, O Ione san was the scholar put forward to recite the congratulatory ode, to play the prim little festival jig on the yet stiff piano, and to lead the musical drill, which always closed the girls' part of the entertainment. It was wonderful to see her and her companions marching in quick step up and down the huge hall, their English teacher walking backwards before them, her Girton gown flying round her in black streamers as she exhorted her pupils to lift their feet and move quickly and together. She looked like an energetic crow trying to marshal a flock of humming-birds.   O Ione did not care for this part of her studies at all, and slipped through the gymnastics without ever having really lifted her foot from the ground, or having once straightened up her slender form from the willowy droop which is the only carriage possible for a high-born damsel in Japan.   She saw no reason to obey her teachers, clever though they might be, when they ordered her to move and stand like a coolie.

No thought of her future — at any rate beyond the end of the term — entered her head as she went day after day to the school near the Houses of Parliament. It was only a little distance from her home, and she en-joyed the walk in the morning freshness, and also in the afternoon when one of her companions would saunter back with her, their two maids — confidential, middle-aged women — chattering together just behind them, and carrying bundles of school-books tied up in violet cloths bearing the crests of the little ladies' fami-lies.   Though the streets were full of school-girls in the morning, people generally turned to have a second look at Viscount Mæda's pretty daughter, tripping along in her brilliant purple "nakhama," with touches of crim-son and rose in her sash and sleeves.   There was more rose and crimson in cheeks and lips, and the eyes were bright and sunny for all their Eastern darkness; and now that her hair, instead of hanging down her back in a long plait, was dressed in a fantastic crest, pinned into place with glittering ornaments, she looked indeed like a human humming-bird, a creature made for sunshine and honey, from whose airy presence the profanities of sorrow and pain should be banished forever.

Now on a day it happened that Lieutenant Sada Takumichi was passing from the Naval College down to the Rokumeikwan, the Nobles' Club, just as O Ione and her maid were returning to their home. He stopped and turned to look after her, as the ponderous iron gates of her father's house were thrown open by a porter, who bowed double as the girl passed in. The servant followed her, the gates swung together, and the lieutenant watched the graceful figure till it disappeared among the rhododendrons of the garden in the direction of the house, which stood some way back from the road. He was not a Tokyo man himself, and stepped up to the gate to ask the porter who was the master of the house.

"Viscount Mæda," the man replied. "That is our young lady who has just gone in."

"Thanks," said the lieutenant. "The viscount is in the Ministry of Marine, is he not?"

"Honourably, so it is," the servant replied. "Did you wish to see him? He is not here at present."

"No," said the lieutenant, and he turned away and walked up the dusty road, apparently lost in thought.

He was a man of middle height and well-knit figure, which showed to good advantage in his close-fitting naval uniform. His small, cropped head and quick, dark eyes indicated thought and determination; the nose, depressed at the bridge, spread slightly at the nostrils, which were wide and mobile; the mouth was

flat and pitiless, with a long upper lip, but this was
partly hidden by a stiff black moustache. His whole
bearing was soldierly and well-bred; his age at this
time was a little over thirty, counted as a year or two
more by Japanese reckoning.

The only son of an impoverished Daimyō, he had
grown up under the influence of the great modernising
movement in Japan, which, beginning when he was in
the cradle, now offered him all the openings to success
and distinction which his ambition could desire. And
in his own way Sada Takumichi desired much. He was
now a rising officer in the Torpedo School, and the
only day-dream he ever permitted himself to indulge in
was that of a sudden outbreak of war with a great
power, when he should have the satisfaction of sinking
the enemy's flagship. He was not married yet, and
had made up his mind to leave all thoughts of marriage
aside for some years to come. He felt that it would
but hamper him in his career, and being of young
Japan, he made light of the old-fashioned obligation of
providing a clever, submissive, nurse-daughter-in-law for
his parents in their old age. But he was by no means
averse to the society of those beautiful and witty ladies
whose business it is to cheer the lives of homeless bach-
elors, without entailing upon them any domestic responsibility; and, off duty, Lieutenant Sada Takumichi was
something of a roysterer, delighting in noisy suppers
and music, saké, and dancing-girls.

For all that he was not a popular man, and was disliked by the subalterns under him on account of his

overbearing ways, and because he never neglected an opportunity of getting them reproved or put under arrest for trifling irregularities, which a good-natured superior would have winked at. Before he left the Naval College, the elder men, although always ready to give him his due for brains and courage (the latter being taken as a matter of course), withheld their final approbation for future reference, and shook their heads over what was whispered of his dissipation and extravagance. He carried out all his duties with the greatest exactitude, so that no one had any ground for remonstrating with him; but if the wisdom of the ancients held true, when did saké and geishas help a man to fight for his country or honour his emperor? No, they told each other, many a youngster would do better than he with half his brains — Omori, for instance. There was a boy whom his teachers might be proud of — bright-eyed and open-hearted, with a temper of gold and nerves of steel, quick to obey, and trusted by all.

Yasu Omori was younger by some years than Takumichi, and though both had passed far beyond the Naval College stage at the time when this story begins, their respective positions had not greatly changed. Omori was running his senior hard in the service, and was always the favourite with officers and men. Takumichi outwardly sneered at the other's easy popularity, and inwardly grudged it to him with watchful bitterness.

There is a visitation of the gods called love at first sight. Of all the fantastic passions that humanity is heir to, it is the most unreasonable, the most incomprehensible, the least useful, and most enduring. The malady is developed in the twinkling of an eye, and generally seizes upon the most unlikely victims, and by its means that cynical little lady, Dame Fortune, delights in upsetting and confounding the plans and ambitions of a lifetime. It has been responsible for many a tragedy in Japan, where the conventionalities are built breast high to keep an extraordinarily impulsive national character within bounds, where love must leap its own wild height to be free, and has to break away at last through rivers of blood and tears.

This judgment fell on Sada Takumichi at the gate of the Mæda Palace. He turned and moved on up the dusty hill like one struck blind, not knowing why or whither he was walking. The blood was hammering like big drums in his ears, his heart, awake at last, beat wildly in his breast, and his eyes saw nothing but that vision of rosy girlhood, radiant with the evanescent grace of dawn, tender with the promise of a woman's perfect day.

As he turned at the top of the hill to look back, he could see, above the massive wall which shut off the gardens from the street, the carved roofs of the palace standing up amid feathery bowers of green, which reached far away behind it to the verge of the second moat. And Sada, who had sneered at passion and laughed at love, stood and swore to himself by the tablets of his ancestors and the honour of his sword that little O Ione Mæda should be his own, by love and marriage if she would — if not, some other way.

He chafed a little at the slow means by which he must reach her, but he thought it best to make his proposal in proper form, and, a day or two later, sent one of his relatives to call on a sister of Viscount Mæda. The employment of third parties to conduct such negotiations is intended to provide the necessary defence against friction or personal humiliation. O Ione's aunt listened favourably to the proposition, and promised to do her best to forward Lieutenant Sada Takumichi's suit. His name was old and honourable, and there was nothing to be said against his character as far as she knew. He had the reputation of being a smart officer and a gentleman, although of diminished fortune. This drawback would probably be reckoned a small one in the eyes of O Ione's parents, who, having no son, hoped that her husband, when she took one, would make her interests his, and in the end administer her large inheritance as the representative of the Mæda family. A bridegroom who would not separate her from them was what her father and mother wished for, and they would not have found him in the person of a man of very large independent means, who would have insisted upon absorbing his wife into his own family.

The few days of suspense which followed this step were the longest and dreariest which Sada Takumichi had ever spent. It was a new thing to him to find that time hung heavy on his hands; a new thing, and not a pleasant one, to realise that his happiness or misery depended on the nod of an unknown person like O Ione's father. He pondered enviously on the foreign methods of courtship, such as had been described to him by those of his friends who had spent some time in Europe. He had little doubt as to what would be the result of his pleadings could he proffer them himself. But that was such an unheard-of breach of etiquette that he meant only to have recourse to it when everything else should have been tried and found useless. He had not even the consolation of watching for O Ione as she passed in the street, for he was ordered down to Yokosuka to inspect and try some newly arrived torpedo boats, and had to leave word with his envoy to communicate with him there.

Meanwhile there had been much pondering and discussion in the Mæda family, many long talks between the viscount and his wife and sister as to whether it would be wise or foolish to accept Takumichi's proposal. It was the first that had been made in form for the hand of the daughter of the house, and, though far from brilliant in some ways, presented certain advantages which her parents were quick to see and value. The lieutenant's family was as noble as their own, and had given warriors and statesmen to the country in times past. At his father's death he would succeed to an honourable title, and Mæda's influence at court could obtain other distinctions for him. Viscountess Mæda said openly that to have her only child taken away from her would cause her a grief which she could not survive ; and she argued that Takumichi would make an ideal son-in-law, inasmuch as he was willing to promise that O Ione should not be permanently separated from her parents, and should, in any case, always remain with them while he was away at sea. His small fortune was a matter of no importance, as O Ione's inheritance was such a notable one. Viscount Mæda, idolising the child as entirely (if not so openly) as did her mother, saw the force of these conclusions; man-like, he made light of the fact that Takumichi was known to indulge in occasional dissipation, and did not confide to his wife what would have been a drawback in her eyes.

O Ione was told nothing of the matter until all the pros and cons had been patiently threshed out; but her sharp young senses caught the stirring of fate's wings, and she questioned her old nurse (who was, of course, taken into the family confidence) so closely and mercilessly that she had very little to learn when at last her father and mother announced to her, with affectionate solemnity, that a gentleman of whom they approved had asked for her hand, and that nothing remained but for her to see him and decide whether his company for life would be agreeable to her.

O Ione was just at the age when youth is longing to see everything, and keeps its wings in a perpetual flutter on the edge of the nest. She had not the slightest wish to be married, and decided in her own little mind that the gentleman would not be to her taste. But the interview with him would certainly mean a treat of some sort; a picnic most likely, or a breakfast for duck-shooting at her father's beautiful place on the river, where she and the aspirant for her hand could have a good look at each other, and even a little conversation; in fact, without once mentioning the affair for which they had been brought together, every opportunity would be afforded them of making up their minds as to whether it would suit them to marry or not. No one would be the worse for the pleasant party, so why refuse a little bit of fun ?

So O Ione, with her eyes on the ground, intimated her willingness to comply with the honoured wishes of her beloved parents, and the viscountess began to look over her daughter's wardrobe, to see if any additions were necessary before she made her first grown-up appearance in society. She and her chief maids spent a whole day in unfolding and turning over soft crapes, and embroidered bands, and " obis " stiff with gold and silver. O Ione, of course, refused to go to school that morning, and sat on the silk cushions beside her mother, enjoying the wonderful display of colour with all her heart. The aunt was present, and two or three cousins, who sighed gently from time to time, and told O Ione that she was the happiest girl in the Province to possess so many beautiful things.

It was the first time that even she had seen all the gorgeous stuffs spread out, for as a rule they were kept folded away in the odorous darkness of the huge lacquer boxes (all over gold dragons and six-winged butterflies — the Mæda crest), tied with heavy ropes of scarlet silk, and locked up in the family storehouse, a fireproof building crammed with ancestral treasures. Thither the winter garments were sent when spring burst over the land, and there the web of spring blossoms was stored when summer permitted the wearing of an iris pattern on a cool, water-green ground. And from thence, when the autumn fired the maples, the fine red wool under-robes were brought out and the delicate white grass-cloths laid by in their place to wait for next summer's heats. The gold tissues and embroideries were wrapped, piece by piece, in soft silk coverings, and then piled in double and treble boxes to keep out the treacherous dampness during the long rains. In very wet weather, fires were kept burning in the "hibachis" in the storehouse, fires fed with sweet roots and banked up with white wistaria ash (impalpably fine and soft), raked into sea-and-cloud patterns by the artist fingers of the fire-girl, who had only this one detail to attend to in the great household, and did it with her whole soul.

Finally a dress was chosen for O Ione to wear on the great occasion. It was one which had been given to her by an Imperial princess some years before; but she had not then grown up to it, and so had never had the joy of putting it on. It was a heavy silk crape shaded from a dazzling velvety blue at the foot to the paleness of a morning cloud on the shoulder; from a sea of foam and pine-needles embroidered thickly round the base, delicate shoots and tendrils crept up its length in honey-suckle tints, and the end of the long sleeves seemed again to dip towards the pines and the foam. Touches of gold gleamed on its supple folds, and the roll of silk which stiffened it at the bottom was of the colour of sunshine. The next robe beneath (for a Japanese lady must wear three, one just showing beyond the other at neck and wrists and feet) was pale green like the young bamboo, and the innermost of all a warm tea-rose, which lay caressingly against the clear white of throat and arm.

The question of the sash occupied the committee for a full hour, while tea and sweetmeats refreshed the worn councillors. O Ione and her cousins were for a piece of scarlet and gold brocade, most gorgeous to behold, but the viscountess insisted on something dark, though stiff with gold, and only allowed the necessary touch of youth's "young red" to appear in the narrow crape girdle which should be tied over all, and in the strand which must be knotted into O Ione's hair with the gold and tortoiseshell roses when the great day should come.

At last the beautiful stuffs were swept away, and O Ione, tired of sitting still so long, led her cousins in a wild dance under the willows and over the red toy bridges of the garden, till they came to the big tank where a hundred fat goldfish rose at her call, jumping and hustling one another, and opening greedy mouths to be fed with lark cakes and rice balls scattered on the water.

II

O IONE wore her beautiful dress, but the "treat" turned out to be of a quite unexpected kind, neither a picnic nor a wild-duck party, but a grand luncheon on board a battle-ship at Yokosuka. The vessel had just arrived, in shining beauty, from a European dockyard, and Japan's Sailor Prince, with the Minister of Marine, and all his staff, and many others, were invited to inspect it. As a rule, ladies did not attend such parties, but of late the Empress, keenly interested in all that touched the country's greatness, had been once or twice to Yokosuka, and had gone over the vessels lying there, to the jubilant delight of officers and men ; so now the great ladies and the officers' relations were following her example, and were charmed to be invited to an entertainment on board the last addition to the Fleet. It was easy for Viscount Mæda, as Vice-Minister of Marine, to arrange that a certain number of officers from the Torpedo School should attend the fête, and Lieutenant Takumichi was privately informed that this was the occasion on which he would be presented to O Ione san. No reference had been made during the negotiations to his having seen her in the street, and it was taken for granted that she was as much a stranger to him as he was to her.

The day broke clear and fine, a thing not always

to be expected in the moist spring months, and the harbour was brilliant with flags and boats, and gay with martial music which mingled with the murmur of the waves. It set O Ione's young blood dancing as she sat beside her mother in the Government barge, which every stroke of the oars brought nearer to the great white ship floating proudly at anchor, dressed with bunting and flower garlands from stem to stern, from bowsprit to topmast, where the red and white flag waved royally, a scarlet sun on a field of silver — the whiteness of peace kept safe by the watchful menace of war.

O Ione looked up and trembled as she realised that those immovable chains of figures high in air were sailors manning the yards, and after that she thought of nothing for a minute or two, as the great guns boomed out their thunderous salute to the prince, and the air was rent with deafening roars of welcome.

The young girl was almost frightened, simple and unconscious as she was, when she found herself standing with her mother amid a ring of fine ladies, who had collected together under one of the awnings. The deck — the attenuated deck of the modern warship — was crowded with uniforms and gay dresses, some Japanese, some foreign. The foreign ladies, of whom there were a few, seemed quite at home among the guns and machinery, and cleverly managed to drop out from the circle and find some man acquaintance to take them about and show them everything. But the Japanese women kept close together like a flock of doves, and only bowed and smiled to their friends, and quite refused to come out from under the awning.

In the strangeness of the scene O Ione had forgotten the reason of her having been brought there, and wondered why her mother broke off a conversation with a neighbour, and turned to look questioningly at her father, who was approaching, accompanied by a young officer. Now O Ione felt shy indeed, for she knew who this must be. If the truth be told, she edged a little behind her mother, and never raised her eyes from the ground when Viscountess Mæda moved aside to allow of the officer being presented to her daughter. The names were spoken almost inaudibly, and O Ione did not catch any distinct sound. She took it for granted that this was Sada Takumichi, and for the moment she was quite satisfied with looking at his boots, which came well within her line of vision, small, close together, shining aggressively in a strip of sunshine that split the shade where two awnings touched overhead.

Then there was a movement all around them, her mother sailed slowly away on somebody's arm, looking back to see that O Ione followed. A pleasant voice said : —

"May I have the honour of taking the O Josama down to the saloon ? "

The boots had wheeled round to her side, and a black cloth arm, ornamented with a badge and gold stripes, now presented itself. The voice was so friendly that she found courage to look up. She saw a face which took her by storm, beautiful straight features, a mouth that smiled on her in simple kindness, dark eyes all on fire with life and youth, and whose light seemed to mean something more than the mouth could say as yet — the face of Yasu Omori, sub-lieutenant, of the Torpedo School.　What wonder that the child's heart went out to him as they stood on the snowy deck? What wonder that as she walked by his side towards the companionway (for she could not make up her mind to bring her hand out from her sleeve and lay it on his proffered arm) she should have thought, " Now this is the lord and husband whom my parents have chosen for me.　Verily, they have chosen well."

So, as in a dream, she came by his side to the stair, and there, because the steps were slippery in their gleaming newness, and because the great ship sighed at that moment, and changed her lie to the waves, O Ione was fain to let him take her hand and lead her down, he going backwards before her, looking up, step by step, from the level below into her sweet face, and feeling it sink deeper and deeper into his consciousness as she descended towards him ; she leaning on his hand and listening to that glad cry in her young heart, " Verily, my parents have chosen well."

The staircase came to an end at last, and O Ione was led to where her mother was already sitting in state on a red velvet sofa, where she had kept a place for her daughter.　As O Ione slipped into it, her father turned, and glanced at her from where he was standing with a group of other men in gorgeous uniforms.　She thought that he looked anxious, so she smiled to him to tell him that all was well, and then he slowly moved from the spot and came towards her, followed by some one whom she had not noticed before, an unattractive-looking man with a dark face and piercing eyes.

Takumichi had been dragged off by one of the officers to inspect a new machine-gun amidships, and had not escaped in time to greet the Mædas on their arrival. He came towards them now in a blaze of suppressed excitement. He bowed stiffly to the viscountess when her husband presented him, and intentionally dropped his eyelids as he turned to her daughter. This was only his second glimpse of her, but he felt as if the fire that ran in his veins would scorch her where she stood.

She shrank back and hardly noticed him, and her eyes went past him to greet Yasu Omori, who was now returning, balancing a glass of champagne in one hand and a plate of sweetmeats from the elaborate luncheon-table in the other. Takumichi had lost his place in the running; in those short ten minutes Omori had outclassed him for life.

Viscount Mæda bent down and whispered something in his wife's ear. She appeared slightly discomposed, but bowed her head quietly. Then, turning to O Ione, she said gently : —

"Look at me, O Ione san, one of your kanzashis is coming out." Then, pretending to arrange the gold pin in the girl's hair as O Ione obediently turned to her, an almost inaudible word passed from mother to daughter, "This is he, not the other."

The pin was carefully planted in the proper place,

and then the two women — for O Ione's childhood suddenly became a thing of the past — sat up, each in her
place, both rather pale, and O Ione with parted lips and
quickened breathing. Takumichi felt that something
had happened, whether for good or evil he could not
tell as yet. It was enough for him just now to be near
O Ione, to try and get her to speak to him, to drink in
every detail of the fresh loveliness which had vanquished him once and for all.

But she would hardly reply to his remarks, and did
so with a coldness and shyness most discouraging to
the proud lover. Omori was still standing before
Madame Mæda, holding her glass of wine while she
pretended to taste his provisions. Takumichi went to
get something for O Ione, and when he returned found
that Omori had shifted his position to the girl's side,
and seemed in no way inclined to give it up. O Ione
san would have none of Lieutenant Takumichi's bonbons, merely saying that she was not hungry, so he was
obliged to lodge the plate in a porthole, where it
balanced dangerously; and then he did what he could
to make friends with O Ione's mother, seeing that
Omori filled the only possible place on the other side.
He, poor boy, knew nothing of Takumichi's affairs, but
understood that he was in black disgrace with his
senior from the glances of newly kindled hatred which
the other bent upon him. What matter? He was so
happy that nothing else seemed of any importance, and
he was making deep calculations in his mind as to
whether he could be considered in any way a possible

aspirant for the hand of this dear, sweet girl. He thought he might ; breeding for breeding, race for race, an Omori could match with a Mæda ; indeed the families were distantly related already, a fact which had given him courage to ask the viscount to present him to his wife and daughter that morning.

O Ione's mother spoke kindly to Takumichi, feeling that her support was in a manner pledged to him. She too had fallen into the mistake of taking Omori for the authorised pretender to O Ione's hand, and was almost as bitterly disappointed as the girl herself when Takumichi was finally made known to her. She thought him unattractive, cruel-looking, and was no whit surprised to see that her self-willed little daughter would have nothing to say to him.

Whatever chances might remain to save the situation were his. Omori was called away to be presented to the prince, an honour which Takumichi had received before, and the latter was left practically alone with O Ione and her mother, until Viscount Mæda came to take them home, when the other guests were leaving the ship. He talked to them of many things, led them about to show them whatever he thought might interest them, and really made himself very agreeable. But O Ione kept close to her mother and would not look at him. Her eyes wandered over the different groups, and did not light up again till just at the last moment, when Omori ran towards her, bringing a parcel of special sweetmeats rifled from the prince's table for O Ione to carry away. Then he led her very slowly down the gangway steps, just as he had led her down the stair that morning, and tried to get her to look at him. She did so once, and dropped her eyes and blushed crimson, and would hardly say good-bye at all. But when the barge had pushed off, and he was watching it wistfully, he saw that she leaned forward and took his little offering out of her father's hands and laid it on her lap with the greatest care. He hoped it was not all for the sake of the bonbons!

Nothing was said of the all-important affair during the journey back to town. The special train was crowded with people, many of them friends or acquaintances of the Mædas. The women talked unceasingly all the way, and by the time they steamed into the Shimbashi station, O Ione, who had never been in a society crowd before, felt that she had heard and seen enough to last her for weeks. It was delightful to get back to the large-roomed privacy of home, to let her nurse take off her finery, and then to sit in her simple house dress at her mother's feet, and talk over the many impressions of the day.

When her father joined them, O Ione was asked whether Lieutenant Takumichi had found favour in her eyes, and the answer was given in the negative with so much decision and readiness, that even she, spoilt darling as she was, had to listen to a parental lecture on the extreme danger and impropriety of a young girl's having a distinct will of her own. But O Ione soon coaxed father and mother back into their usual mood of smiling indulgence, and to tell the truth, neither of them had been so favourably impressed by Takumichi as greatly to regret her verdict.

Meanwhile Yasu Omori, who had also returned to town, dropped in at the Nobles' Club for a game of billiards before going on to his own home, where he was to spend a few days with his mother.   He was so pleased with life this evening that he wanted to talk and laugh with other men, simply to let off his exuberant spirits.   His play was wildly unsuccessful; but it was all one to him, and he lost the game with smiling equanimity.   Then he watched others playing, and backed the loser, and cared for nothing till he heard some one mention the name of Mæda.   He turned quickly, and saw two men standing a little apart near the fire.   He knew them slightly; one was a cousin of Viscount Mæda, the other a minor clerk in the Ministry of Marine.

"Yes," one was saying slowly, as he blew smoke rings from his cigar, "yes, my cousin is a man of progress, much in favour of the new ideas.   I saw that he took his daughter to Yokosuka to-day.   I consider such gatherings too public and crowded for young girls."

"Ah, but there was a reason for that," the clerk exclaimed, delighted to be able to give details about the second chief man in his office.   "I have it on good authority that the young lady was taken there for family reasons — in fact, to meet Lieutenant Takumichi of the Torpedo School."

At this point Omori joined the speakers, who bowed to him without interrupting their conversation.

"Is it honourably so?" said Mæda's cousin, with a lifting of the eyebrows. "None of the relatives of the family have been notified of such a proposal."

"It is, however, true," said the clerk, "and I have no doubt that Mr. Omori, as a friend of Sada Takumichi, can corroborate the statement that that gentleman has made a proposal for the hand of Viscount Mæda's daughter."

Omori stood dumb, for this was the worst of news for him. He turned eagerly to Mæda's cousin, who spoke somewhat scornfully in reply to the other's eager expression.

"In truth, I am surprised at what you honourably say. It seems strange that my cousin should choose for his son-in-law a man of small fortune and dissipated life. I hope that you may have been misinformed."

But, alas! it seemed only too true. Yasu Omori remembered, one by one, all the events of the day; his surprise at seeing O Ione on the ship, Mæda's slight reluctance to introduce him to her, the marked way in which Takumichi had been brought forward, and he himself spirited away by O Ione's father to be presented to the prince. Of course, the meaning was clear now. But he would not give up hope yet — the hope of a happiness which he had not desired or dreamed of till that morning, when he had seen the fairest of girls standing in the full blaze of the midday sun on the deck of the battleship, her country's flag fluttering over her head, and the bright waves dancing below, as the trumpets pealed out the National Hymn, and every heart on board thrilled high in gallant answer.   Would life say " No " to him after that ?   Ah, never !   Besides, O Ione's smile, her shy glances, the hesitating touch of her slender fingers, had surely meant something which could not have been half so well expressed in words. He was sure she liked him, and he was sure that she had not liked Takumichi.   All was not lost yet.

So he went home a little later, sobered, but not really discouraged.   His house lay in the northern district of Tokyo, in the half-deserted gardens of the old Omori " Yashiki," whose great guard-houses and magazines, dismantled when the Daimyōs were shorn of their power, still shut the place in from curious eyes, and gave it an air of aristocratic seclusion quite wanting to the gorgeous Europeanised palaces which so many of the nobles have built in the fashionable quarters of the town.

There is no shame in not being rich in Japan, and among the upper classes money is never spent on mere display, which is rightly considered as the mark of the upstart.   It was no humiliation to Omori to live in the old palace which stood so sadly in need of repair. Heavy gateways of the beautiful " Torii " shape guarded the entrance from the road.   These were fretted deep with carvings, and had been brave with red and gold in their day.   Now they were dimmed and darkened, and only gave out a sober splendour when the sun shone after a sudden rain, and gilt their juts and curves and bold, soaring crests with rainbow glory. Then the flocks of pigeons that built in their hollows

would whirr out in hundreds as the after-rain wind
swept their eyrie, and wheel a dozen times in the sun,
blinding white on the rise as it caught their breasts,
dark on the fall when earth drew them down, to strut,
and coo, and flutter on the broad terrace inside the gate,
and tell each other astonishing stories of flies caught,
and marauding crows put to flight. The old porter who
lived in the gatehouse knew them well, and connected
them with the souls of Yasu's ancestors, whom his own
fathers had served for hundreds of years, so they never
missed their daily feed of maize and lard biscuit, and
were treated with unfailing respect. Beyond the porter's lodge the road divided to embrace a little hill
crowned with camellia and bamboos, which made an
effectual screen within the gate. Then it ran past a
pond and an old garden pavilion smothered in wild rose
creepers, across quite a stately bridge, and finally up to
the house itself — a long, low building, framed of costly
woods toned to grey uniformity by age, and surrounded
by small fir trees set close together. The entrance,
a kind of open vestibule approached by three broad
steps, was at one end, and in it hung a huge bronze disc
covered with ancient characters, which served as a bell
when struck with the camphor-wood hammer which
swung beside it on a silken string.

But there was no need for the Kurumaya to strike his
gong when the master of the house was returning.
The porter had run before him and given the signal,
and as his jinriksha drew up beneath the archway, the
gilt screens at the top of the inner steps were pushed

back with a flourish, a smiling servant ran down to help the master descend, three or four girls within bowed their heads to the ground repeating, " O Kaeri, O Kaeri," (literally " the honourable return "), and his mother stood on the upper step waiting to welcome him.   She was a pale, high-bred-looking woman, dressed with the severe simplicity suitable to her age, but her dark grey gown was of thick home-grown silk, and its sweeping length showed that she was of the most noble birth. Her face was that of a brave lady who had seen heavy trouble, and who would not quail if she saw it again.

There is no embracing among relatives in Japan. Mother and son exchanged deep and solemn saluta- tions, which might have marked the meeting of com- parative strangers, but when those were over, Yasu's mother laid an affectionate hand on his arm, and accom- panied him to his room, where she helped him to lay aside his stiff uniform and don a loose robe — the "yucata," which is the Japanese gentleman's dressing- gown.   She would ask no questions about his day, nor encourage him to talk, until he had plunged into the little ocean of warm water, slippery with iris leaves and milky with starch, which the bath girl had made ready for him.   The beautiful bathroom was cloudy with steaming moisture, which set free all the fragrance of its perfumed woods, carved in a hundred airy pat- terns suggestive of ease and freshness.

" Was my lord weary ? " the girl asked.   " If so, the blind Masseur was in waiting for him, ready to rub all fatigue away."

But Yasu needed him not to-night.   He would make haste to rejoin his mother, having many things to tell her of, and others on which he needed her counsel.

It was not long before he came to her, fresh and cool, with a smile on his lips, and an eager light in his dark eyes.   To her he seemed the goodliest youth in all Nippon, and the worthy descendant of a house which numbered a hundred generations of warriors and gentle-men.   All the lines of sorrow passed out of her face as she gazed on him, and she looked the proudest and happiest of women.   Pure love is a woman's silver, love in grief her gold, but love in joy over her beloved, a hovering glory of sunshine and diamonds and dew for which we have no name here.

Yasu had to be served with all his favourite dishes, she taking them from the servants, and waiting on him herself.   He, too full of other things to care about mere food, did what he could to show his apprecia-tion of all the little dainties, but at last said, smiling : —

" Nay, my mother, no more !   I have eaten, and am satisfied, and thank you for all.   Now, send the girls away, that we may speak more freely."

So the maids, mostly daughters of old Samurai, re-tainers of the house, slipped away (to come back like a flock of pigeons at the first clapping of the mistress's hands), and mother and son were left alone.

" And now, Yasu san," said she, " what is it that makes your countenance so bright and yet so startled to-day ?   If it is joy, let me share it ; if there is sorrow, let me take it all."

"My mother," replied Yasu, "it shall be joy or sorrow, as you will."

The phrase was a conventional one, but the tone was full of kindness and respect.

"When I wish you sorrow, my son, Fuji shall be floating on the bay. Of all my children you have served me most faithfully, loved me most truly. What is there I would not get for you if I could? Whose daughter is she?"

"Now, how did you know what I have told to no one?" cried Yasu, amazed.

His mother laughed a little, and took his hand, where it rested on the low table, and held it up.

"That told me," she said; "see how it trembles! And your eyes, and your sending the girls away. There is but one malady whose first stages are all joy. Tell me her name."

"How clever you are," Yasu exclaimed admiringly; "it is true, indeed; and her name is O Ione Mæda."

He spoke the soft labials with a kind of rapture. His mother turned sharply and looked at him.

"Mæda?" she said; "the daughter of Viscount Mæda, who has the house in Azabu? But she is a great heiress. They would try to adopt you; I could never consent to that!"

"Nor I," said Yasu, proudly; "my name and my mother are treasures I would never barter away. But O Ione! O Ione!—"

He broke off, and turned his head. His mother

thought that she had made an impression, and, woman-like, hastened to weaken it with trivial considerations.

"And she has been brought up with so much luxury. Even if she would come, how could you bring her to our old house, to our frugal life? What a daughter-in-law would you give me, Yasu, one of whom I could never ask the simplest service! They say she is spoilt and wilful, and has been brought up chiefly by foreigners. Oh, my son, choose elsewhere!"

But Yasu now turned his face towards her with an expression of resolve, such as she had never seen there before. It reminded her of his father, who had been a man of power and determination.

"You are mistaken, Okkasan," he said slowly; "her mother is a true Japanese lady, as gentle and dignified as you yourself, and O Ione san is as good as she is beautiful. You would — you *will* be proud of such a daughter-in-law, and I, prouder than any man living. If her parents will consent, O Ione shall be my wife. I do not desire her riches," he added, in a fine heat of youthful generosity.

"She could not live without them," moaned his mother; "she is a hot-house flower, like one of the Empress's beautiful orchids, which die if the sun is too hot or the glass house gets cold. Oh, my boy, choose a wife who will be a fitter mother for a warrior's sons."

"She comes of a soldier race, even as I do," said Yasu; "and where could I find a nobler or more beautiful girl? She is so young and sweet; oh, mother, I know you would love her in time, and she would love you — almost as much as I do.   You see it really must be O Ione or — nobody.   So now, my dear, honoured, clever mother, you must find means to arrange it all. Did you not say you would give me anything in the world?"

Then he took her hand, and smiled into her face, and her heart melted to this beseeching from the idol of her life; and she was conquered, as a poor woman always is, by the victor whom she has trained for such conquest from his cradle.

III

ALL is fair in love and war, says an axiom often quoted to excuse transactions which bear very slightly on either of those great subjects. Omori's determination to marry O Ione came honestly under both headings; so doubtless the slight duplicity which made him withhold from his mother all knowledge of Takumichi's attempt in the same direction was permissible. Had she known of it, she would not have raised a finger, even to help Yasu, until the first comer's suit was honourably disposed of, he being a brother officer of her son, and on friendly terms with him.

Viscount Mæda had an interview with his sister as soon as possible, and requested her to have the family's refusal conveyed to Lieutenant Takumichi in the most kind and respectful manner. If any explanation were asked, his cousin (who had made the application for him) would be told that it was not based on any personal grounds, but merely on the fact that the young girl had entreated to be allowed to remain with her parents for a little longer. Indeed she was but a child still, and had much to learn, her father said; and then he went down to his bureau, and put the whole matter out of his mind.

A few days passed quietly by. O Ione had suddenly lost all interest in her classes and lectures, and asked to be excused from going to school any more. Surely, if she were old enough to be married, she was too old to be doing lessons, she said ; she was rather pale and listless, and seemed to need change, so her mother took her down to their villa at Numadzu, the warmest, brightest spot on all the coast. The spring was sharp and changeable that year, and Doctor Herz, the great authority in Tokyo, said that O Ione had been working too hard, and must shut up her books for some months at least.

But though the books were left behind, and the sun shone warm among the Numadzu pines, O Ione did not at once recover her rosy cheeks and high spirits. There seemed to be a hush on life for her just then, and a new experience was growing silently into it and filling it more and more. She had her first heartache, and cherished it tenderly, as women always cherish that which shall be their pain. She missed something when with her mother, and found it again when she was alone — the brooding over the recollection of that glorious day which had suddenly shut her off from all her past — the drawing out of her memory every line of a face which had dazzled her so that she seemed to see nothing else wherever she looked. She wondered that others did not see it, too ; that day in, day out, her mother never mentioned Omori's name. She longed to ask some questions about him, but dared not, lest some tremor in her voice should tell her precious secret. Would she never, never see him again ?

She was destined to see him soon, but the meeting

came to her as a surprise. Yasu's mother went very quietly to work; but she had put some powerful machinery in motion to help her son's cause. She had friends among the imperial princesses, and was rather closely related to one of them, who had been chosen as the bride of a prince from among the ranks of the old Tokugawa nobility, to which she herself belonged. This gracious lady was much younger than she was, and might, perhaps, be induced to take a friendly interest in Yasu Omori's love affairs. So to her she went, having first sent a present of some exquisite old lacquer which she knew the princess had been coveting for years. She knew also that the Mædas had received many kindnesses from her, and that O Ione had always been a favourite with the royal lady. Indeed, it was from her that the present of the beautiful dress had come; and O Ione was not so absorbed in her dreams as to be unable to rejoice when she was told that she would soon have an opportunity of wearing it again at a garden party given by *her* princess at the Hamagoten Palace.

She and her mother came back from Numadzu for the event, and O Ione had not been five minutes in the gardens before she found herself face to face with Yasu Omori. Her heart had been beating quickly already, for the profound salutation to their gracious hostess was a matter not easily accomplished; but now the poor little life-clock leaped up in a flutter and dyed her cheeks with the crimson which had paled of late. She could not answer a single word to his eager greeting, but her mother was able to supply her deficiencies, and was very kind to Lieutenant Omori, allowing him to stay at her side most of the afternoon. Madame Omori was not there, for she never showed herself in the world now, but she had placed the affair in the princess's hands, and most ably she conducted it.

Without any appearance of particularity, Viscount Mæda was told of the state of affairs by a lady-in-waiting, and was then brought to H.I. Highness to be coaxed into giving his consent, which he, of course, could not refuse to the royal pleader, only premising that the suitor should find favour in O Ione's eyes.

"Well," said the princess, smiling, "look there on your right !"

Mæda turned and saw Omori in gay talk with Viscountess Mæda, while O Ione, flushing like a happy rose in the sunshine, watched him from under her mother's parasol, and seemed to drink in every word he said. They would not tell her of his request until they had reached home, but Viscountess Mæda was also made acquainted with the situation, and had very little doubt as to what O Ione's answer would be. As the princess was about to withdraw, she called O Ione to her, and laying her hand on the girl's shoulder, said kindly and earnestly : —

"O Ione, child, I wish you to do everything that your honourable parents command. Only so will you be always happy."

Then she broke a long twig from the fringe of a willow and put it into O Ione's hand.

" See," she said, " the emblem of a good woman. Tender, pliant, strong, must she be, binding the family together as the willow binds a hundred sticks in one bundle. May a thousand happinesses be yours."

O Ione's graceful head bent low in acknowledgment of the honour done her, and she brought the little green branch home in her hand and kept it for many a long year.

Takumichi tasted the most acute bitterness when he learnt that his suit was repulsed. No politeness of wording could alter the fiat. O Ione would not have him. It was the first time that he had loved a woman. Till now he had merely amused himself, and had never met with the opposition which might have fanned a passing fancy to the flame of passion. This was more than fancy, and had elements of duration not often accorded to mere passion. He had felt that it would be a turning-point for him. If she would love him — even only enough to marry him — he thought that he could attain any distinction, scale any height. It was all that was wanting to him — the tender, faithful companionship of a beautiful woman, his alone. He could not reconcile himself to believing that it was true that he was refused. He felt that there must be a mistake somewhere ; he probably had an enemy who had prejudiced the Mædas against him. But no, O Ione's parents had consented to the proposal, had brought her to Yokosuka to meet him. It was the girl herself who would have none of him. Ah, she was young — but a child ; he could not wonder that she was frightened at the idea of marriage.   He would wait ; she might come to think differently of him if he could cultivate some friendship with her people.   Surely there would be a good chance for him later.

His pride made it possible to 'hope against hope, impossible to despair entirely.   In this mood he lived for the next few days, turning patiently over in his mind the plans which presented themselves, and feeling angry and sore at having to take such a world of trouble about a matter which should have been simplicity itself. That he, who as yet had succeeded in every undertaking of his life, should now have to wait for a girl's favour — it was humiliating and absurd !

" Give it up," said Pride.   " There are others as fair and sweet as O Ione Mæda ! "   But it was something stronger than pride which had taken the mastery of Sada's heart, and merely to say her lovely name, to remember her face and form, set him weeping burning tears of love and desire, drew oath after oath from his dry lips that neither life nor death should come between him and her.   She should be his in the end, come what might.

It may be imagined that during these days Takumichi was anything but a cheerful companion.   Fortunately there was a good deal to do, for the first rumour of war in Corea had swept over the land, and though nothing was certain as yet, all armaments were being inspected and brought up to fighting value.   He saw his advantage in it, and hoped ardently that hostilities would break out.   With even ordinary opportunities for distinguishing himself, he could do something which should cover his name with honour, and he argued rightly that the surest passport to a young girl's fancy would be the homage of one whom she could call a hero.

One day when he had had an interview with some of the authorities on matters of business (for he was looked upon as quite worth consulting on special points), he was passing out of the entrance hall of the Marine Bureau, and met Omori coming in, his hand full of papers which he was to take up to Viscount Mæda, who was just now employing him as his private secretary. He stopped for a moment to speak to his superior officer, and he looked so triumphantly happy that Takumichi was seized with the strongest desire to strangle him. He had always disliked the boy, who appeared to win all desirable things with careless ease. Omori seemed in no mood for talking, and moved on, while the other stood and watched him for a moment, wondering why he felt more than usually bitter towards him to-day of all days. That Omori looked radiant while he was miserable seemed a poor reason to give himself; but there could be no other.

He finished his business, and avoided having any personal interview with Viscount Mæda, not feeling calm enough to carry it out with dignity as yet. Then he returned to Yokosuka, where the torpedo flotilla was stationed, and threw himself with energy into whatever he found to do.

On the third day came the news, brought by some

one who had been up to town, that Viscount Mæda's daughter was to be married, almost at once, to Yasu Omori.   Then Takumichi's misery found sudden relief in the very conviction of its reality.   Here was some one to hate — a tangible enemy to be swept away. He understood now why he had always disliked Yasu, and why the dislike had instinctively strengthened of late.   He laughed bitterly when he thought of O Ione's excuse for not accepting him.   The shy child who was unwilling to leave her parents had accepted this other man with alacrity, had probably singled him out before Takumichi had ever seen her.   Then he fell to cursing the new ways which gave a girl a will of her own, which made her parents defer to her silly whims and fancies, and gave her an opportunity of actually select-ing a husband for herself, instead of meekly accepting the one chosen for her.   He could value the blessings of progress and enlightenment where the efficiency of naval armament and the education of men was con-cerned ; but as to the women — the old modes were the only reasonable ones, and they were as old as the world itself.   And now — how was he to crush Yasu Omori ?

Yasu had also been ordered down to Yokosuka, and had gone with rather a bad grace, so he received rather a sharp reprimand for attempting to shirk his duties. It was easy for Takumichi to discredit him by tales half told and shakings of the head when his name was men-tioned, but he found that Omori had made a powerful friend in Viscount Mæda, and also that some whisper of his own frustrated intentions had got abroad, for some of the elder men openly taxed him with jealousy. Meanwhile the date for the marriage was fixed for the early summer, and only a short time must elapse before it was celebrated. What could be done to stop it? Again and again Takumichi found himself dreaming of the good old days when a man of his rank would have ordered out a few hundred armed retainers, with whose help he would have stormed the Mæda Palace, and have carried away the girl in triumph, asking no one's consent. He would gladly have paid for that joy by a lifetime of fighting, such as certainly would have ensued, but — who would have cared? In his eyes the prize would have been well worth the fighting, if indeed that had not been an inducement by itself. Alas! those times were over forever, and unless he could have Omori removed, or draw him into a fatal quarrel with himself, events must take their course. A personal quarrel would not have helped Sada Takumichi either with O Ione Mæda or with the authorities, so that had to be ruled on one side. The other alternative was a possible one — for life is still cheap in the sunny East, in spite of progress and its imposing strides.

It is not often that love enters into marriages in Japan; but when it does, it is accompanied by all the divine follies which have marked its path since the world began. Yasu and O Ione were as much wrapped up in each other as Hero and Leander, and Yasu, at any rate, chafed bitterly at the short, ceremonious visits which he was allowed to pay during his betrothal, and which were the only occasions granted him to gaze

on his beloved.   Her mother was always present, and
O Ione, as a rule, hardly spoke at all.   Now and then
he would catch a glance from her bright eyes, and a
smile which told him that all was well.   She and her
parents had made a solemn visit to his mother, who had
returned it the next day, and he thought that the
mutual impression had been a favourable one, in spite
of his mother's regret that he had not chosen a less
richly dowered bride, who would have been willing to
take and occupy the place of the dutiful daughter-in-
law for whom she longed.   All was going quietly
and majestically, and the happy day of his marriage
was not far off; but Yasu was chafing impatiently at
all these restraints, and at last vowed that he would
see O Ione alone, if only for five minutes — he had
so much to say to her, and he was longing so intensely to hear some of the many things which she
certainly must have to say to him.

After some deliberation he decided to take his foster-sister into his confidence.   She was one of his
mother's maids, a bright, clever girl, entirely devoted
to his interests.

"O Také," said he one morning, as she entered his
room with his carefully brushed coat on her arm, " I
want you to do something for me."

" Command me, master and brother," she replied joyfully.   "This is a happy day for your servant !"

" It is this," he said ; " come near that I may tell you
quietly.   I wish to have a meeting with O Ione   san,
alone.   Now — manage it for me."

Také's face fell for a moment, and she spoke gravely.

"That is against the custom of honourable families, dear master. For a common worm like me it would not matter, but for a great man's daughter — a noble lady — it would bring her scorn."

"Now, that is foolishness, O Také, and you are too clever to believe it, even while you speak. She is to live with me alone — forever, after the next few weeks. How can it hurt her for me to speak five minutes with her now? I respect her so greatly that I would not touch her little hand — nor would O Ione san allow it — but I love her, O Také, and I must once hear from her own lips that she loves me. Do you understand?"

"Then you will be very good and quiet, dear master, and not say or do anything to frighten her, and never let our lady know a word about it, if I help you?"

"Never a single word, O Také, on my honour. Now, how will you bring it about?"

"I think," she replied, "that you have never sent any present to O Ione san's nurse. Send her a nice gift to-day, by my hands, and I may have news for you when I come back."

"A good thought, my sister," said Yasu; "there, take money, buy what you think she would like, and so also buy me a great joy."

"Then I may tell our lady that you sent me out, danna san? I may not go without permission."

"Make haste, then," said Yasu; "yes, of course. Who should I send to the European shop for collars and gloves but my clever, kind little sister?"

O Také was away for some hours, and returned towards the afternoon with a bitter complaint about the "European shop," where she had gone to fetch the master's gloves.   They had sent her from one place to another till she was ready to drop with fatigue, and had had to spend as much as fifty sen on jinrikshas.   But there were the gloves — she had found them at last; she would go in and show them to him to make sure that they were right.

Yasu greeted her eagerly.

"What news?" he cried, as she knelt and touched the floor with her forehead.

She raised her head and smiled, putting her finger to her lips, then came and knelt down beside him, holding out the gloves, and said very low: —

"O Sudzu sends you word that O Ione san goes to feed the goldfish every evening towards sunset. The tank is far from the house, and by it is an iron gate, opening on a lonely road. The gate will be unlocked to-night and to-morrow night for an hour after sunset."

"Does she go alone?" asked Omori, in a joyful whisper.

"Yes," said Také, "unless her cousins are with her; but they are not expected to-day."

"Dear, kind Také, what shall I do to reward you?" he cried, forgetful of listening ears and paper walls.

"Nay, my lord," she said, looking round hurriedly; "it is nothing. I am glad I found the gloves at last." Then she added in lower tones: "To see you happy is my best reward, beyond all deserts of mine, but I entreat you to be careful.   It would be bad talking if this became known."

It was a long day to Yasu, but its closing hour came at last.   With a beating heart, for he was not quite sure how he would be received, he climbed the long shady lane which bounded the Mæda gardens on the south.   It was the moment when in those warm spring days all the town comes out to breathe and rejoice in the freshness of the twilight.   The morning had been somewhat sultry, but now a fresh breeze was sweeping up from Shinagawa and the sea; the new-grown foliage on all the leafy hedges was rustling and rejoicing in it, the birds in the wide gardens were singing their evening songs and disputing tenaciously the best roosts in the pine trees.   The Mæda Palace lay on the higher slopes of the Azabu, and from the streets below the voices of children at play came up clear and sweet on the air.   But on the road that led to the back of O Ione's garden Omori met no one.   It was a deep-set lane between the boundaries of two large properties, whose pine and maple trees almost intermingled their leaves and branches overhead.   He had brought none of his own servants with him, fearing their gossip, but had dismissed a hired jinriksha two or three streets farther off; and, as he passed under the odorous bloom of a white-laden elder tree close to the iron gate, he congratulated himself on the complete success of his venture, so far at any rate.   But at the gate he paused, peering eagerly through the bars and listening for any possible sound of voices.   A nightingale was singing in the hedge that crowned the bank; otherwise all was still. He could not see the pond from where he stood, and would have to enter to find out whether O Ione had come or not. Very cautiously he tried the gate, and found that it gave to his hand. Old Sudzu had kept her promise of leaving it unlocked. It creaked a little as he pushed it open, but in a moment he was inside, his feet on the yellow gravel of the garden path. He turned to the right boldly, rounded a full-leaved shrub, and met his little lady face to face with a suddenness which left them both dumb.

She had finished her task of feeding the goldfish, and, tempted by the cool greenness of the garden, was sauntering along with a bundle of rushes under her arm, while her fingers were weaving their ends into a tiny basket. Her soft, clinging robes were the colour of the twilight, tall dark pines rose behind her, and overhead a young moon hung low in a rosy sky.

She uttered a little cry and stood still before Yasu, while her rushes fell in a heap at her feet. But her face was rosier than the sky, and her eyes shone with joy.

He advanced with hands outstretched.

"O Ione san . . . don't be angry," was all he could say. "I . . . was passing and heard your step."

She took command of the situation at once, as a woman will if the man gives her three seconds to snatch it in.

"But — I am very angry, Yasu san," she said, trying to look severe, though her eyes were beaming the tenderest welcome. "I thought you were a robber. How did you get in?"

She was not shy or afraid to speak any more, since she was alone with him at last. His presence was joy and safety, and sweetness untasted till now.

"Never mind how I got in," he answered, laughing happily at that which he saw in her eyes; "I have a million things to say to you. I have never thought of anything else for a moment, since that morning on the ship, and I cannot live till our wedding day unless you will tell me something."

"Are you ill?" she asked, looking anxiously up into his face, which was bending close over her now.

"Not ill — but dying of hunger," he said, taking her hands in his. "Tell me, little empress of my heart, do you love me? Are you glad you are going to be my wife?"

"I — don't know what you mean," she whispered, reddening.

"I will show you what I mean," he cried, suddenly opening his arms and drawing her to him. "Here, listen to my heart! Every beating says O Ione! O Ione! Let me hear the answer in yours."

She lay there for a moment like a gathered rose, and love's high tide sang deafening pæans in her ears. Then she broke away from him and fled, crimson-cheeked, into the green dusks of the garden, and he was left alone in the gathering night, with her iris leaves scattered at his feet. He had learnt what he came to ask, every questioning had been swept away forever in the minute's ecstasy — how was it that his hunger for her sweet presence was a thousand times more mighty, more imperious, than before?

Verily, love is a strange passion — from West to East, the whole world round, it is ever the same, that which should still its longings but intensifies its hunger, and the day that its hunger is appeased love must die.

IV

WHEN Sudzu the nurse crept up, with something of
guilt on her conscience, to lock the iron gate, she saw
no signs of Lieutenant Omori. He waited in the
dusky walk for some time after O Ione had fled, hoping that she might return, but all was silent, and he was
fain to go without another glimpse of her. The night
had fallen when he turned out of the gate into the
deeply shadowed road. It was one that he had never
passed through before, and he hesitated for a moment
as to whether he should turn to the right or to the left.
His memory did not serve him at once, being so full of
those radiant moments with O Ione.

Suddenly he was confronted by a man who appeared
to be carrying a load on his back, and who jostled him
roughly, causing him to lose his balance and fall against
the grassy bank. He was on his feet again at once,
but to his amazement saw the gleam of steel in a hand
raised to strike. With the quickness that came of long
training in the " Jiujiutsu " school he ran in under the
weapon and knocked out his adversary's wind with his
head, catching him round the waist and throwing him
heavily backward. The man, who seemed to belong
to the coolie class, dropped his knife and fought fiercely
to break free. He slipped at last from Yasu's hands,

leaving his blue cotton jacket behind him, and ran, half naked, into the darkness.

The whole thing had happened so quickly that barely two minutes elapsed after Yasu came out, as in a dream, from the garden of his paradise, till he found himself standing covered with dust, his coat torn, the coolie's jacket in his hand, and the blade at his feet. He stooped to pick it up, expecting to find the woodman's sickle with which his assailant had been cutting the bundle of sticks which had rolled across the road in the scuffle. But to his surprise he found that it was a knife as long as a short sword, of great temper and fineness, ground to a murderous edge, with a handle of bronze — altogether the last weapon that he would have expected to find in the hand of a wretched road-side thief, driven to rob by want and hunger, as he at first supposed his assailant to be. He realised that this had been a deliberate attempt to murder him, and an attempt made by some one who was either informed of his movements or who had followed him from his house. The sensation was an extremely disagreeable one. An open enemy was rather an added joy to life for the descendant of the fighting Daimyōs; but a skulking cut-throat, waiting in the dark — no gentleman would feel complimented at such an addition to his acquaintance.

He walked on briskly and soon found himself in the more populous thoroughfares. He wished to avoid remark, and the aspect he presented in his damaged uniform, carrying a bare blade of such peculiar character, was certain to attract it; so he sprang into the first empty jinriksha that he met, and bade the man raise the hood, which sheltered him completely. He stopped the runner a few yards from his own gate, and when he passed through it, handed the blade to the porter in a careless way, telling him that he had picked it up in the street — it was to be taken to his own room.

For the best of reasons, he told no one but Také of this adventure. She was, as has been seen, a woman of resource and intelligence. She questioned him closely as to what enemies he might have made, and reproached herself bitterly with having let him run into such danger. She knew nothing of Takumichi's reasons for wishing him ill, or she would, after the manner of her class, have at once assigned the cowardly crime to him. Yasu Omori was incapable of suspecting that a brother officer could fall so low, and repulsed the mean suspicion with scorn when for a moment it presented itself. Také put away the blade, shuddering, and could not imagine why he did not send for the police inspector and tell him the whole story at once.

"And how about O Ione, and the iron gate?" asked Yasu, smiling. "No, Také, we cannot tell our story to any one, and you must be quite silent about it, as you know so well how to be, where my affairs are concerned. I have had a happy escape."

"You have indeed, beloved master," she said, "and the next time I have leave to go out I will take an offering to Kwannon in thanksgiving for her merciful protection. Had you died, I would have audaciously taken the liberty to die also.   Pray condescend to take care of your honourable self."

"I am not going to die yet, Také," said Yasu; "but when I do you must make many prayers for my soul, so you will have to go on living, you see."

"No living for me — then," said Také, under her breath; "my soul with yours, my brother, to wait on you there as here."

And she slipped from the room, pale and silent.

Omori was a good deal envied in these days by the other men, who were working hard and who had no beautiful *fiancée* with an indulgent and powerful father to get constant leave for his future son-in-law.   It was owing to Viscount Mæda's influence that Omori, without losing any seniority, was allowed to remain on shore while a part of the torpedo flotilla, accompanied by two cruisers, went down to Ooshima.   Takumichi's boat was one of those ordered to Ooshima, so that Omori did not meet him again after his little adventure in the lane; and he himself was so taken up with the thoughts of his marriage that there was room for little else in his ardent heart and brain.

Matters had been satisfactorily arranged as to the future of the young couple, who were to live in a house of their own, after the foreign fashion; O Ione's father had bought for them a beautiful house near the Mæda Palace, where O Ione would be mistress and Omori would be master, and both mothers-in-law could come and go as they pleased.   Even this slight separation filled Viscountess Mæda with grief, but she had to consent to it, since Omori's pride forbade him to accept the position of a man adopted into the wealthy family of his wife.   O Ione seemed so happy in the prospect of her marriage that her mother, who knew how seldom any personal feeling entered into the great life contract, could not set herself against it, but she kept her daughter very close to her side in these last weeks, and talked to her long and earnestly on the duties of wives and mothers.   It was hard for her to give her cherished darling into any man's hands, however noble and loving ; but she knew, as every mother knows, that only so can woman fulfil her life, come to her fairest bloom.   She often spoke to Yasu, whom she suspected of having been brought up in the strongest conservative convictions, as to all that affected family life ; and she knew that her child, educated in the freer atmosphere of modern school and modern home, would never take the place of mere smiling slave to husband and children assigned to the wife in old Japan.   The love and the faithfulness, the heroic loyalty, of the traditional Japanese women would never fail O Ione's husband, for the child's heart was pure gold, and she came of a noble race ; but they must let her walk upright, must let her feel her feet and even use her wings in the sunshine of freedom and love — her heart would never fly from home.

All this was entirely contrary to Madame Omori's ideas, and caused her much uneasiness.   She had found her life rich and full both of joy and sorrow, and could not imagine that any woman could need a wider sphere than the one she had filled in the stately seclusion of the Omori Yashiki; but Yasu belonged to the younger generation, and saw, with the generous quickness of youth, that there were far more chances of good for everybody if the women would move with the times as well as the men; besides, was not his first object in life to be O Ione's happiness? So he repeatedly told Viscountess Mæda, who came to have a strong affection for the warm-hearted, intelligent young man, and he in his turn promised to be everything to her that her own son could have been, had she had one.

To the viscount it was a real pleasure to talk with Yasu, to take him about with him, to tell him of many a plan for the future or experience of the past. A daughter is the flower of home, but a son is as a trusty staff on the road of life, and Mæda had no son of his own.

Madame Omori sold the whole year's crop of her finest rice-farm in order to provide the presents of ceremony which her son was to offer to his bride, his bride's relations, and even her servants. She resolved that nothing should be wanting to their magnificence, and the family "godown" or store-house was ransacked to provide lacquer caskets and rich wrappers in which to convey the piles of silk and crape to the bride's dwelling. All these would be acknowledged by O Ione in presents to her bridegroom's family and dependants after the wedding.

Yasu, a little ashamed of his impetuousness, had not made any other attempt to see O Ione alone; indeed,

Také quite refused to help him along that dangerous road, and preached patience whenever he gave her an opportunity. But neither he nor O Ione forgot the twilight meeting, and the little secret shared seemed to draw them wonderfully close together.

A Japanese wedding ceremony is a patriarchally simple affair. All pomp and display are reserved for the feast which is given later in the day. In a small chamber of the Omori Yashiki (for the ceremony takes place in the bridegroom's house), fitted with fine woods and utensils for the poetic ceremony of the " honourable tea," O Ione and Yasu plighted their troth. It was towards evening, and the sunset breeze came in with fitful freshness from the garden, all one burst of peonies and roses in honour of the day. The tablets of Yasu's ancestors had been placed in the niche of honour, and fragrant incense was burning before them, while graceful groups of the lucky flowers, red and white peonies mingled with branches of pine and bamboo, rose on either side from bronze dishes full to the brim with limpid water — a sign that summer had come indeed, for water in any quantity is considered too chilly to look at in cold weather. The princess, the real maker of the marriage, was represented by her maid of honour, who stood near the ancestral tablets. Yasu Omori, a few steps in advance of her, waited in silence for the advent of the bride. He looked a worthy descendant of a line of warriors, as he stood, his hand resting lightly on his sword, his dark eyes afire with expectation, and joy illuminating every line of his handsome face, as the setting sun outside was reddening every flower in the garden. A young girl, one of O Ione's cousins, held the silver cup from which bride and bridegroom must drink the sacrificial wine. She and the princess's lady were in their beautiful national dress, and the whole picture was strangely typical of the Japan of to-day. In the purely Eastern room, the young officer, in the smart naval uniform, was to wed his bride in a ceremony whose simple details, whose archaic worship, are much the same as they were before Lars Porsenna marched on Rome.

The screens were pushed back, and O Ione, delicate and brilliant as a June rose, and clad in sweeping robes of golden magnificence, was led in by her mother, who, contrary to custom, had insisted on being present.

Yasu's heart leapt at the sight of his bride, and she was trembling all over when he took her hand and led her close to the tablets, before which she bowed down in her first act of homage to her husband's forefathers. Then the other young girl came forward, and standing between them held up the strangely shaped silver cup. Yasu put his lips to it on one side, then O Ione on the other; nine times they drank that mystic wine of the joys and sorrows of life, and their eyes met in dumb vows of immortal constancy across the silver brim.

And that was all. When O Ione withdrew her sweet lips, moistened with the wine of that bowl of love, she was Yasu Omori's wife.

His mother was far too proud, and too tenacious of the customs of her class, to allow the wedding feast of the first day to take place in the bride's house, as Viscountess Mæda had wished it to do. Of somewhat more ancient family than the Mædas, Madame Omori would not yield an inch of precedence to their great riches or their high position at court. She strained every nerve to render her son's wedding feast one worthy of his name; for the strong sense of self-respect, which in Japan forbids unnecessary display among people of the middle and lower ranks, makes it incumbent upon the representatives of great old houses to fall no whit short of that which consorts with their ancestral dignity.

So the old Yashiki was laid out anew, and planted with flowers in bloom and trees at their full growth. The scars in the buildings were repaired, columns painted in scarlet and gold, woodwork renewed, and sweet-smelling mats laid fresh in all the principal chambers. Madame Omori had called together all the old retainers of the family, Samurai whom the new order of things had scattered to farm and shop and counting-house, and the wedding guests were properly impressed by the sight of a couple of hundred of fine-looking men lining the entrance and ante-chambers, wearing their beautiful old costume and carrying the two swords, the long and the short, which had been the emblem of their rank. There were dancers and singers to amuse the guests during the banquet of purely Japanese character, where no traditional delicacy was wanting, and when that was over, a display of the ceremonious "No" dancing closed the indoor part of the entertainment. This, being almost a religious function, is witnessed in respectful silence by the audience, and even the most light-minded are awed into admiration by the extraordinary perfection of an art in which every national triumph has been embodied and commemorated for countless centuries by the same families of artists, who permit no stranger to enter their sacred ranks.

When it was all over, O Ione stood with Yasu, bareheaded under the stars, waiting in the fragrant garden among the marshalled guests for the final display of fireworks, which would give the signal for departure. Her hand was in his, shy but confiding, and close to her on her other side stood her father and mother, exchanging speeches of overpowering courtesy with Madame Omori.

Even the outburst of the rainbow glory could not turn Yasu's eyes from his wife's face, shadowy pale at first in the almost darkness, then lighted and flushed with sudden pleasure as the rustling flame darted from point to point of the framework, firing it into a jewelled globe for a few seconds, and then lining the sky with a wonderful rain of blossoms, trails of peach bloom, crimson and white, golden lilies and ruby roses, all opening in quivering radiance against the purple of the summer night.

.   .   .   .

When Lieutenant Takumichi returned, looking rather gaunt and ill, from his trial cruise with the new torpedo boat, he learned two things — that O Ione Mæda was married to Yasu Omori, and that war was declared against China.

While Yasu and O Ione had thought of little but each other, events had been hastening along the path laid out for them, and Destiny, laughing as she turned her wheel, flung her careless verdict forth — the first great naval struggle of our day was to be fought out between Japan, the darling of the ages, and China, her early teacher, decrepit now and dying, as the aged die, unconsciously. Dressed as a mere matter of ceremony in the perfection of modern armour, China was to meet in the death grip a nation of warriors who have made every weapon their own, who have thrown themselves passionately, with the joy of discoverers, into every intricacy of modern warfare, — looking upon these innovations, not as destructive of their old fighting spirit, but as the means of playing their favourite game with science and success in the arena of the world. And yet Japan did not, as is popularly supposed, force the war on China. With a patience admirable in the eyes of the few who watched the inner course of the negotiations, she gave her old enemy chance after chance of making terms which would have been equally honourable to both disputants. China, ill-advised by those who should have been better able to gauge her weakness, scorned any suggestions of compromise and returned insulting answers to all overtures made in the cause of peace.

With anything like an honourable compromise to offer the nation, the Ministry would have been able to avert the war, and were honestly anxious to do so. But Ito, Oyama, Yamagata, were not the men to ask the country to accept an insult, and had such men been found in Japan they would have been swept aside like chaff before the fury of public opinion. Never did that democratic force take such deep root, and come to such rapid growth, in any soil as it has in the country, grimly in earnest, which people used to call "dear little Japan." Let her glean the wisdom of democracy and restrain its follies ere it becomes her master!

Yasu and O Ione had been married just six weeks when the blow fell. All the festivities and ceremonials, the visits, and the present-giving were over for the time, and these two young creatures were drinking draughts of happiness so deep and pure that they might have known that they were being fed and fortified against bitter grief. But grief seemed a thousand miles away, and O Ione, wandering in the garden by her husband's side, waiting on him with a perfection of courtesy which honoured the giver as much as the receiver, listening for his return from the office, whither he now accompanied Viscount Mæda every day, standing at the head of her household to greet him as he entered — O Ione, in fact, with her head among the stars, and love whispering the divinest stories in both her ears, walked in a dream of joy far too perfect to last — as the world now stands.

It may have seemed strange that Viscount Mæda, who knew well what might be expected, should have allowed his daughter to marry a sailor — on the eve of such a war; but he was a sailor himself, and would always have chosen a naval man for his son-in-law, in preference to any civilian; and besides, his devotion to his child was not of the kind which would have deprived her of the perilous honour of being an officer's wife. There had never been a woman in either family who had hesitated to give her all and her best for the country's need. But he kept Yasu near him until hostilities with China had actually broken out. A great press of work was thrown on the administration in those days, and Omori had become his right hand in many ways.

But now the order had come for Yasu to proceed to Yokosuka at once to take command of the torpedo boat which had at last been assigned to him. The poor boy felt that one human heart was too narrow to carry the throb of exultation with which he hailed his appointment and the agony of parting from O Ione. His mother was forgotten, and yet she would suffer more from the separation than the proud young wife, intoxicated still with the first triumphs of love and life.

Yasu rushed home to tell O Ione of the coming parting and his new glory before any word of either should reach her through others. In the doorway he met Viscountess Mæda, and stopped in all his excitement to salute her affectionately. She was frightened at the emotion in his face, and asked what had happened. When he told her in a few hoarse words, she turned a little pale. Although she had known vaguely that war was inevitable, she had not expected it so soon.

"My poor O Ione!" she gasped. "Let me tell her, Yasu. I fear — I fear for her."

"No," he cried, the patriot suddenly mastering the lover, "it is a proud day — a good day when I go to fight our country's enemies. She will be glad for me. Is she not a Samurai's daughter? I will tell her myself."

"She is your wife — since so short a time," sighed the mother, and then she turned to follow him, for he ran past her.

He had come home at an unexpected moment, and O Ione had been waiting as usual to greet him; but a servant ran to tell her that he was there, and she came quickly, with heightened colour, and made her deep obeisance before him. Then she looked up in surprise, for he and her mother both stood without returning the salutation, and one face was pale with fear, the other flushed and working with emotion.

"What is it, my lord?" she asked slowly. "No misfortune — has come to my honourable father?"

"No, O Ione, no," her mother answered quickly, "Yasu san has come home suddenly to tell you — no bad news."

"Good news, dear," said Yasu. "A Samurai's wife should rejoice over such news. I am given the command of a torpedo boat, and the chance of winning much glory! We are even now at war with China!"

O Ione staggered a little, and put her hand against the lintel of the door to steady herself. Her world was darkened for a passing instant; but then she drew herself up, and said, with white lips: —

"My lord speaks well, and this — is — a good day — since he calls it so."

It was his turn to salute her, and he laid a hand on her shoulder, and bowed his head as he spoke.

"You are indeed a Samurai's daughter, my honourable wife, and I thank you for your courage. It will help me slay a thousand foes."

O Ione's mother had withdrawn from them a little. A throb of exultation stirred her heart, as she realised that her spoilt darling had suddenly grown to woman's height, and henceforth would be one on whom husband and parents could lean safely in their need.

In the short and hurried hours which followed before Yasu left her, O Ione never gave way to grief, but busied herself with preparing everything which would be of use to him in the campaign. Indeed, both she and his mother sent so many cases of wine and delicacies of all sorts down to his ship that the poor steel little vessel would have been able to carry nothing else, and they were sent across to the hospital ship, of whose existence, with all its grim possibilities, the loving women at home knew nothing. O Ione was quiet and busy up to the last moment; but when Yasu finally tore himself from her, she swooned in her mother's arms, and lay for long hours in a state of merciful half-consciousness. Not even her mother could guess what the wrench had been. The next day she insisted on being taken to see Madame Omori, and spent some time with her, alone. When she left, the elder woman accompanied her to the door, and took an affectionate leave of her, returning to her own apartment with a little of the desolation lifted from her heart.

O Ione had told her something which had comforted her, and it was a joy to find that she was a worthy wife for the cherished son.

Yasu had forgotten to say good-bye to Také, but she got leave to rush after him to Yokosuka by the next train, with a consignment of small personal properties which had been forgotten. That which is convenient is always proper in Japan. Nobody saw anything absurd in his mother's sending a servant after him, and so Také was the only one of the family who trod the low deck of the ugly little vessel, on which he had already taken up his quarters, when she arrived. Alone with him in the tiny cabin, she gave him the " honourable mother's " last messages, stowed his things away in the lockers as if she had been at sea all her life, entreated him to remember that he had a dozen new silk handkerchiefs, and then broke into a storm of weeping, her head on his feet.

" Dear Také — kind sister," he said, his hand on her shoulder, " do not weep. I shall come again safely. Take care of my mother . . . and of my son — if I ever have one. I may be kept long away! "

" Too long, too long! " wailed the poor girl. " Either you or I will die, for I shall never see you again! Oh, Heaven forgive the words of ill-omen! All happiness go with you, my lord and my brother! "

Then she gathered herself together and touched his feet three times with her forehead, and crept ashore at last, despair in her heart, and an old torn sock of his, which she had found among the good ones, lying above it.

V

Convoying transports and watching for an enemy who never appears is dull work, and by the middle of September Yasu Omori began to be heartily weary of both occupations, and to long for an active engagement — for some spice of risk to give a flavour to the cramped life on his little torpedo boat. She was, of course, the pride of his heart, and ranked only next to the very chief objects of his affections; and on that account he longed intensely to try her in a great action — to see his beautiful "steel babies" flying from her tubes and making splendid rents in the Chinese warships, as he knew they would do. His finger-tips had tingled with envy when he thought of the men who had been present when the *Nani-wa* sank the *Kowshing*, the only real action, if such it could be called, which had taken place at sea as yet. Comrades in arms on shore had had their share of fighting already — would his own day never come? The inaction was galling in many ways, for Takumichi had been placed in charge of the torpedo flotilla to which No. 29 belonged, and it is never pleasant to have your only enemy become your official superior.

Without at all transgressing the rules of official etiquette, Takumichi made life very trying to the commander of torpedo boat No. 29. It was one of the

most efficient in the flotilla, and whenever there was
a disagreeable job, which would bring no one any glory,
to be carried out, the lot fell to Omori. The slowest
transport was always made his care; if any of the
boats had to cross a bar in shallow water — the curse of
navigation on these coasts — No. 29 was sure to have
the most favourable position for sticking in the mud,
whence she must be tugged — with opprobrium — under the admiral's eyes.

Sometimes Yasu could not have three hours' sleep in
as many nights, for his sub-lieutenant was inexperienced, and the warrant officer both coxy and stubborn;
so that in plying to and fro as escort to the heavy transports and their precious freight, days went by without
Yasu's being able to change his rough suit and heavy
oilskins for any more restful garments, and his narrow
bunk by the cabin table saw very little of him at any
time. Not once in all these weeks had he caught sight
of any Chinese vessel more warlike than a red-eyed
junk, labouring along like an ill-packed basket on the
tossing seas. The weather was squally and changeable,
and the approach of the equinoctial disturbances was
already making itself felt.

Yasu had good news from Japan, however, and that
kept him gay and cheerful in the midst of much grime
and discomfort, the worst point of which was, to him,
the impossibility of getting a warm bath, — or any bath
but a salt one, — the supply of fresh water being far too
limited to be wasted on washing. Once, when he
received a box of little comforts and dainties from home,

the memories they roused of O Ione and the old ways of life brought a sharp pang of pain. He felt for an instant as if nothing mattered except to see her again, to move with her through the stately, airy rooms, the secluded garden, of their Tokyo home. The little things she sent — perfumery and fine linen, books and cigarettes — seemed so pathetically out of place in this grimy, oily, salt-drenched little vessel, a mere shell of thin metal, which the slightest blow from the enemy would probably send to destruction. The mood only lasted for a moment, then he shook it off, with a flush of anger at his own weakness, and began immediately to smoke some of O Ione's cigarettes, and found great comfort and solace in so doing.

The poor child would hardly have recognised her brilliant, handsome husband in the dark-skinned, rather hollow-eyed man who looked through the openings of the conning tower, or strode up and down on the black deck of the ugly craft. His foster-sister — O Také — would have wept at the sight of him.

At last all the troops were successfully landed, and were being concentrated on Phyöng-yang, and there was nothing more for the torpedo boats to do for a few days. They were ordered to lie in the Tai-dong, quietly out of harm's way, until further orders; and Omori, leaving No. 29 safely at anchor, rowed down to the mouth of the river where the main squadron was lying, to get the coveted bath and a dinner (somewhat more civilised than anything that his signalman cook could produce) on board the *Shizuoka*, a small cruiser commanded by a friend of his.

It was a still evening, and the signs of coming autumn were on hill and valley on either side of the broadening stream. The air blew softly off the brilliantly green rice-fields, where the last crop of the year was swelling for the harvest. Beyond the plain, on his right, rose a wide horse-shoe of hills, rolling up in beech and oak woods, all mellow and golden in their deep foliage, till they suddenly broke out in towering flame when the sun touched the crest — a leafy ridge of scarlet maples — red as any Dago Zaka azaleas in the spring. The most beautiful moment of these latitudes is the one when summer, drowsing in careless slumber over the sun-steeped land, is waked to defiant life by the first crystal touch of autumn. The river ran blue and peaceful, ever widening, to the sea, and Yasu, sensitive as all Japanese are to every mood of Nature, drank in draughts of rest and refreshment in the sunset calm.

He had left his sub-lieutenant in charge of No. 29, and meant to stay away from that tyrannical little mistress as long as possible.

He and the commander of the *Shizuoka* (whose small deck seemed enormous to Yasu after the twelve-foot beam of his own vessel) had a very cheery dinner together, and were smoking in long chairs on the quarter-deck, watching the stars come over the hills of that strange land, when a signal was sent up from the flag-ship; another followed quickly, and the two men sprang to their feet, thinking that some Chinese vessel must be in sight. Their excitement subsided when the order proved to be one to make ready to put to sea at daybreak.

"I wish I were going with you, Ikemoto," said Omori; "you are always in luck, you people. They have not said anything about the torpedo boats, and there we shall be left to stick in the Tai-dong for days and days."

"Wait a bit," said the other, "my first lieutenant is in hospital, and I lost two petty officers in the *Kowshing* business. I cannot go to sea short-handed in this crawler. She is a capital vessel, but the slowest in the squadron. I will apply for you to fill Inosuke's place, if the torpedo boats are not to come along."

"I wish you would," said Omori; "but they will never give me leave. Still, the admiral is always kind. You might go and try."

He waited alone on the *Shizuoka*, pacing the quarter-deck in the cool darkness, and thinking of many things. In about two hours Ikemoto returned, the splash of the oars breaking the stillness as his gig drew near.

"It is all right," he said, as he stepped on the gang-way. "We are going to have a look at Hei-Yang Island, and come back again. The admiral hopes to see the end of a pigtail somewhere on the horizon. That is where they always go when we heave in sight. There will be no fighting, but you may come with me in Inosuke's place."

"How did you persuade them so soon?" asked Yasu.

" I thought I should have to let Takumichi know, and he is up the river."

" No, he is not," said Ikemoto, "he is on the flag-ship, in the admiral's packet, and he is going to have a look at Hei-Yang, too.   I don't know how he has managed it."

"What did he say ?" asked Yasu, quickly.

"Oh, nothing much," answered Ikemoto, turning away.   "He did not seem pleased, but he never does, and I got the private secretary to ask before he knew anything about it ; so when the admiral said it was all right, and looked at him, he had to bow and say it was all right, too.   I am glad you are coming.   It will be horribly dull there in the river till we get back."

Omori despatched a man in one of the harbour boats with a note to his sub-lieutenant, telling him of what was occurring, and requesting him to send down a few things, as they might not return for a day or two.

Then in the chill dawn they ploughed their way out over the grey and heaving sea, the detached squadron leading, the main squadron following soberly, with the little *Shizuoka* lagging somewhat in the rear, but only a decent distance behind an unarmed transport, the *Tokyo Maru*, and another gunboat, somewhat smaller than herself, but slightly faster.

Twenty-four hours passed in reaching Hei-Yang Island, in steaming round it, and having it explored by parties of officers and blue-jackets, and the order had been given to proceed to another island, Tahi, also lying off the mouth of the Yalu, when, one by one, long wreaths of smoke come up over the horizon. In breathless silence they were watched from the Japanese fleet — watched and counted, till ten great vessels lay in sight, and the admiral knew that he was face to face with his enemy at last.

The Chinese ships formed in a somewhat irregular line, evidently expecting that they would be met in line and engaged in a colossal hand-to-hand duel of the old "hit hard" kind. Their flag-ship and her twin stood proudly together in the centre, and the weaker vessels lay, four on this side and four on that, the smallest at the farther end of the line. Two of their number, with the torpedo boats, were still in the Yalu when the combatants sighted each other, and these hurried out to join the Chinese fleet, too late. They could only hang on its outskirts and try to keep out of danger when the Japanese squadron began that beautiful and complicated series of manœuvres which marked its admiral as a naval tactician of the first rank. Without precedent of any kind, and having hardly an hour in which to compose his plan, he fought from noon to sunset without making a single mistake or losing a single vessel. Every opportunity was made the most of, every attack warded off, as the two Japanese squadrons circled round and through the Chinese fleet in evolutions of easy perfection, sinking, burning, putting to flight, wielding their yet untried ships and arms in this maiden fight with the patience, valour, and sagacity of veteran heroes.

The Japanese admiral, seconded by the perfect discipline and indomitable gallantry of officers and men, reduced the Chinese fleet by half, and won a victory which alone would have decided the course of the war, and this he did weakened by the absence of the torpedo boats, and hampered at every turn by the feebleness of three of his vessels, and the necessity of protecting them, which never seems to have been absent from his mind for a moment. Why these three weak vessels were included in the main squadron is even now a mystery. Their presence threatened, as the event showed, to be a serious danger to the splendid fleet, but was turned into an added triumph by the astonishing resource displayed in their protection.

It would be hard to say how Omori chafed at finding himself lagging behind on the poor little *Shizuoka* instead of racing to the front in the glorious great *Yoshino*, the foremost of the detached squadron. The *Shizuoka's* highest speed was twelve knots to the *Yoshino's* twenty-three, and the leader of the splendid line was already rounding the Chinese right, leaving one of their ships on fire, when the *Shizuoka* first came within reach of their broadsides, which were fired in quick succession without exact aim, but with deadly plentifulness and rapidity.

Omori stood beside Ikemoto, trembling with restrained excitement, trying hard to see in the clouds of smoke how the fleets stood.

"We are the last," said Ikemoto, quietly; "we may not reach the flank. The torpedo boats have got out of the river, and are rounding over there to starboard."

"I wish I had No. 29," said Omori, savagely. "To think of a fight like this, and not one of the black beauties in it. Was there ever such bad luck?"

"There goes my best petty officer!" Ikemoto exclaimed.

A man fell three feet away from them, all but cut in two by a piece of shell. His commander stooped over him as his lips seemed to be forming words.

"Never mind, Takeda," said Ikemoto, kindly. "I'll tell the Emperor you were the first on board to die for old Japan."

"Honourable thanks, Augustness," gasped the man; "would I had lived to see our victory!"

Ikemoto sprang to his feet as the man's head fell back, and, taking a sudden resolve, gave the order to make for the enemy's front.

"Going to attack the Chinese all by ourselves, Ikemoto?" said Yasu, smiling rather grimly.

The poor gunner's was the first bloody death that he had witnessed, and he was feeling sick and revengeful.

"We must," said his friend, quickly, "but it will be shorter this way. They are such fools that we may get through."

As the little vessel deliberately turned and headed for the Chinese line, she was met by a hail of shells and bullets, which lashed the sea into hissing foam all round her, but she came on prosperously till she reached the very mouth of the passage she had chosen, between the *Ting Yuen* and the *Chen Yuen*, this being as the chord to the arc which the Japanese squadrons had described. The *Shizuoka* carried a few small Krupps and two machine-guns; these were worked with admirable effect, and fortune seemed to be favouring the brave attempt. But as she passed within five hundred yards of the *Chen Yuen* her topmast was carried away, and poor Ikemoto fell dead at Omori's feet. Yasu was hardening rapidly in the fiery furnace of war. He was quite calm now, and found time to be glad that his friend's death had been quick and painless. By this time the air was impenetrable with smoke, and stifling with gunpowder and the smell of burning ships. The crash and thunder of the guns was so awful that many of the gunners were bleeding from the ears, and no order could be given by word of mouth more than a foot away. The decks were slippery with blood, and those of the men who could do so were discarding their shoes. According to the Japanese custom they had all dressed themselves in their smartest clothes as soon as the Chinese vessels hove in sight, so as to meet death or victory with proper dignity.

Omori had the captain's body taken below, and assumed the command of the vessel, as had been arranged between them before the engagement began. His first act was to plant a bamboo spar bearing the flag on the stump of the mainmast, his second to return the *Chen Yuen's* fire with all the strength left to him by his crippled resources. The *Shizuoka* was badly damaged when she finally broke through the line and joined the main squadron beyond, but she was still sound enough to be very dangerous at close quarters, and she had had the supreme joy and pride of sinking one of the smaller Chinese vessels quite as effectually as any of the big ships could have done.

The main squadron by this time had worked on in single column, steaming round to the starboard of the Chinese vessels, but the detached squadron, led by the *Yoshino*, had turned back to protect the *Taikio Maru* and the *Akagi*, who were in danger from the cruisers and torpedo boats.

Omori was congratulating himself on having got his poor friend's ship safely through the lines, and was pushing on in the wake of the large vessels, when he realised that he was being chased by the *Lai Yuen*, a Chinese vessel of far greater size and speed than the *Shizuoka*. For a few minutes he ran before her, hoping to reach the protection of the main squadron; but the Chinaman gained on him with every revolution of the screw, and, after a quick glance about him to see that he had a fair field, he determined to round on the enemy and fight it out.

For a moment the firing ceased, and the *Lai Yuen* seemed to be watching for his next movement. When it was seen that the *Shizuoka* meant to fight, a yell of joy went up from her enemy, and in a moment the guns were working as hard as before. A shell struck the deck and exploded, killing several men, but Omori reserved his return fire till within three hundred yards of the other. Then, bidding his men take clean aim as the smoke drifted a little, he fired a shot which was marked by two or three heavy explosions on board the *Lai Yuen*, and the next moment she put about and fled, with flames dancing along her decks. But a Chinese torpedo boat came into view as she retired, the *Shizuoka* having already turned to follow her original course. In a very few minutes the torpedo boat caught her up, and it seemed as if nothing could save the Japanese vessel from being sent to the bottom then and there. Omori's available ammunition was all but spent. He fired a round and missed, then turned to present the stern of the *Shizuoka* to the attack. But before the manœuvre had been completed, the torpedo boat let fly, and Yasu sent his thoughts back to bid little O Ione farewell, for it seemed unlikely that he would ever see her again.

And then a strange thing happened. The torpedo suddenly dipped and struck the water at about a hundred yards from Omori's vessel. He waited, breathless, with his blackened, bleeding crew, expecting to be struck under water. No, the *Shizuoka* tossed unharmed on the swell, and a cry from the other side of the ship made him move across to see what portent had taken place. The torpedo had dived, and had come up harmlessly on the other side, where it was bobbing up and down with an odd see-sawing movement.

"Something wrong with the balance chamber," said Omori to himself; but he wiped his brow, and felt strangely relieved.

It was now about half-past two, and the main squadron had been doing terribly effectual work, while the detached squadron darted back and forth, like a shuttle in the loom, ever obedient to the watchful signals on the *Matsushima*, the Japanese admiral's flagship. A few minutes later a yell as of a world in agony rent the burdened air, and even drowned the ceaseless crash and roar of cannon, as the *Chao Yung* sank with all hands in deep water. The flag-ship herself was one frightful scene of carnage, redeemed by such heroism, discipline, and self-annihilation that the hideousness of the bloodshed may almost be forgotten when history writes the story down. A shot from the *Ting Yuen*, herself in flames, exploded a heap of ammunition on the deck of the *Matsushima*, killing enormous numbers of her men. When most of the gunners were slain, even the bandsmen came forward smiling, and asked to have the honour of taking their places. Dying men refused the assistance of the surgeons, entreating them to help the less severely wounded, who might still be of use in the battle. In the absence of the surgeons, who were otherwise busily employed, one or two amateurs were trying to assist the poor fellows who lay bleeding in the temporary ward, where a shell had just burst among the wounded. Then from under a heap of dead and dying a ghastly apparition crawled out and gasped, "Don't give them that — it is the wrong bottle — get the blue label; but be careful, there's not much left," and the speaker, a doctor, swooned in his own blood. A man blown overboard by the explosion rose to the surface, dyeing the water crimson. "*Nihon Bazai* (Japan forever)!" he shouted to his comrades, and then sank and died.

Takumichi and Omori did not even catch sight of each other, for the three weaker vessels had been convoyed into safety by the detached squadron before the last and heaviest engagement of the day, when the Japanese fleet and their enemy had, figuratively speaking, fought one another almost to a standstill. The most powerful of the Chinese fleet made their escape, and at last the admiral called his exhausted vessels back, and set about preparing the despatches for Japan. Takumichi, as an officer of well-known ability, was called in to advise the admiral concerning the minor details of the engagement. This may have been the reason why the *Shizuoka's* exploits were summed up in a few contemptuous words.

"This vessel suffered a great loss in the death of her commander, Captain Ikemoto, early in the day. She was left in charge of Lieutenant Yasu Omori, of the torpedo flotilla, a young and inexperienced officer, who very wisely refrained from taking her into any avoidable danger."

Towards evening the Chinese were in full flight for Wei-Hai-Wei, and the Japanese fleets had been recalled from pursuit. The smoke cleared off, and as the sun sank the air grew calm and still. The officers had gathered on the quarter-decks, and were talking over the day's work, while, by some secret accord, all eyes were turned towards the eastern horizon, all hearts towards the beloved country lying far beyond its rim. Suddenly a great wave of song burst from a thousand voices, and on their red ships, standing above their dead, officers and men joined in the triumphant notes of the national hymn. In an instant the band of the flag-ship took up the strain, and over the rose and silver of the twilight sea rolled forth such a tide of victorious melody that it seemed as if its echoes must be wafted to Japan across the water. As if called by the music, a beautiful falcon swept down from the sky, and alighted with outspread wings on the topmast of the *Takachiho.* All could see the wonder, and welcomed it with intense emotion, while the last chords of the hymn were still quivering in the air.

The emblem of victory had found its rightful home.[1]

[1] The main incidents of Chapters V. and VIII. of this story are historical, little having been altered except some names of officers and vessels.

VI

On the day before the battle of Hei Yang Island the Emperor transferred the headquarters of the army from his palace in Tokyo to the port of Hiroshima, in order to be nearer the scene of action, and to superintend all active business in person. Here the descendant of the sun goddess, the being who in youth was considered too sacred to do the slightest thing for himself, and who had never been allowed to walk until after he was sixteen, when the Revolution gave him his birthrights of liberty and responsibility, worked for many hours a day, living in two small rooms, and utterly absorbed in the cares of administration. The court accompanied him in a body, and all the noble women who could do so left their beautiful homes and followed their Empress into the hospitals of Hiroshima to perform the most menial services in attendance on the sick and wounded, who were always sent home to be nursed.

Most of the great houses in Tokyo were shut up. Great ladies dismissed their servants, and did the washing and cooking for their families themselves in order to save money to contribute towards the expenses of the campaign and the comforts of the men. A regular service had to be instituted in the very beginning of the war, to convey to the troops the enormous numbers of presents which the people sent to their soldiers. Clothes and bedding, delicacies of every description, books and tobacco, were the favourite gifts, and the ordinary means of transport were found entirely insufficient to deal with them. It may be noted in passing that this burning, active patriotism went far to help a poor country through the terrific expense of such a war.

Viscount Mæda had of course accompanied his sovereign, and O Ione and her mother, with Madame Omori (towards whom Yasu's wife felt strongly drawn in their common anxiety), spent all their time in the hospital wards, vying with each other in care and kindness to the poor fellows who were brought in in crowds after the great battles on sea and land. The Empress's love for the sick, and her tender care for them, had in a way set the fashion in that direction many years before, and her Red Cross Society had spread far and wide among Japanese ladies the instruction and good will necessary for such work.

The few months that had passed since O Ione's marriage had made a woman of the laughing, slender school-girl. When the cherry blossoms were in bloom she was still going to her lessons, playing with her schoolmates, looking at life and its cares with an incredulous smile. When autumn set loose the chrysanthemums, with all their fireworks of red and gold, O Ione knew the ache of separation, the burning anxiety, and the just pride of the woman whose best beloved stands in the forefront of a great war. For the sake of that pride, for the sake of her parents, who watched her every look, for the sake of Yasu's son, whose face she hoped to see, she gave way to no pining grief, but smiled bravely on Fortune, was always busy and occupied in whatever they would let her do, and only rebelled when her mother, anxious for her health, tried to keep her away from the pitiful sights of the hospital.

"Stay away from our soldiers, from my august husband's comrades, in their need!" cried the generous girl. "What would he say to me when he returned?   What good is a cowardly wife to a brave man, a cowardly mother to a Samurai's sons?   No, my mother, do not ask that, for I cannot obey you. Am I not right, oh august mother-in-law?" she said, turning to Madame Omori, who stood beside them.

"You are indeed right, my daughter," replied that lady, and her eyes kindled with a pride and tenderness that O Ione had never met in them before; "you are worthy to be the wife and the mother of a Samurai!   Come, let us go in."

This conversation had taken place in the corridor of the hospital established in the old Hiroshima palace, the Emperor having given it up for that purpose.   The wounded from the battle of Hei Yang had just been brought in, those of them, that is to say, who had survived the journey.   They were lying still on stretchers in the great central receiving hall, while their places in the wards were being assigned

to them. A letter which had reached O Ione by the
same ship had filled her heart with gladness, for she
knew that her husband was safe, and rejoiced with him,
now that it was over, in his having had an opportunity to be of service. He had spoken very lightly of
his own share in the work of the day, which had really
been a considerable one after poor Ikemoto was killed,
since he had sunk a Chinese vessel, set fire to another, and brought the disabled little *Shizuoka* safely
out of the action. Viscount Mæda, having already
heard that his son-in-law, by some strange chance, had
been in command of a vessel, expected to see his name
mentioned in the despatches and was bitterly disappointed when he found the admiral's short and
scornful notice. He was comforted by hearing from
some one who accompanied the wounded men that
the *Shizuoka* had done excellent work, and had been
thoroughly well handled, and he knew that he should
have plenty of opportunities of putting Omori right in
the eyes of the Emperor and his staff. He had said
nothing to O Ione of his disappointment, and she went
to the hospital unknowing of the cruel calumny.

Many were coming and going, all eager to see their
heroes as they fondly called them, and the pale faces
of the men lighted up with pleasure at the hearty
welcome. People brought them offerings of tea and
tobacco, and some women knelt and fanned the poor
fellows, for the heat was still oppressive and the
place was crowded. The three ladies stopped for a
moment, bewildered by the bustle, and then O Ione

suddenly moved from her mother's side and sank down on her knees by one of the stretchers, whose occupant had attracted no special notice as yet.   He was a bright-looking fellow, scarcely more than a lad, and had a cradle over his leg, which had been frightfully shattered.   On a ticket attached to the stretcher was his name, Sato Mimura, and that of the ship from which he came, the *Shizuoka.*

"You are from the *Shizuoka,*" said O Ione, eagerly. "You saw my husband; tell me about him."

"What was his name, honourable elder sister?" said the boy, in a weak voice.   He used the peasant form of speech, and had never addressed a lady before.

"Omori san," said O Ione.   "If it does not hurt you to talk, tell me of him.   He took command of your ship when the captain was killed."

The man's eyes brightened.

"Oh, yes, I saw him, O Kami san.[1]   I stood very near him till almost the end.   He is a most valiant gentleman — as brave as Hideyoshi."

"Oh, happiness to you for speaking of him," she cried.   "And is he well?   Here, drink some tea," and she stopped some one going by with a tray, — "then you will tell me all that happened.   Was he in danger?"

The wounded man smiled, and sipped the tea which she held to his lips, passing her other arm under his head to raise it a little from the low pillow.

"Nobody was out of danger on that day, O Kami

[1] "Mistress," — literally, the honourable person of the hair, the dressing of which is the distinguishing mark of women's costume.

san, but Omori san played with it. He is very brave. He is not hurt."

"I thank you for the word," said O Ione, paling a little. "What happened?"

By this time she had been joined by the other two women, with the faithful Také, who followed her mistress closely in these days. They all bent forward to hear, for Mimura's voice was weak and husky.

"The mast was severed by a shell," he said, "and the flag fell with it. Omori san fastened it to a bamboo, and the bullets were dancing round him as the 'buyos' (mosquitoes) dance over a ripe rice-field. And he fastened the flag up on the stump of the mast and saluted it. As he raised his hand to salute, a bullet passed between his arm and his body — nay, O Kami san, do not be frightened; he was not hurt."

O Ione had dropped her face in her hands, and shuddered violently. Také came and knelt down beside her, putting her arms round her tenderly.

"And then?" said Madame Omori, hungry to hear of her son's exploits.

"He brought us out between the two biggest Chinese ships," the man went on, "and when a torpedo was sent at us he smiled, and told me drowning did not hurt. But the torpedo went under us. We did much harm to the enemy, and as soon as we had passed through the line, he had the dead put down below with great respect; and we washed the decks, and made the ship ready for action the next day. Omori san was pleased with us. The Emperor will reward him surely, for we sank a ship and burnt a ship, and we were always in danger because of the slowness of our ship.   Ikemoto san was a brave man too, but he was killed too soon."

Here the surgeon approached with some of his assistants; he bowed to the women, and then gave orders to raise Mimura and carry him to his place in the ward.

"Do you wish to accompany him?" he asked them, seeing that they were dressed in the hospital caps and aprons worn by those who were privileged to help the nurses.   "I can find plenty for you to do.   We had not expected so many by this vessel, and are short-handed — and you — and you," he said, turning to Madame Omori and then to O Ione, "are occasionally of some use!   But you must not make the poor fellows talk.   They will all have temperatures to-night after the fatigue of the journey."

The nurses were all occupied already, so O Ione held the basin and Madame Omori the boracic lint and the fresh bandages, while poor Mimura's leg was dressed and made comfortable for the night.   When at last they came downstairs, faint with the atmosphere and the sad sights of the ward, they found Také, with Viscountess Mæda and seven or eight of her friends, wrestling with heaps of blood-stained, travel-soiled garments amid fumes of disinfectants in the hospital wash-house.   They went on the principle that every volunteer diminished the sums paid out for labour, and this, the hardest work of all, was constantly done by ladies.

It was late that evening before O Ione and her mother were able to tell Viscount Mæda what they had heard. He looked pleased and then troubled.

"I am afraid he has an enemy," he said. "Nothing about this was said in the despatches. I hear that Lieutenant Takumichi was in the *Matsushima* acting as the admiral's secretary after the engagement. It will be terrible if he tries to make mischief for Yasu san. He is his commanding officer just now."

"Why should he make trouble for him?" cried O Ione. "Yasu san has never done him any injury. How wicked that they should not have told of his brave deeds!"

Angry tears came into her eyes, and she felt as if she could kill the detractor, whoever he was.

"I will write to the admiral," said her father; "he must know all about it now, and then I can show his letter to the minister, and even to the Emperor if the lying rumour has got so high, and so far. Yasu had better have stayed by No. 29 in the river than have got himself mentioned in that way, poor boy!"

In a few days the admiral answered in an autograph letter, to Viscount Mæda's inquiries, that he had eventually discovered that Lieutenant Omori had behaved with signal bravery in very trying circumstances, and had done more than could possibly have been expected of him to help to win the day. Takumichi had been questioned and had disavowed all intentional slight to Omori. His excuse was that the details of the *Shizuoka's* actions had not been supplied when he gave in his report.

Madame Omori was very bitter when she learnt what had first been written of her son, and though she said proudly that the praise of fools was more hurtful than the blame of wise men, and that a Samurai would certainly do his duty regardless of either, in her own mind she put down the injustice to the filtration of the new ideas, which would lead each man to seek his own advantage regardless of loyalty to friend or foe.

During the next few days O Ione was very busy in making up a box to send to her husband, full of dainty gifts and warm things for the approaching cold, which, they were told, was already sharply felt on the Yalu, where the torpedo boats had now joined the squadrons.

The taking of Phyöng Yang had been simultaneous with the naval triumph at Hei Yang Island, and the campaign in Corea was closed when the Chinese, after these defeats, retired beyond the Yalu, on whose eastern bank the Japanese massed their troops in preparation for the invasion of China.

It was understood that there would be a slight pause before any further movement was made, and advantage was taken of this to send transports with ammunition and stores of every description. So O Ione chose and packed her little wares with the greatest care, consulting her mother-in-law at every turn as to what would best meet the tastes and serve for the comfort of the much loved man on torpedo boat No. 29. In spite of their wealth, the Mædas were experiencing a moment of some embarrassment owing to their very generous donations to the war fund, and O Ione had the joy of selling some of her splendid silks, and even some jewellery, to obtain the sum required for a magnificent fur overcoat, which she was anxious to send to Yasu before the winter came on. When it was finally packed, the pockets were full of warm gloves knitted by her own fingers, fleecy socks and woolly comforters filled up the corners of the chest, whose bottom was heavy with concentrated soups, tobacco, and packages of tea. With great hopes that he would use it, she put in a spirit-lamp and kettle, bought in a foreign shop in Yokohama, and then, there being still a little space on the top, packed in her own wadded silk coverlet, made in the shape of an enormous jacket higher than the head, longer than the feet, and wide enough to roll a man round and round in. How she envied the thing after she had stuffed it in. This senseless bit of silk would hold and warm him — far away from her. Would it tell him how her arms ached to clasp him once more? She buried her face in the yielding folds and for once wept her heart out for her short, short happiness, her long loneliness of separation.

" Do not weep, dear lady," said Také's kind, low voice, and she raised her head to find Yasu's foster-sister kneeling beside her; "do not cry so. It would grieve our lord so deeply, and it is bad for you. He will soon come now."

" Indeed he will not," O Ione answered sadly; " the real war is but just beginning, they say, and many months must pass before he returns. Oh, I cannot bear it!" she cried, in a sudden outburst of rebellious

grief.   "What is this war which takes him from me?
I will go to him," she said suddenly, springing up, and
clasping her hands.   "Také, dear, let us go to him;
I must see his face again."

"No, you cannot go, beloved mistress," replied Také,
gently; "there is no place for you among the guns
and the machinery and the raw, rough smells.   It
would kill you and break the master's heart.   Men
among men . . . women with women . . . so the gods
always order it when great things are happening.   O
that I were a man!"

"If I were you, Také," said O Ione, excitedly, her
eyes still brimming with tears, "if I were you, and had
only myself to think of, do you know what I would do?"

"What would you do — that I will not do, august
lady?" asked Také, with flashing eyes and a tremor in
her voice.   She defied any one to love the master better
than she did.

"I would go," said O Ione; "I would cut off my
hair and steal a man's dress and get taken across in a
transport, and I would find him, and stay with him,
serving him night and day!   Oh, why am I not free to
do it?"

She wrung her hands and began to weep again.

"Nay," said Také, "you are needed for the greater
honour of building up his name — you will bear him a
son to be the pride of his age and to inherit the dignities
which will surely be conferred upon him.   But I will
go in your place.   I will see him face to face, and give
him all your messages; and if he needs me not, I will

return to you here, and tell you that I have seen him."

"My poor Také," said O Ione, "I spoke wildly — you cannot do it. How will you ever get them to take you on those ships so full of men?"

"I can do it, indeed," said Také, crouching low at O Ione's feet, "if you will help me, dear mistress! Think what a comfort it would be to us both to know precisely how he is, how he looks!"

"But what will my mother-in-law say?" said O Ione, touched by the intensely fervent expression of the gentle, homely face.

"She must not know of it, Augustness," replied Také ; "no one must know but you — and I — whom forgive for mentioning together with your honourable self. I will ask for a short holiday in which to visit my sick mother, whom we left in Tokyo. The noble mistress will forgive me afterwards, but she would never let me go if she knew of it."

"True," said O Ione, "though I am sure she would have done it for her husband when she was young and strong!"

For a full hour did these two loving creatures sit on the same mat, hand in hand in the twilight, arranging all the details of a plan by which Také could carry out the bold idea. O Ione was willing to take all the responsibility towards the family should the facts be discovered, and the happiness of sending this trusty, if humble, friend to her dear one was so great, that she put aside all envy of Také's joy in seeing Yasu again, joy which to her own hungry heart would have been as rain to the rice-fields in the summer droughts. So simple are the lines of thought in O Ione's country, that no doubt entered either her mind or that of the servant as to the reception which the latter would meet with on board the torpedo boat. No action is considered ridiculous in Japan, if its motive be a deep and serious one; and the claims of affection rank as the most serious of all motives, except the love of country. Také's romantic expedition had its roots in both, and would need no other excuse in her master and foster-brother's eyes.

When at last Také rose and slipped away to begin her preparations, O Ione smoothed the folds of her coverlet in the box with a little scornful movement of the hand.

"I am sending you something better than silk and tea and furs, my beloved — something better than the seven preciousnesses of the gods! a loving heart to cheer you, a loyal tongue to speak sweet words of home — to tell you how I love, and love, and love you, my hero, my Samurai, my heart's own heart, and my poor life's lord. Oh, Yasu, beloved, come back, come back!"

VII

THE winter set in with great severity, and Ta Lien Bay with its leaden sea and chilly sky was not an inspiring spot. But it was, after the taking of Port Arthur, the base of all operations, and the troops were concentrated there, as well as the squadrons, previous to the attack on Wei-Hai-Wei — that "leaf of China's gate," as the Emperor of Japan called it. The troops on shore really suffered much less than did the men at sea, and even in the bitter cold would often strip for a long wrestling bout, in spite of a freezing temperature such as they had never experienced in their lives. Every one was cheerful, for it was understood that a great blow would be struck as soon as all preparations were complete; but the waiting was bitterly cold work on the ships, where the cramped space precluded all real exercise, and where, rolling at anchor on the grey and icy swell, it was impossible to keep warm. The harbour was crowded with vessels — fifty transports were waiting to convey the troops across the narrow strip of sea, and they were to be accompanied by the whole of the fleet, including the three torpedo flotillas.

Yasu had been walking up and down his little quarter-deck, counting the lights as they flashed out from the forts on the shore. The short day was over, and darkness was settling on the sea, while icy blasts came whistling down from the frozen lands to the north. Yasu shivered, and, plunging his hands deeper in his pockets, turned on his short beat, and then stood still, peering out into the encroaching darkness.

A boat was nearing the vessel, tossing wildly on the swell. It seemed to contain a large white object, and was being pulled by one rower. A second figure soon became visible, crouching against what now proved to be a packing-case of considerable size. The boat was hailed by the lookout, and the man who was rowing explained that she was bringing a box for Lieutenant Omori; the other passenger did not speak, but sprang up the steps as soon as the box had been hauled on board, and came, with some hesitation, to where Yasu was standing. He was pretending to be quite indifferent about the parcel, but his heart was beating gladly; he knew that this must be a token from O Ione, and the wintry sky became warm with invisible sunshine.

Then he was aware of a young man, in the dress of a servant, standing and bowing low before him. The Omori crest showed on the shoulders of his loose black coat.

" Who are you ? " asked Yasu, quickly.   " Who sends you ? "

" Augustness," replied a strangely familiar voice, " I am Kato, the brother of Také, and the noble lady, your wife, sends me to bring these things, and to inquire for your honourable health."

"It is strange that I never saw you before," said

Yasu, carelessly.   " Now tell me quickly, how is O Ione
san — well, and gay, and happy?"

"Not gay," said Také's new brother, "but well, yes;
and happy when she thinks of your return.   She sends
you many things in this case — and a letter by my hand."

Yasu had the chest taken below, and stooped over it
under the light which hung from the low cabin ceiling.
The messenger was keeping out of the circle of rays,
and leant back against a bulkhead, gazing at him
with hungry eyes.   Yasu thought he was alone, and
caught up the first thing he found, O Ione's silk quilt,
and pressed it to his cheek and hid his eyes in it in the
wild longing for her presence which the sight and perfume of it called up.   When he raised his head, he saw
her letter lying on the table, and tore it open.   As he
read it hastily, its thin folds slipping from his left hand
to his right, his face lighted up with pleasure at all the
tender things he found there.   Suddenly, however, joy
gave place to surprise, — indeed, something of dismay was written on his features as he looked up, strode
towards the trembling creature in the corner, and drew
her into the light, holding both her hands.

"Také!" he cried; "but, my poor girl, this is madness.   How did you dream of coming here?"

"Oh, do not be angry," she entreated.   "The Okusama wanted so much to come, but she could not, and
I said I would come and see you, and tell her just how
you were.   It made her so happy to send me," she
whispered, looking up into his face, "and no one need
know."

"You poor, brave, silly girl," said Omori, trying to seem severe, but quite failing of success. He was so glad to see her, to see anybody from home, that even this wild flight must be forgiven. He looked to the door, and then came and made her sit down beside him.

"Quick," he said, "I shall have to send you back to shore — tell me all about her. Some one may come down — I have no place to myself, you know."

"Oh, my brother," said Také, "I only live again now that I see your beloved face! Yes, I will tell you all you wish to hear."

She sat with him for a full hour in the little cabin, pouring out a thousand details in his hungry ears. All that the dear women at home had been doing for the sick and wounded, their encounter with the blue-jacket from the *Shizuoka*, their sweetness and self-denial, their constant talk of him, and their eager looking for his return, — "As if," said Také, "there would rise no sun for any of us till that day, and then he would never set again."

As he listened (for word had gone out on board that the commander was shut up with a messenger from his home, and no one came near to disturb them) his worn face, which had seemed to Také to be bitterly sad when she first beheld it, shone and glowed with warmth and happiness, and the poor girl, who had braved a hundred perils and discomforts to get herself brought over with a shipload of volunteer coolies, felt that she was a thousand times repaid for all. There were messages from O Ione which never could have been trusted to paper; words too loving and precious to come through any medium save that of a faithful heart. When at last Yasu jumped up, as eight bells rang out on deck, he was warmed and comforted, wrapped round again in love's mantle, and strengthened as with new wine.

"You must have something to eat, Také," he said, "and then you must go back; I cannot keep you here — and oh, my sister — you have cut off all your beautiful hair. Poor girl — poor, brave Také! What will you do?"

"What does it matter?" she said.

But this had been, as Yasu well knew, the greatest sacrifice of all. Také would feel disgraced and unsexed in the eyes of her kind. She was quick to see her advantage in his sympathy.

"Please, please let me stay with you," she implored. "I do not mind where I sleep or what work I do. You see, my lord, I cannot show my poor face among women now; so let me be a man for a little while!"

But Yasu had to be stern, for here the question of discipline came in. There was no place for a stowaway on No. 29.

"No, dear and faithful sister," he said, "there is a steamer going back to Nippon to-morrow with sick people, who must be taken home, and you must indeed obey me and go back in her, and tell no one who you are. See, if you did not go, who would tell O Ione san all that she most needs to hear? You are a bird of good omen, Také — a faithful carrier-pigeon, bringing us good news of each other. How we shall cherish you always! You shall be next to the Okusama in the house, and our children shall honour you as a second mother. Come, dear," he said, " we sail to-morrow for Wei-Hai-Wei; it is late, and the wind is rising. Have you money for all your needs?"

"I have everything . . . that I do not want," she said, with a pale face and lips that tried not to quiver; "and what I do want . . . to stay with you, my lord . . . I may not have. But I will obey you. Now, tell me all that I must say to the Okusama, and look at her presents before I go, that I may be able to tell her that you liked them and were pleased."

Nearly another hour passed before she got away and was rowed back to shore, laden with messages, and carrying one or two curiosities of coral and silver Corean work which Yasu sent as tokens to his wife. She shed a few tears, salt as the icy spray of that unfriendly sea, when her boat bore her away from him. But she knew that the chief part of her mission was fulfilled, and Yasu's kind words, his warm hand-clasp, the joyous change which those two hours had wrought in his face, all told her that her effort to bring him comfort was not thrown away. Her last glimpse of him had been a happy one, so she dried her tears and peered out bravely for what might still be seen of the torpedo boat.

But the winter night had wrapped it in darkness, and the cold alien sea rolled black and mountainous before her eyes; the driving gale howled angrily, sweeping down from the frozen deserts of the Pole.

The gale of that night was as a gentle zephyr compared to the one which the fleet encountered a few days afterwards, just as a united attack of land and sea forces on Wei-Hai-Wei had been planned. The ships were necessarily scattered to different harbours of refuge ; the disappearance of the torpedo boats caused the admiral intense anxiety until, when the two days' storm abated, the irrepressible flotillas gathered again in their full number. Yasu thought that he really owed his life to O Ione's fur coat, which had, in some measure, protected him from the frightful cold. The decks, armour, and rigging of most of the vessels were an inch thick in ice; the mouths of many of the guns were completely blocked with it, and the fury of the storm, causing some of the vessels to roll to an angle never attempted before, had proved most exhausting to the men. As they gathered again, the officers glanced with grim fury at the Chinese fleet, riding safely at anchor inside its glorious harbour, protected by islands, and forts, and the boom.

It was the boom which had baffled them. But for that combination of steel hawsers, ponderous baulks, floating chains, and embedded anchors, which closed the natural gates of the harbour on either side of Liu-Kung Island, the Chinese vessels would have been brought to bay long ago ; but the boom defied all efforts to break it up, and was absolutely impassable.

At least so it seemed, till at last, after many failures, a small portion of its extreme eastern end was destroyed by the Japanese explosives, and a narrow passage was cleared which would just admit a small torpedo boat if carefully and adroitly handled. The final struggle of the war was to be carried out by these useful little scorpions, as if in compensation for their having had no part in the first great naval battle. Here the great warships were of no use. The little vessels must attack what remained of the Chinese fleet alone.

It was late in the afternoon when the captains of the torpedo flotillas were summoned to the flag-ship to receive their orders. The gale was over, but there was still a heavy sea, and half-frozen snowflakes drove in the officers' faces as they approached the *Matsushima*. It was a gaunt and battered group which saluted the admiral as he approached, but he looked at them with almost tenderness in his eyes; they were the flower of his salt flock, and he was about to send them to almost certain death. His address was short and to the point.

"Gentlemen," he said, after he had returned their salutation, "I have sent for you to tell you that work, peril, and honour are waiting for you to-night. You are no strangers to all three. I have decided that it is impossible for us to delay any longer in the vain hope of wearying our brave enemy into submission. He has been summoned to surrender, and his answer has been what yours and mine would have been in the same circumstances. All the nations of the world are watching the issue of this war, and if we do not crown it by the victory of Wei-Hai-Wei they will say that our other successes were accidents, and that we were defeated at last by a few yards of steel cable and a couple of damaged forts."

He knew well how to touch the spirit of his officers. They listened to his words with flashing eyes and quick, short breath.   The admiral continued : —

"Many attacks have proved unsuccessful, but will probably ensure your success now by the increased experience they have afforded.   To-night, after moon-set, such torpedo boats as can pass by that small opening" — he pointed towards the broken end of the boom — "will enter the harbour, destroy enough of the boom to allow the fleet to pass, and then torpedo the Chinese vessels."

He stopped speaking, and the senior captain, Sada Takumichi, stepped a little forward to reply in his own name and that of the others.

"We will do our best, sir," he said; "yet as the breach in the boom is so very narrow, the torpedo boats which get in may very possibly be unable to return. If you have no objection to this, we shall be quite ready for the attack."

"There is no other way," said the admiral.   "If any boats are lost, their officers' names will be written in flame on this page of our country's glory.   It would grieve me unspeakably to lose you, but there is no other way."

He glanced round the group, and was met by a happy smile on every face.   Just then the clouds were rent asunder; a sudden flood of sunset glory broke over the sea and shed a dripping veil of gold over the tall masts and rigging of the *Matsushima*, and the wind lifted the white and scarlet flag and spread it wide in the air. The admiral glanced up at it.

" A good omen," he said.   " I perceive that we understand each other.   Now, Captain Takumichi, what dispositions will you make?   The smartest torpedo boat in the hands of your most experienced officer should enter the breach first.   The rest, of course, I leave to you."

Takumichi, looking grim and pale, in his worn and stained uniform, produced a note-book from his pocket and quickly made a diagram and wrote a few numbers. He showed it to the admiral.

" This," he explained, " being the eastern end of the harbour, I have three boats which are small enough to enter the breach, Nos. 8, 14, and 29."

The admiral glanced at the sketch and nodded approvingly.

" While one of them is engaged in destroying the boom, the other two can discharge their torpedoes at the Chinese vessels.   We will blow up the boom with heavy grapnel charges."

" You have assigned that task to No. 8, I see," said the admiral, looking up.

" My own vessel is too large to enter, sir," replied Takumichi, whose face was working with some suppressed excitement; " otherwise . . . but that is of no importance.   With your permission I will, however, make an alteration.   I should prefer to send No. 29 in first, and let her break the boom.   She is light and small, and will attract less attention."

" Her commander is . . . ? " asked the admiral.

" An officer of great talent and courage," replied

the other, with something like a sneer — " Lieutenant Omori."

"He will require both those qualities," said the admiral, in a grave voice, while he glanced sharply at Takumichi. "I presume that it is on account of them that you have given him the post of honour . . . and danger?"

"All my officers have talent and courage, sir," said Takumichi, quietly, "and I do not wish to make invidious distinctions. No. 29 is the best boat for the job."

"You are the best judge of that," said the admiral, politely; "and now," he held out his hand, "good luck go with you all and with your gallant boats. When you succeed — the war is over, and China in our hands. If we should not meet again — farewell. Brave men are never forgotten."

They clasped his hand one by one, and then went to prepare for their dangerous task with jubilant rejoicing. This was something worth living for in their eyes.

Takumichi could not rob Omori of his fierce satisfaction when told that he was to be put in the forefront of the battle.

"I have given you the post of honour," said Takumichi, looking at him coldly from under half-closed lids, "that you may retrieve your reputation. I hope you will make a better use of your opportunities than you did at Hei Yang Island."

Omori saluted, came a step nearer, and answered: —

"If I do no worse, my captain, I shall be satisfied."

VIII

WOULD the moon never set? After nights of storm and darkness she was riding in a frosty sky, and it seemed as if all her rays were glorified icicles, so intense was the cold where the torpedo boats lay dark and quiet on the silver sea. The attempt which they were about to make seemed as if it must be fatal for some of them, although of enormous importance to the fleet. Takumichi had ordered all charts, reports, instruments, and signals to be consigned to the care of the battleships, not wishing them to fall into the enemy's hands. Even lights were not to be used, only a small hand lantern being allowed on board. The situation seemed so grave that he had advised the commanders of the boats to put any valuables, documents, or other things which they would wish to have preserved for their families, under the care of friends serving in the squadrons, and to take nothing with them which was not absolutely necessary.

No love was lost between Yasu Omori and the captain of his flotilla; but the younger man was too generous not to admire the cool, well-considered courage of his elder. After all, as Yasu told himself, it was no wonder that Takumichi did not exactly love the rival who had borne off the prize refused to himself. Yasu sat down and wrote a letter to O Ione, and confided it, with many a dear token of hers, to the care of a comrade on board the *Matsushima*, only to be sent to her in case he should not return. He made one request to the friend for himself, that if he were killed; and his body could be recovered, it should go home to lie in Japanese earth. He added that he hoped, in consequence of the constant intercourse by different steamers with the mother country, that this request would not give trouble; but if it appeared that it would do so, it was to be disregarded.

Although he made all his dispositions very carefully, they were mere matters of duty, and did not impress him with any gloom. He took a far less dismal view of the work before him than did older and more experienced men who had less to lose. The visit of his foster-sister, O Ione's messenger, had cheered him inexpressibly, more than anything in the world could have done, except O Ione's self; and he felt warm at heart, and full of hope and courage during those last hours at anchor, while he and his sub-lieutenant paced the deck and talked in low tones of that which must be done between moonset and sunrise. The junior was a distant cousin of his, and had come to feel a warm friendship for his commander, who returned the liking heartily. They had been inclined to disagree in the early days of the war, but had arrived at a thorough understanding now, after all these months of shared work and privation and danger.

The bright half-moon had set at last. It was close

on two o'clock in the morning, and the cold was breathless. Omori had the tubes examined to see that they were not blocked with ice, and then, as quietly as possible, steamed out from behind the larger vessels, followed at a short distance by No. 8 and No. 14, all very narrow boats, which, it was hoped, would be able to enter the small breach at the end of the boom.

All was still as death. Not a gleam shone from the forts, and the Chinese vessels showed never a light where they lay, black monstrous forms on the dark waters of the harbour. By daylight, Omori had made them out, with their guard-boats in a line before them. He had watched every rise and fall of China's ancient dragon flag, flapping listlessly on the breeze, fit emblem, Omori told himself, of an empire so corrupt that all the heroism and devotion of its many brave defenders could not save it from destruction. But even the flag was invisible now. Steaming slowly so as to attract no attention, No. 29 drew nearer and nearer to the boom, farther from the dim and silent Japanese squadron, whence her commander knew that his movements were watched with breathless interest, as far as sailors' eyes could follow him. It seemed to him, in that most silent hour of the night, that the rushing of the water beneath his screw was loud enough to rouse every fort or vessel for miles around; but no sound came from the enemy, and he was already passing through the narrow opening when the first shot flashed out, followed by its sharp report, from one of the line of

picket boats, some 1500 yards away. No. 29 was just
between some sunken rocks and the chains of the boom.
It seemed as if the trembling of an eyelash would drive
her on those or hang her up on these. But Omori
knew that he could trust his cockswain, who was steer-
ing with the calmness of a planet on its course. Not a
man on board stepped from his place, hardly drew his
breath, until they were safe over in the deep water of
the harbour, when they put about and made for a point
about two cable-lengths from the entrance. The cold
was so intense that a film of ice had formed over the
harbour, and No. 29's movements were notified to her
foes by the cracking of the ice before her bows as she
rent her way through it.

The enemy's guard-boats were all awake now, and
in a few minutes a continuous fire was being poured out
in the direction of the boom; but here Yasu found the
advantage of No. 29's small size and low freeboard.
She was almost invisible, and carried no lights, so the
shells fell round her harmlessly, and no one paid any
attention to them. The Chinese guard-boats seemed
to be coming no nearer, and Omori, elated at having
passed the channel so well, thought that he would have
time to carry out his work successfully before his position was made clear enough to be interfered with.

Now came the effort of the night — the night which
saw the downfall of China's last stronghold. The excitement among the men was intense, but the deadly
work was done in the most deliberate and business-like
manner. Under Omori's supervision, several heavy

charges of gun-cotton were made fast to the boom, an operation which would have been difficult at any time, but was rendered trebly so now by the hail of shells and bullets which accompanied the delicate manipulation required to get the whole thing into position.   Just as all was ready and the torpedo boat withdrew to fire the mine, an accident occurred.   The wire connecting the explosive with the battery was cut by a fluke of the anchor.   Without a moment's hesitation the cockswain sprang forward, caught hold of the severed ends and repaired them with copper wire.   But something had gone wrong; the precious mine refused to explode; time was passing, a shell might strike No. 29 useless at any moment, and Omori ground his teeth.

"Fresh charges," he said shortly and unwillingly.

The men went rapidly to work, and in a few minutes three heavy charges were prepared.   Both the sub-lieutenant and the cockswain volunteered to clamber out on the boom, and make them fast to it, but this Omori would not permit.

"My work, Sakura," he said to his cousin.   "You shall have a try if I don't succeed.   You are frozen, man," he cried, as by chance he touched the other's fingers.   The fire of excitement in his blood was keeping his own hands warm.   "Here, put on my coat — catch hold!"

In a moment he had stripped himself of O Ione's gift, and had thrown it on his cousin's arm.   Then, while the cockswain steered the boat as close to the boom as he dared, Omori crept far out on her bows, hung over them, felt in the icy, dark water for the timber baulk, and sprang off on it. In the twinkling of an eye he had thrown a rope round the beam, and then with feverish haste and extreme care made first one and then another of the explosives fast to the boom.

"Now for the third," he cried. "Take care of this roller! Keep off the water as long as you can!"

Some caprice of the ocean was sending a great crest of foam along from the west. Sakura, who was holding the third charge, hastily wrapped it in Yasu's precious cloak, and passed it out to him. What did cloaks matter? No one would get out alive. More than one poor fellow's blood was freezing, unseen, on the deck. Yasu found this charge far easier to lash than the naked ones, and did not realise the sacrifice till too late. Then he said to himself:—

"Better so. Our boats and our bodies are the enemy's; my wife's gift shall not fall into their hands!"

Then he climbed back into his ship, numb and sick with cold, but the task was accomplished. A few minutes later a rending explosion shook the forts on the islands, set the great vessels quivering where they lay, and tore out a hundred feet of the boom, flinging its wrecked fragments up like the eruptives of a volcano.

"Now," said Yasu, as No. 29 settled to her stride after the shock, "we will show our people what to do when they get inside."

He did not wait to see the rest of the torpedo boats enter the bay. The forts on Liu-Kung were thundering unceasingly, their shells almost crossing those from their own ships, all directed against the boats of the flotillas, which were darting here and there, and hissing out their terrible missiles like things with a will of their own.   Save where the guns made lurid rents, sky and sea were one sheet of blackness; but Yasu Omori knew how to reach his prey.   Long before moonset he had marked the position of the great battleship in the northern corner of the harbour, somewhat apart from her mates.

"Steer for the flashes of her guns," he said; and they did so.

Soon her enormous bulk became a conviction, a solid blackness against the inky sky.

By this time the Chinese machine-guns were filling heaven and earth with bellowing thunders, which crashed out sharp on the sea, and rolled back in muffled roars among the hills.   The rush of torpedoes, the riot of hurtling shells, their crashing explosions every few seconds, made hell's own hurricane over Yasu's head; but there were sadder sounds close to him, which he felt more clearly than he could hear. More than one of his crew had "missed the number of his mess," more than one death-groan had been stifled in a brave man's throat for fear of disheartening his comrades; and as the commander gave the final order to bring his amidships' tube into position, he swore to his father's soul and his father's sword that for each of his men gasping there in the darkness a hundred foes should drown in the bay.   Not a thought of love or life was with him then; only untamed hate and hunger for revenge, heightened to fury by those choking sounds at his feet, and the smell which came raw to his nostrils in spite of pouring smoke — the smell of his country-men's blood.

He was close in now, not more than thirty yards from the Chinese flag-ship, whose shells flew far over his head, but whose machine-gun bullets were pattering in pitiless hail on the thin steel deck. Then No. 29 achieved her mission, and did at one blow what the whole fleet had been unable to accomplish without her. A torpedo crashed forth on its errand, struck the enemy on her beam, and rent her life out through the gash. Yet, like a thing in agony, she snapped at her slayer. As the torpedo boat swept rapidly past, a shell burst on her deck. Sakura and Yasu were struck, one by a splinter and one by a bullet, and staggered back against the wall of the con-ning tower shoulder to shoulder.

Two blue-jackets who had been lying down abaft the funnel, working the machine-gun, ran to their officers' help, but were motioned back to their post.

Sakura sank down in his place, but Yasu found his feet and was almost unconscious of the lead in his lungs. The engines were still working, and he gave the order to steam hard aport, where a second huge bulk had become visible. Springing over a groaning heap, he reached the bow torpedo tube, where a tor-pedo lay, waiting the touch on the firing lever. He caught at it, had time to wonder whether it was blood or water which made his hand so wet, and then was momentarily dazzled by an intolerable glare thrown full on his face. The enemy's search-light had found him. He reeled on the slippery deck, gripped his numbed fingers round the lever, and pulled — heard the winged death rush forth at his bidding, heard a million thunders clash on the riven night, felt the tortured sea shudder once more beneath him, and then fell heavily back on a heap of chains. A shell struck the boiler. It burst with a shattering roar and hissings of steam, stifling the short agony of the men who died in the scalding flood.

When No. 29 shot out from under the dense cloud, she was a hopeless derelict, piled with twisted machinery and dead bodies. As her impetus weakened, she rose and fell meekly on the lessening swell, the last she would ever scar across the sea's breast. Where the search-light lay on the water, one or two black objects were visible for a moment — men who had fallen overboard in the shock. For a few seconds they kept up, trying with feeble strokes to reach the boat; but the cold took them, and before the light was withdrawn, its rays showed an empty path of water, fast filming over with ice, between No. 29 and her sinking foe.

Inexorably, consciousness took the dying man in its hold, and bade his spirit comprehend its own despair. Back from the painless blank of his swoon a slow, tingling agony dragged him limb by limb to life — if that could be called alive which could neither move nor speak, but lay dumb, wide-eyed, on a rack made of chains, whose frozen links scalded their way into the yet sentient body as surely as if fire and not ice had forged their power to torture.

When Yasu knew certainly that he was in his death-pains, and alone, a red rebellion seethed up in his pulses, and sent the failing flame back to his heart. One thing he must know — whether he had done his work or not. The sky was grey for dawn. If he could raise himself he could see what had been won or lost. With all he had of strength he turned a little, pulled his right hand (his left was useless) from where it lay under him in scorching, grinding contact with the iron, and in spite of excruciating pain, raised it to the top of the torpedo tube by which he had fallen, and pulled himself up, an inch at a time, till he could look at the sea once more.

The water was glassy already with the winter dawn, glassy as the eyes of the dead. To the east Liu-Kung and its fort swam black and dumb, with never a flash for all its last night's thunders. Before him a dark wall of hills rose between pale sea and paling sky, and he saw, halfway to the shore, a sunken mast rocking a little; farther on, one side of a huge hulk, turned blindly to the sky, where the flag-ship had foundered in the mud.

The last flash of earth's joy shone in Yasu Omori's eyes, and he found strength still wherewith to turn and look behind him. The harbour was scattered with wrecks and wreckage, but the *Matsushima* and the *Yoshino* and all their glorious train rode on its breast, near the great gap in the boom. On his own vessel there were only stiff and purple corpses. He was alone with his dead crew.

"It is enough!" he murmured through parched lips, as he fell back on his iron death-bed with closed eyes and something like a smile on his streaked and blackened face.

Then the roll of the vessel shifted the chains, and he looked round once more. Was there no one — no one to bring him a drop of water? Not one. Thirst suddenly became a specific suffering. He could not move again — his left hand was frozen to the lever already.

Suddenly he opened his eyes and his face glowed with rapturous joy. The pupils became distended — he raised his right hand as if to reach out for something.

"O Ione, love," he gasped, "you have brought . . . the wine of life!"

His hand fell, and his head sank back. They found him stark and frozen when the full day broke. Death had kissed the smile into his poor face forever.

"Dead at his post — his hand on the lever — his blood on the ice," they told the admiral, when he came to inspect the wreck.

The great commander spoke not till he stood over Yasu Omori where he lay.

"A gallant gentleman," he said, uncovering; "his work has crowned the war and led us to our final victory." Then, turning to the officer beside him, he continued, " Let his body be taken back to Nippon, that his spirit may watch over his country."

.   .   .   .

On a cloudless day in the early spring, the *Yoshino* steamed into port, all traces of warfare effaced, colours flying, bands playing, sunlight shimmering on her rigging and dancing on every point of burnished brass till she seemed like a second sun herself, moving over the face of the waters. Dense crowds lined the shores, and as she dropped anchor by the quay, ten thousand throats sent up a rending shout, the just acclaim of welcome to the first and greatest of the returning conquerors. Who stopped to think of one silent victor lying in his narrow bed where the sun shot down the mainmast 'twixt sheet and awning?

The Emperor stepped on board, and the national anthem pealed out and was taken up by the crowds on shore. A few equerries followed the sovereign, and then Viscount Mæda, and O Ione, pale and proud, crossed the gangway. An officer had been waiting for them, and at once addressed her.

" Madam," he said to O Ione, and she turned on him eyes that saw nothing yet. " Madam, I have a message for you from the admiral. May I give it now ? "

Mæda glanced anxiously at his child. She bowed her head in sign of assent.

" He bade me say that your husband died covered with a glory which shall never fade away. And he prays you, as your husband's heir, to take the thanks

of his commander and his comrades for his noble conduct, and the country's thanks for signal service done."

Twice O Ione tried to speak before the words would
pass her lips.   Then, —

"I am repaid," she said; "take me to him."

She followed, walking upright and alone.   He led to
where, on the snowy deck, guarded by a single sentry,
Yasu's body lay.   On that spot he had first looked into
her eyes . . . last spring.   The flag that had floated
over her lovely head that day lay in pure folds over
his coffin now, white, save where Japan's blood-red sun
covered his quiet heart; still, save when raised gently
by the scented wind from shore which he would never
breathe.   The waves danced silver-glad beneath her feet,
now as then, but him they rocked in the eternal sleep,
and O Ione's heart was frozen in her breast, and her
feet would be leaden all her days.

She sank slowly to her knees where she stood, and
bent her widowed head to the ground in profoundest
homage.   Then, white and rigid, she rose, came a few
steps nearer, and prostrated herself again.   Mæda and
the other men looked on, almost terrified at the un-
yielding strength of the stricken girl.   Mæda turned
and found himself face to face with Takumichi, who
stepped forward, his arm in a sling, the lights of hope
blazing in his eyes.

"I beg to offer my sincere condolences," he said,
bowing; "you and . . . your daughter have suffered
a great loss."

Viscount Mæda returned the bow, and then drew

himself up, and went three paces back. From there he looked full into the other's eyes, and said in a clear voice : —

"Captain Takumichi, I and my daughter refuse to accept condolences from you. You have done all that lay in your power to injure my son-in-law; you gave lying reports which robbed him of the honour which was his due ; you sent him, as I have little doubt, to his death, and left him to die unaided when he had achieved his task. We give him to our country, and with him the hopes of his house and ours; we give him without a murmur for his sovereign's need — but from you we take neither condolence nor friendship. You are unworthy to serve the Emperor."

A terrible change had come over Takumichi's face as Mæda spoke. He seemed to see some awful vision beyond and behind his accuser. Footsteps had approached, but the speaker had not heeded them. He was looking sternly and scornfully at the deathly countenance of the man before him. As the steps came close — halted — Takumichi suddenly became very pale, and a glassy horror filmed his eyes, which never moved from that vision of judgment. He tore the sling from his wounded arm, made a step forward as if to strike, shuddered violently, and turned staggering to the companionway. Mæda wheeled as some one touched his shoulder.

Behind him was the Emperor, with his attendant officers, standing uncovered before Lieutenant Omori's coffin.

O Ione had reached it now, had sunk beside it, hiding her face on the flag above her husband's breast. The contact was too much for her broken heart, and with a wild cry she fell forward insensible. As her father sprang to her side a pistol shot snapped out on the sunny air.

Takumichi had ended his dishonour and his life.

.   .   .   .

Years have passed since that day. The greatness of her grief has helped O Ione to bear it; for a grief crowned with supreme honours is hardly a grief any longer, and O Ione rose from the first crushing shock of her husband's death with that sense of strength that only an ennobling sorrow can give. And the brightest gift is hers, for Yasu's son smiles in her face, keeps her hands busy and her heart warm, and as the years go on, will almost fill the empty place at her side. No mother is really a widow. O Ione feels as if her life's lord had but gone on a distant journey, leaving her their boy to train for him. When her son follows her to the quiet room where she daily places flowers and food before her husband's portrait, the child sees no anguish of sorrow, no floods of tears, for O Ione can look on the picture with a calm brow, and eyes where love and hope have long conquered despair.

In the few radiant weeks of her life with Yasu, there had not been one unkind word to remember, one look or tone that was not all truth and tenderness. No faintest shadow of hurt ever dimmed the warm glory of their love-tide, and its memory, passed with him beyond the ebb and flow of earthly circumstance, is hers forever now in the reality of eternity.

With that white flame at the soul's core, with her little son at her side, and the love of parents and friends all around her; above all, with her hero's nâme graven deep on his countrymen's hearts, O Ione is rich in the truest of all happiness, that which cannot be touched by time.

SEALSKINS

Sealskins

(A TRUE STORY)

RTIE jumped up and crossed the room without looking at me. Then he stood before a great map, and began to run his finger over it, while he hummed an offensive refrain : —

"Alfonso was a sailor,
And he served aboard a whaler !"

"I don't see what that has to do with it," I said gruffly, for I was rather annoyed with Artie. We were old friends — very old friends, in fact. Artie had done me numberless good turns, and it was a habit of mine to say that if ever the day came when I could do any- thing for him, etc., etc. The day had come. Artie had just asked me to do him a great favour which, he said, would cost me very little trouble, and I was extremely annoyed. The trouble might seem little to Artie (whose real name, Archibald Bartie, was invariably shortened to this tender diminutive), accustomed as he was to toy airily with such potent engines as Government cyphers, Consular seals, red tape, and Chancery stores. I had often watched with secret admiration his cool method of sweeping all such venerable lumber into one deep drawer in his battered writing-table, turning the key, and then tossing the bunch in the air before he ran out for his lunch. It was not lunch-time now, but nine o'clock in the morning of a November day, and I was destined to lose a little of my respect for the consular regalia before its close.

"It has a great deal to do with it," replied my friend. "It means that a man who can do one thing well must be able to do a few others tolerably. Why can't you take care of the office for one day? You're cleverer than I am, by long chalks. Nothing is going to happen, because it is really a holiday, and my chief and all the other fellows' chiefs are up at Negishi at the races, and they think I am there too. If anybody does ring you up, say 'Yes, sir,' and answer all questions — well, evasively, *you* know — you are not a newspaper editor for nothing; but nobody'll ring — ta-ta! I'll be back before dinner, honour bright!"

And the heartless boy left me to catch the 9.30 train to Kamakura, where he would spend the day, metaphorically speaking, in the arms of his betrothed — a blooming young missionary of American extraction. It was very wrong of him, for he was just then in sole charge of the Consulate in a port which it is quite unnecessary to name, but which is of paramount value to British trade in Japan. As he had not been engaged more than a fortnight, perhaps he was excusable for feeling that a day in the society of his *fiancée* was a matter of paramount value to him. After all, as he said, it was the first day of the local race meeting, and most of the community were already trooping off to the race-course behind the town. I should probably have a few undisturbed hours in which to work up some trade statistics that had baffled me the night before, and I spread my papers out on Artie's table and tried to take a hopeful view of the situation. An uncomfortable reflection presented itself at the end of the first row of figures. If Artie was so certain that no one would want anything, why was he so coldly determined that I should remain in the office? Why not lock the door and hand over the key to the constable? No, Artie feared complications, and had left me there to take care of them for him.

When I realised this I gave up the statistics. I tried to remember what I had heard lately as to any weighty negotiations pending between the port, the seat of Government, and distant "home," whose blessed old Union Jack was flapping away in the sea-breeze outside. I began to feel less depressed and more hopefully important. Perhaps I should have a chance of helping to make a bit of history! I looked out over the bay, where the warships of a dozen nationalities danced at anchor, close enough for their men to exchange greetings, but separated by great currents of interests that would keep them apart forever. There, a few hundred yards from the Bund, was a huge Russian vessel, dark and sullen-looking, as if she resented the presence of two dazzling white British ships, who flaunted their beauty on the blue waters of the harbour, as if the whole Pacific were theirs by right.   There were yellow ships, grey ships, black ships; and one old American tub, so decrepit and shaky that she never will cross the ocean again, but has her crews sent out and exchanged where she lies.   And among all these the crowds of harbour boats came and went: graceful junks, with huge square sails; foreign yachts; Japanese coast steamers, crowded with passengers; ocean liners disgorging their cargo or filling themselves with coal; hundreds of sampans plying to and fro and scurrying out of the road when some screaming steam launch came rattling and snorting by.   All the life of the port seemed to be throbbing out there on the short blue waves under the morning sunshine, and what I could see of the Bund looked deserted by contrast.

As the clock struck ten, a sharp call of the telephone bell rang out in the quiet room.   I turned round in dismay, and had to look about me before I could make out where it was placed.   As I got to it the strident call was repeated.   My interlocutor was in a hurry.

"Are you there?" came the first — quite unnecessary — question.

"Yes," I replied boldly.

Then came an inquiry I could not make out.   The voice, very far away, seemed to be saying: —

"Is Auntie taken?"

"Auntie — taken," I repeated to myself.   "Oh, *worse,*

I suppose. I wasn't brought up in his family. How should I know? I must answer something, though. Here goes," and I shouted down the wire, "Slightly better, I am glad to say."

The answer surprised me, and it was given with evident irritation.

"Do you think I am wasting Government funds and my time in asking after your beastly cold? Where's — *Artie?*"

"Now," I thought, "we are getting at it. Artie is down in Kamakura with Miss Minnie Spang. I must answer evasively." So, with all the persuasion I could throw into my voice, I replied, "Just where he should be, sir," for I began to feel little thrills of authority along the wire, as if possibly the Head of Things might be at the other end of it himself. In that case — but here I had to listen again, and this was what I heard.

"Have I got a man or a maniac at the other end of the line? *She should be at second boy!*"

I sank down in a chair and gazed at the machine in dismay. It looked sober, well-regulated, almost religious, in its square case, and yet it had certainly given voice to this amazing statement. O dear me, second boy! *She!*

These were evidently family matters, but what on earth could Artie have to do with them? Oh, why did I ever let him go?

At this point my reflections were broken in upon by a sound of voices in the outer room — a kind of corridor, where a Japanese employé had his desk, and where the juniors occasionally interviewed callers when the Consul was too busy to see them. Suddenly there was a lurch against the door, which opened to admit a strange seafaring creature, with a face like mahogany, eyes of childlike blue, and a voice like a foghorn.

"Consul?" it said, and taking a step into the room, added, in an enormous whisper, "*Antarctic!*"

Then I remembered, and with the remembrance came the explanation of those extraordinary remarks at the other end of the telephone. I had presence of mind to close the door and debar the Japanese servant from sharing our colloquy, and then I sat down in the nearest chair and laughed hysterically. The *Antarctic* was a sealing schooner, which rumour said had fallen into the hands of a great European-Asiatic power who patrols the waters for a considerable distance out from Vladivostock.

"What's the joke?" asked my visitor, his blue eyes almost disappearing under some weather-beaten eyebrows which suddenly came into prominence as he scowled at me. "Seems a pretty poor kind of joke to laugh at a chap who comes to you in a fix — a b——y bad fix too, papers and all took away — sixteen hundred skins mooning round outside the bar, nary a paper to land 'em with, and that," he pointed out to the sulky black warships in the bay, "waiting to swallow 'em whole if you try to run it."

Then he put his great scarred hands in his pockets and turned round to look at me, with the scowl gone from his face and only profound and simple trouble

written all over it. I was so sorry for him that I felt
impelled to offer him a mark of my deep sympathy
before going any farther.

" Have a drink," I said, and pulled a square bottle
and two glasses out of the archive cupboard. Besides, I scented " copy " from afar.

" Thank you, sir; with you," he replied, brightening
visibly at this proof that he had lighted on a man and
a brother.

As he put his glass down, the telephone rang sharply.
I had forgotten the Head of Things up in Tokyo. I
sprang forward to reply, but paused on the way.

" This is about you, I expect," I said. " Are you
the captain of the *Antarctic?* What am I to tell the
authorities about the schooner?"

" I am the captain, right enough," said the man.
" My name's Frost. You say I'm here, and I've got
the schooner safe if they can get her in."

I obediently repeated his statement, and am quite
certain that I heard a long whistle of triumph come
down the wire before the next words were spoken.

" Keep the man — shall be with you shortly," said
a delighted voice.

" Who is it?" asked Captain Frost, with some
anxiety.

" British minister up in Tokyo — he's coming down
directly."

" That's good enough for me," said my new friend.
" Say, those are British vessels out there, aren't
they?"

I did not answer at once. I was looking at a time-table and calculating how soon the Head of Things would walk into the office and — discover that I was not Artie. The distance was twenty miles, and the dangerously rapid express train took just an hour to cover it. I would send Artie a frantic wire bidding him return, and in any case I should get my "copy" from Mr. Frost before I was handed over to Constable Wilkin to be locked up in the consular gaol, on a charge of fraudulent misrepresentation of a Government official. I poured out another drink for the *Antarctic's* captain, and asked for his story. He looked hard at me for a minute, then raised his glass and smelt the whisky. It was the best — Artie does himself much too well for a junior — and evidently turned the scale in my favor.

"I suppose you couldn't manage to make out my papers first, sir, could you?" he asked. "I'd just get 'em aboard with my mate in case he got overhauled, and I could come and explain things to you afterwards."

I could not have made out his papers for him if my life had depended on it, so I shook my head sternly, and said that such a proceeding would be distinctly illegal. I must hear the whole story first.

"Well, it was like this," he began, setting down his glass and moving it round and round on the table. "It was in April that we got our papers from the British Consul in Shanghai, me and the captain of the *Shadow* — we generally seal together, being old messmates, and knowing each other's ways and the

seals' ways pretty thoroughly. The ships ain't British
— that I know of. Guess they've sailed under most
of the flags by now, changin' hands, as they do, every
two or three years. Brandon and me, we were 'Meri-
can last year, and Swedish the year before, 'cording
to taste and fancy and the sort of crew we picked
up. But this year we heard the Rooskies had put
on three more patrol ships, and would be doing a
devil of a business along Vladivostock way when the
nor'westers began to blow the sealers beyond the
neutral belt; so I says to Brandon, 'Sonny, the old
Union Jack's the best of the rags to sail under when
there's trouble about. You and me'll be true blue
British sailors for the next six months.' So we got
our papers all right from the consul, and we hoisted
the old bit of bunting and made for the hunting
grounds. Now, I tell you the old flag brought us
luck. If she pulls me out of the fix I'm in now I'll
never hoist no other. The seals were plentiful, the
weather fine, and the sea fairly dancing with light,
day after day. You could see a herd anywhere this
side of five miles, and the boats came back at night
bows all but under water with the weight of dead
seals. At last we had about sixteen hundred skins,
half on the *Shadow* and half on the *Antarctic*, and
Brandon says to me, as we counted the take one
evening: 'Mate, it's enough! Don't wear out your
luck! I smell a gale, and it'll only blow us into the
track of those patrol thieves up there — us and the
skins! I say, back to port and trade with the take!'

"I saw he was right, more by token the sea had changed colour that day, and was all running in streaks, pale grey and dirty brown, and rags of breakers quarrelling with both — that meant no more fair weather till next year.

"'Right you are,' says I; 'we'll make for Yokohama at daylight. It's a prime catch of seals, and we shall be the first in the market, I believe.' Well, I suppose we had tired out our luck, as Brandon said, for that night a gale came along such as the schooners don't meet once in five years — a sou'-easter, by all the contrairies! Instead of helping us down where we wanted to go, it got us into its gullet and just spit us into the track of the Roosky patrol ships; and what with the dirty weather, and what with their natural desire to lift a few hundred skins, if such came handy, I tell you those b——y patrol ships were a hundred miles south of their proper beat, if such skulking sea-thieves can be reckoned to have one at all.

"It had turned pretty cold. We were trying to keep clear of each other, and of what we thought was another sealer. In the darkness her lights came and went, and she was much nearer than I liked, when suddenly she came nearer still, and all but boarded the *Shadow*, which was tumbling about not far from us. The wind had fallen a little, and Brandon was trying to hoist a few feet of sail to steady her. Well, that third ship wasn't a schooner at all, but a great hulking Roosky gunboat; and the minute she had Brandon in tow she bore down on me.

"It was all Brandon's fault. What did he want to

go talking about such things as smelling gales and wearing out one's luck for? Downright b——y blasphemy and unreligiousness I call it, after such a season as Providence had sent us. In a quarter of an hour after she'd nabbed Brandon, two of her great boats were alongside of the *Antarctic* ordering me to hand over my papers and eight hundred skins — you see they couldn't take two of us in tow, and they wanted to make sure of the skins. I thought for a minute I'd train the gun (we all carry one or more up there) on the boats; but even if I had sunk 'em both I shouldn't have gained anything by it, for the black thief had plenty more; so I gave in — as far as I had to. We got up the skins in bundles, and strung them on long rope-ends for easier handling, as I said to my mate; but I winked at him, and he suddenly laughed out loud, for he saw that I didn't mean to give them up so easily. You see I knew they couldn't tow two schooners in all the way to Vladivostock, and I knew they wouldn't want to crowd up their nickel-plated battleship with a lot of stinking otter skins; so I wasn't surprised when I saw them all put on board the *Shadow*, where I knew Brandon would do what he could to save them, but that wouldn't be much.

" In that sea it took a powerful time to get them all on board, and under cover of the darkness I got word to Brandon to have the skins ready for me when I should be ready for them. Then I took the Roosky commander's orders very respectful, and most uncommon confiding orders they were.

" ' You follow close, you d——d poaching Britisher,' says he, ' and if I see you trying to get away I'll sink you to hell to-night instead of letting you wait to get there in proper time.'

" ' Oh, I'll follow,' says I, ' till I get what I want.' But he didn't hear me, bless you. He was that full of triumph at having got our sixteen hundred skins, he didn't even put a Roosky on board the *Shadow* to watch them.

" Well, off we steamed, with the *Shadow* tumbling along behind him, and me behind the *Shadow*, made fast to her stern by a great steel hawser that Brandon threw out to me. It grew darker and darker, and now the wind was lessening and the rain came down in black sheets, and that was just what we wanted, for along that hawser, in the dark, every single bundle of sealskins was slipped along on its rope, me and my mate hauling 'em up over the side, and two of the hunters stowing them down below as fast as we hauled them up ; for the sea was running high still, and it would have been a poor joke to have 'em all washed overboard. It took just two hours for the job, and at the end of them the patrol thief was steamin' along in grand style, as if she had the whole of the British fleet at the end of her tow rope, when she only had an empty schooner without a single skin or a single man on board. When the last man (he was the Chinese cook, and a good plucked 'un too) had come scrambling up the side, we cast the hawser loose, let the patrol thief steam a bit farther into the night, and in half an hour the wind had changed, and the *Antarctic* — I

could cram on the canvas now, for she was pretty
deep in the water — was racing S.E. under most of
her sail.

"Lord, how we laughed, Brandon and me! There
was only one thing we'd lost, and that was the sight of
the Rooskies' faces when they found what they were
towing! You can't have everything in this world, can
you?"

"I don't see what you've got to complain about, Mr.
Frost," I said, rising to mix him another drink, which
I thought he had honestly earned. I am something of
a Russophone myself.

"Well," he said, returning to his professional manner
at sight of a four-finger peg, "when I said we hadn't
lost anything but a laugh, I forgot the papers. Sir, a
schooner full of sealskins, and no papers to show, is
like a woman with a family and no wedding ring!
There ain't no room for her in this fallen world!
Luckily, I'm flying the Union Jack, and that keeps
me safe on the high seas, but I can't stay there forever.
I want to trade, and I want to provision, and I want to
pay off my men. I can't sell a single skin or let one
of the hands on shore till I have my papers all right.
The harbour authorities can confiscate the ship and
clap us all into gaol. See?"

"How did you get on shore?" I asked.

Captain Frost looked at me for a minute without appearing to have heard my question. Then the corners
of his mouth twitched under his ragged moustache, and
one eye closed in a slow, portentous wink.

"Swam," he said shortly; and finished his laugh inside his tumbler, which answered with a friendly gurgle.

Before it had ceased, the traitor Artie, wild-eyed and breathless, broke into the room. I seized him by the arm, trying to explain.

"Oh, stow it all," he gasped. "Put away the whisky while I get things out and make the place look business-like. The Minister'll be here in three minutes. I saw him at the station, and sent Martin to buttonhole him while I came on here."

Martin was the local bore, always good for ten minutes' delay when he once got hold of you. Long before the Head of Things reached the office all Artie's tools were spread out on the table, the Glenlivet had returned to the archive cupboard, and the fraudulent young official had donned a ragged coat kept for working hours. When everything was in place and the scene set, I retired gracefully, quite willing to wait for the rest of my "copy" till the evening. I had no desire to explain my presence at the end of the telephone to the Head of Things just now.

The sequel to Captain Frost's adventures will be found in the following fragment of a letter written by the Minister's wife to some crony of hers at home. It came into my hands in the course of time, and represents the Tokyo point of view:—

A small and curious international complication has just taken place, in which a little scamp of a sealing vessel, called the *Antarctic*, came very near being the

cause of a three-cornered quarrel. She and a consort
(they generally hunt in couples) had gone up as part of
a sealing fleet into the northern seas, which may roughly
be divided into three zones, Japanese waters, neutral
waters, waters of a — European-Asiatic Power. The
neutral waters are the happy hunting grounds of innu-
merable otter and seal hunters, who pick up a rich harvest there every year. The Japanese hardly need
patrol their own waters, since the seals go farther
north, but the European-Asiatic Power keeps up a
lively system of sea police, and pounces ruthlessly on
any wretched vessel that gets driven too far that
way.

Well, one morning, a few days ago, the Minister of
the European-Asiatic Power turned up here looking
very ill-pleased, and rather peremptorily demanded an
interview with the chief.

The first person he met was Jack, who had only arrived from England a few days before, and who was
enjoying his holiday, schoolboy fashion, with a cigar-
ette and a novel, in the biggest arm-chair in the study.
His father was out, and he undertook, rather shyly, to
entertain the visitor. But the visitor would not be en-
tertained — he did not want cigarettes, or arm-chairs, or
schoolboys — he wanted the British representative, and
a British vessel. As soon as the chief came in Jack
bolted, and our indignant colleague made his surprising
request.

" Would his Excellency kindly instruct the Japanese
Government to hand over a certain sealer which was

now lying in Japanese waters, well away from the European-Asiatic gunboats in Yokohama Harbour?"

The chief's amazement at this cool request made itself visible and audible. Hand over a British vessel to the Japanese authorities to give away to one of their friends! I am afraid something was said about seeing the European-Asiatic Power and all the others farther first, and then the whole pathetic story came out. Two wicked, immoral, little sealers, flying the British flag, were caught poaching in the waters sacred to the sea police of the European-Asiatic Power. The sea police raided them, seized all their papers, took one with sixteen hundred skins on board in tow, and told her consort, the *Antarctic*, to follow. As the *Antarctic* had now no papers they knew she could put into no port without being seized by the authorities, and even the sea-police ships cannot tow two schooners at once.

Well, it was a very dirty night, and though at first the *Antarctic* kept obediently near, the police ship lost her somehow in the darkness, and never caught sight of her again. It also lost sight of all the skins which were supposed to be in the prisoner schooner. When day dawned the prisoner rode nice and light on the chopping sea. The *Antarctic* had disappeared with the loot, and it is said that, as she dropped southwards, her skipper was seen making a very rude sign at his late captors through the fog.

A few days passed, and then a little schooner, flying the British colours, was noticed by one or two incoming steamers, puzzled at seeing her lying so far out at sea and making no attempt to enter the harbour. Her skipper, however, seems to have known what he was about. Out there in Japanese waters no one could touch him; but inside the harbour, crowded with foreign warships, with the foreign settlement looming up on shore, who could tell what might happen? As for landing without papers, of course that was impossible; so with many precautions the skipper got himself brought to shore in a small boat, and crept into the Consulate at Yokohama to explain the situation and ask for new papers. It seems that the Vice-Consul, uncertain how to act, was about to refer the case to the chief, when the warships of the European-Asiatic Power heard of the *Antarctic's* arrival, and notified their representative in Tokyo.

He at once applied to the Japanese authorities to have the schooner handed over to him, but when the vessel was described as sailing under British colours, the authorities politely declined to have anything to do with the matter and most kindly begged that his Excellency would ask for something else. It was at this point that he came to us and preferred the same request (with a good deal of peremptoriness, if the truth be told), to receive in another form the same reply. Then there was a little threatening — if the just claims of the European-Asiatic Power could not be considered by her friends and allies, well, it would be easy for her to vindicate them herself. As the action of seizing any vessel in Japanese waters would be a just cause of war, no great apprehension could be felt on that point. Still, the *Antarctic* could not lie out in front of Tokyo Bay forever, with sixteen hundred sealskins on board, especially now that the winter was setting in; so the chief and I went down and lunched with the admiral on board the flag-ship, and the *Antarctic's* fate was settled over the cigarettes after lunch. They were such long cigarettes. The two arbiters walked up and down, up and down for quite an hour, and every time they came near to where I was sitting with some of the officers, little scraps of their talk showed which way the argument was going. The admiral's dear, handsome old face was black as thunder, and the flap of his coat-tails as he crossed his hands behind him was a protest in itself.

"What had he to do with a d——d dirty little poaching schooner?" he asked indignantly. "Let her go to pieces her own way — the sooner the better!"

The chief was quite of this opinion, too, but — since there was that stupid piece of blue bunting in the question — she should go to pieces under British protection anyhow!

And so it had to be. Long before dawn the next morning H.M.S. *Meander* slipped from her moorings and went steaming out to sea. Her errand had somehow become known, for the sad plight of the *Antarctic* was by this time eliciting much sympathy and comment in the excitable little English community of the port. People went down to the Bund to see what would happen, the club steps and windows were full of men with spy-glasses, and even the official quiet of the war vessels in the harbour seemed ruffled, with the happy expectation of a row. Then a great shout went up from the Britishers on the Bund, for there came the stately *Meander* towing in the poor little culprit, with her colours flying, right past the bows of the great Russian man-of-war, past all the sentinels of the port, to drop anchor safely at last within a hundred yards of the Bund.

And the skins? Well, that is the strangest part of the story. Not a tail or a paw of all those sixteen hundred sealskins was on board. They had all been smuggled off and sold before ever the skipper came to report his sad case to the Vice-Consul. Somehow, I could not help fancying that the skipper must have been there before. It is not in nature to be born so clever as that.

AFTER

The sea of Time
Divides the present from the golden past.
We gaze across the glittering cloud-swept film.
The curtain's falling fast.

The measureless way,
Opening before us, inch by inch, no more.
We climb, and hope the path may lead again
To that blue, sun-kissed shore.

A moment's rest,
And up we start, climb to the cloud-crowned brow;
And thence gaze down, awed by the steep descent,
Hope merged in triumph now.

The Lives that crossed,
Met for a moment, stopped, and went their way,
Join hands once more along the clear white road
To an eternal Day.

H. C. FRASER.